The Thursday Appointments of Bill Sloan

Sometimes your therapist is crazier than you are

by

Timothy Gager

ISBN: 978-0-9904872-0-3

Printed in the United States of America

Parts of *The Thursday Appointments of Bill Sloan* have appeared in various forms in *Night Train, Pure Slush, Red Fez, Poor Mojo's Almanac, Referral Magazine, In Between Altered States, The Legendary, Not Just Air, Tuesday Shorts, Metazen, Zygote In My Coffee, Negative Suck, Thunderclap, Further Fenway Fiction* and *TV Guide*.

Also by Timothy Gager:

The Shutting Door
Anti-Social Network
Treating a Sick Animal: Flash and Micro Fiction
These Poems are not Pink Clouds
this is where you go when you are gone
We Needed a Night Out
Short Street
Out of the Blue Writers Unite
The same corner of the Bar
Twenty-Six Pack
The Damned Middle—Life in a Drunken Slumber

Big Table Publishing Company
Boston, MA
bigtablepublishing.com

For my family, my children Gabe and Caroline, and all others involved in the process. Thanks to the good people that attend Dire, The Davis to Porter Group and the fine folks at Scrawl. Special thanks to Teisha Twomey who never lets me get down on my writing, as I tend to do that. Very personal acknowledgments to Rene Schwiesow, Rusty Barnes, Christopher Reilley, Sue Miller and Ned Vizzini. Additional thanks to television, my babysitter as a child, and to Phil McGraw.

I also offer gratitude to a fellowship which saved my life and made The Promises come true, and to a HP, which I understand.

To my Dre friend and awesome panel for host. Thanks for driving long-long to help me celebrate-

Tim

Prelude: Brad, Last seen on Thursday, R.I.P.

IN THE CORNER near the cheese cubes, Brad's ex-girlfriend Hannah and Brad's best friend Randy were louder than was suitable for a funeral, speculating that Bill Sloan's attendance was an attempt to discourage a lawsuit. After all, he'd been Brad's therapist. Shouldn't he, of all people, have known that Brad would kill himself?

"Idiot shrink wrap," Randy said to Hannah. "Brad saw the guy every week, for Christ's sake."

Hanna sipped weak punch. "I think with Brad it was a chemical imbalance. He should have gotten a lot more out of those appointments."

They shushed as the shrink in question headed over, but neither pretended not to be pissed. "Out of sandwiches?" Bill asked, his eyes on the empty platter.

"Just pasta salad left," Hanna said.

He sighed. "That'll have to do, I guess. Where are the plates?" Earlier, he'd given the eulogy: *"I had no idea. But if I had known, I certainly would have hospitalized him."* It was a guess, an ultimate second guess, because his first guess, as it turned out, was wrong.

So here they were, Randy feeling the act was selfish, Hanna thinking it was strictly a chemical imbalance, and the shrink annoyed that there weren't sandwiches. Randy told him to beat it and go find the plates himself.

"Brad was under his professional care! I wonder how that fucker lives with himself?" Randy asked Hanna as Bill slunk off, sandwich-less.

"And the eulogy... what a fucking cop out! Like some cheesy speech on television or something. Like back in school after that kid Pete Comealy died, remember? And they sent a counselor in the next morning so we *might* be able to deal with our grief. All I thought about was how I hung out in the field next to his parent's house. I hardly knew Pete at all."

"Yeah, what good is trying to deal with things, if you didn't know the victim or the incoming counselor? Such a waste."

"I don't think therapists know the answers either," Hanna said. "They just give you new questions. If you don't like the new answers, then what have you got?"

"I don't think there are any answers," Randy replied.

"Maybe God?"

"Nah, He doesn't know anything."

They went out for a smoke, and Randy let one burn down to his finger. Hanna sat on a wooden bench, legs crossed, and flipped through photos on her phone as tears rolled, forming blobby, and dark black circles on her dark blue dress. Her eyeballs looked thick; shellacked and about to burst, and her lower lip quivered. Randy watched her, mesmerized. Her black hair shone in the sunlight, as perfect as if nothing had happened, but Randy erased it from his mind, because *everything* had happened. Her lips were full and round and he wanted to settle them against his mouth. The afternoons were getting cold and her lips warmed him.

"Randy..." she looked up at him.

"What?"

"I just want someone inside me."

He sat next to her, and kissed her softly, then more forcefully. Her hands slid under his shirt, gripped his chest muscles and moved around to his back. "Take me away from here."

They held hands in the car and Randy counted the traffic lights—eight total, but only five were red. They were at his house quickly.

In the morning, the bed was full of condoms. "What's his name?" she asked.

"Who?"

"Brad's therapist."

"Sloan," Randy said. "Bill Sloan. Don't you have to pick up your son?"

"He's fine. I left him with my mom."

Inside the Mind of Brad's Therapist

MY LIFE'S DREAM is to have my own television variety show, but right now I'm a therapist dealing with the shattered dreams within the lives of others who pay me to solve all their disappointments. I, too, am disappointed. It's ironic that in my dreams I was to go far in life, but instead I'm still living in Massachusetts, the place I was born. The only time I left for any decent period was to receive my Masters of Arts degree at The American School of Professional Psychology in Sarasota, Florida. I had the diploma framed in my office but when things went bad between my wife and me, she came in, pulled it off the wall, and smashed the glass into a million pieces. It seemed each sharp edge that fell onto the carpet was mocking me for the time I've wasted in my life. I haven't spoken to her much since, which I know pisses her off, but I can be a real stubborn bastard if I put my mind to it. Plus now it's sort of become a habit, not speaking to her.

Sometimes I wonder if I should work on my inflexibility. Maybe, I too, need a therapist. Maybe my life would be easier or better. But what's the use? At this point in my life, I can't see what good it would do. It seems every day is the same, and the best way to get through the routine is not to give much of a shit.

I'm talking about my clients, of course. People don't change that quickly, and sometimes they don't change at all, which

9

frustrates me. I have one client, who is only nine, who I might be able to help, but as for the rest of them, basically I just sit and listen, and get paid.

I didn't always feel this way. After I got my PhD, I planned on helping others. I was going to be the caring, sympathetic, insightful therapist who succeeded where all others had failed. I don't have a specialty because I agree that variety is the spice of life, and also it minimizes boredom. I work with bi-polar disorder, multiple personality disorder, substance abuse, anger management, personal evolution, codependency; with men, women, children, groups, and families. I don't want to focus on any specific personality type, disorder, therapeutic technique or treatment, because what I really want, besides being a television star, is to just be free from it all.

As far as seeing both men and women, experts suggest male therapists should see only male patients, and female therapists should only see women. My ex-wife strongly suggests I not see women *period*, but I try not to follow suggestions. I enjoy and respect strong women. At one point, I thought my ex was one of those, but strong women, and for that matter strong men too, are not found in my office. I've got the flawed humans who act out in some way, aggressively or sexually. I'm there to help them realize when this is happening, but it's not my job to prevent any of it. I feel the same way about substance disorders. I know addicts are going to do whatever they are going to do. Who am I to say what is right or wrong, since I engage in some of these activities myself. There is help and a solution for them if they want it, but I'm not going to shadow them to break up drug deals or slap a drink out of their hand. Besides, drinking and drugging may be the only thing that is familiar in their lives. Days pass much quicker if you do things the same way, at the same time each hour, each day, each week and so on. Without predictability we'd all be crazy; which is why I love having a routine so much.

Some of my clients have major anger issues. One is court ordered to see me. I don't know how the courts got my name, but I don't feel I'm the best choice in matters such as this. The courts are pretty stupid, because they ordered him to get treated for his anger problem, but he's not required to show any progress to them. In all likelihood, he won't show any, as he's not coming here on his own free will, nor is he desperate for change. I don't like him very much.

I too, have anger issues.

Who am I? Why can't I have what I want? If Dr. Phil has a show, then why not me? Why not *The Bill Sloan Show*? Last night, I dreamed I was a solid block of concrete with rings of energy flying around me, and the light from the energy was causing all this concrete to crack. I'm not a believer in the meaning of dreams, but when I awoke, I found myself thinking that there is much more in *that* world than in this "real" one, and that if I could crack my blocks wide open, things would be better. Right after that realization, I went back to sleep until the alarm woke me at 7:22 AM. When I got up, I no longer felt the impact of what I had dreamed, which left me feeling angry. The reality of today is that I am tying my tie, tighter and tighter—so tight that it constricts my airway.

Part 1: The Notes

CONFIDENTIAL CLIENT RECORDS

Central Services: 25 Saniford Street, Boston, Ma, 02114

Client Profile: BRAD FLAGG

Brad Flagg is a twenty-five year old male who has been seen previously by Dr. Patrick Sullivan. Brad is a successful businessman in the investment field, is physically fit and is considered attractive. Brad tends to escape reality through negative imagination and depression when his goals and desires are not fulfilled. This contributes to his urgent need to control his environment in the short-term, with no direction in his life. It should be noted that Brad is very guarded and not forthcoming with information. Brad should open up and not be as guarded, as he may be a ticking time bomb about to explode in some way or another. Brad came here because his fiancé, at the time, asked him to go. Now that they are on the rocks he displays a very strange detachment from her and their situation.

Referral Source: Brad was referred to this office by Central Services after he reported that his fiancée, Hanna Sertin, demanded he get help for his control and anger issues. Brad and his fiancé have a son together and they have discussed marriage, but this seems to be on hold until his issues are manageable.

Addendum: Brad has been transferred to therapist Bill Sloan.

CONFIDENTIAL CLIENT RECORDS

Central Services: 25 Saniford Street, Boston, Ma, 02114

Client Profile: KATE HUMMINGBIRD WARRIOR

Kate Hummingbird Warrior (legally changed name) is a bright, attractive, and cheerful forty-year old woman, who is a survivor of sexual abuse (father/deceased) and a mental breakdown. Kate reported to Central Services that her mother suffers from treated and untreated mental illnesses, but there is very little contact between them at this time. Kate has been treated for PTSD. She has been involved in the field of meditation and spiritual healing, after studying the teachings of Reiki through Martial Arts.

Kate's goal for therapy is to discover the effect her childhood had on her current behaviors. Overall, she seems happy and tries to avoid conflict. She smiles inappropriately and feels that everything can be overcome with love and spirituality. Kate also states she wants therapy in order to make contacts for her business. Her self-proclaimed title is, Love Sharer.

Referral Source: Central Services for general services. Assigned to Bill Sloan, who Kate reports is the Universe's preference.

CONFIDENTIAL CLIENT RECORDS

Central Services: 25 Saniford Street, Boston, Ma, 02114

Client Profile: THOMAS MERCER

Thomas Mercer is a forty-seven year old man who referred himself to Central Services after a court ordered him to receive Anger Management therapy. After reviewing court paperwork, a diagnosis of Antisocial Personality Disorder was obtained. Thomas is no longer employed at his construction job because of a physical altercation at a site.

Thomas has an affect that is jagged and dangerous. In the past, he has said that he's avoided tickets and criminal charges because the police are scared of him. During the altercation at the job site, five police were called in, but he willingly gave himself up. This shows his ability for sound reasoning. It should be noted that someone ordered to get help is usually not successful, because this choice is not based on their own initiative.

Referral: Court referral for Anger Management. Assigned to Bill Sloan.

CONFIDENTIAL CLIENT RECORDS

Central Services: 25 Saniford Street, Boston, Ma, 02114

Client Profile: PEARL SLOANEY

Pearl Sloaney is a forty-eight year old woman who reports she is having trouble with her husband. Her husband no longer talks to her and it is affecting their children. During the intake process, Pearl was very agitated and wanted to be seen by a specific clinician, Bill Sloan. Her agitation grew when intake had to check if Mr. Sloan had any openings for new cases, and Pearl revealed paranoid thoughts that the clinician was trying to avoid her.

Pearl's conversational skills are disjointed. She talks about her children, their dog, her husband, her ex-husband, and shopping randomly. Other clinicians were available, but she demanded to see Bill Sloan and no one else.

Referral Source: Central Services through self-initiated call, for family, possibly multi-person/group therapy. Assigned to Bill Sloan, with trepidation.

CONFIDENTIAL CLIENT RECORDS

Central Services: 25 Saniford Street, Boston, Ma, 02114

Client Profile: ETHAN MCGRATH

Ethan McGrath is a nine-year old boy who is treated in a specialized program at Waysworth School, East Bridgewater, Massachusetts, during the day. He is receiving excellent services from a psychologist and psychiatrist there, as reported by his parents. Ethan suffers from Childhood Bipolar Disorder, which manifests itself in manic episodes and obsessions about jumping out of windows and being able to fly. In a depressed state, he has suicide ideologies, which manifest themselves through obsessions about jumping out of windows and not being able to fly. When treated, he exceeds in school and has a calm and delightful demeanor. Ethan's mother suffers from extreme Bipolar Disorder and has had multiple hospitalizations. When treated, she presents well also. Ethan's father is seeking additional support, as he feels that Waysworth is not forthcoming with information regarding Ethan's care.

Referral Source: Central Services through call by guardian, for children's therapy. Assigned to Bill Sloan.

Part 2: The Appointments

Chapter 1: Thursday, January 5

7:22 AM: Alarm clock
Hit snooze button three times
7:43 Get up

8:45 AM: Hanna Sertin, Age 28 (former fiancé of Brad Flagg)

No show. I could have slept an extra hour. Note to self: Call Hanna after 10:00 AM. Might not be a morning person.

9:45 AM: Kate Hummingbird Warrior

I don't know why Kate sees me. She says she solves her own problems sitting in the woods. Kate tells me she wants to make love everyday under a canopy of trees. She thinks she is a tribeswoman and would like to mate with a tribesman. Sex makes her angry when she's finished. She twirls her thick golden hair when she tells me she thinks we should go to the woods together, because I'm a tribesman. I suggested she see a female therapist and her response was, "I've had a few intimate relationships with women." She says she was out in the woods the other day and spoke to a squirrel. What did it say? All it said was, "Hi." She told the squirrel she loved it and placed it on her lap. "Why can't people be like that squirrel?" she wanted to know. It's clear that she related to the squirrel better than she did to people, and in fact, she had a dream that night in which she and the squirrel were lovers.

10:45 AM: Thomas Mercer

Thomas can't commit to anything. He's lonely, yet he pushes people away. He's funny, but has a mean streak. He gasps for love the way he gasps for air. He has asthma. Thomas only wants women he can't have. Thomas should live in a protected box. He feels if he makes love to a woman at least every three months, he'll be fine. Thomas doesn't realize that women might develop emotional attachments. During sessions, Thomas says, "fuck it" or "fuck me" a lot. I can see why Thomas has scars over his eyes; he's been in a few battles. Sometimes he confronts me about his lack of progress in therapy. Thomas doesn't realize healing should all come from within. Thomas doesn't realize, within him is a soulless black hole. He always uses phrases like, "when I finally hunker down..." Thomas is rugged but he's a big baby. I'd like to kill Thomas.

11:30 AM: Lunch—sandwich, apple, juice box

12:45 PM: Pearl Sloaney (new patient)

Real name: Stella, but she used a fake name to get past the intake screeners. I recognize her, and her less than creative last name, too late to do anything about today's presence—"Pearl" is my ex-wife. She is taking this hour to speak to me since I've not returned her calls in months. She needs a favor. This summer can I take the kids and the dog for a few months? She rescued a greyhound for our kids. The dog is driving her crazy. I can take the kids but don't want the dog. She stomps her foot. The kids tell me the dog ate the television remote. The dog needs its own therapist. It is crazy. The kids are 19 and 22 years old, they should be able to be by themselves AND take care of the dog. "If you had only blah blah blah, they'd have learned about responsibility, blah blah blah." Mind wanders: What would it be like to be in a good relationship?

Sweet, like a pacific island. Pearl, I mean Stella, recently got re-married, and is just back from her honeymoon. I tell her to call me soon.

2:00 PM: Ethan McGrath

Ethan is the youngest patient I've ever had. Everything about him seems out of sorts, except for his hair, which is thick and straight. He has been brought to me because he told his teacher he thinks about suicide, and his parents want more than what he is getting in the therapy at school. Ethan is very specific when he fantasizes about flying and jumping off bridges. I fear I am helpless to prevent this. There are bridges all over Boston and his private school is located very close to them. His parents come in during the last fifteen minutes of his appointment each week. The mother is also bi-polar. Usually one of them cries. Ethan reminds me of my own brother, who once he took a handful of our mother's valium and washed it down with some Old Crow from the liquor cabinet. When the ambulance came, the red lights flashed and rotated throughout our living room. I remember because I counted the seconds by them. I just want to grab Ethan and either hug or shake him and say, "Please don't do it!" Sometimes, after he leaves, I cry too. My brother was only fourteen, for Christ's sake.

5:15 PM: Heavy traffic, listen to Jay Z
6:45 PM: Home

Meanwhile, outside the office...

Kate: There is so much people don't know

Kate had an abusive father, a crazy mother, a daughter who was stillborn, and the ability to see what's inside people when she uses her hands to heal them. Bill Sloan doesn't understand any of

25

this, and she lets him view her at her most basic—a wacky girl whose gift is mocked in the same manner as Big Foot, alien abduction, and The Bermuda Triangle. But when it comes to outward perception vs. inward peace and love, who is she to correct any of it? Everything can be fantastic, wonderful, and fabulous as far as she's concerned. She knows that by saying those things, the Universe gives her positive energy, which she tries to give to others.

In contrast, Bill Sloan couldn't see his hands if they were two inches from his face. It's going to take some time. She did the work on herself, and people should take the same responsibility in understanding themselves, as well as everyone they share the planet with. There is so much people don't know. Kate finds that people will love her no matter what. Whatever is going to happen is going to happen. Bill Sloan is going to need her when the shit hits the fan. Bill Sloan is blind to the world.

When her daughter was delivered with tiny lips and blue skin, Kate heard the words: *I love the sea; I die in the sea; I drown in the sea and the water*, and with that, her daughter was not born. "You will be with me always," Kate said, saving the knit cap, the blanket, a sweater, and a pair of shoes.

The shore Kate walks has smooth flat beach stones that warm the bottoms of her feet. Each year she buys her daughter a new bathing suit, and hears her daughter laughs in the sound of the seagulls, the breaking waves and the sand shifting in the ocean breeze. "What should we do? What should we do today, Baby Girl?" Kate asks her baby. "Today will be best day for it."

"I think we should swim." her tiny voice calls to her.

"Swim? I'm afraid I would drown."

"I think you should try."

"But it will hurt."

"It won't hurt, unless you think there are things out there meant to hurt you."

"Baby Girl, I love you more than all the sand on all the beaches everywhere. Most people only feel love as a single grain of sand."

"This is a beach full of them. Now go on."

And Kate walks into the water.

Thomas: A little slice of

It's only been half an hour since Melissa arrived from Las Angeles, and already she's climbing on top of him, and then they're thrashing under the sheets. He can see her ribs, her spine, and her sharp shoulder bones. The last time they were together there was more to her. Ten minutes later, he's distant. He's not used to sharing himself and his house with anyone, but she insisted on coming over. It's 10:00 in the morning, and as Thomas twists open a bottle of rum she says, "Thomas, perhaps you drink too much. Perhaps?"

He waits for the carbonation to settle from the coke in his glass before he answers, adds the rum. "Perhaps," he answers sadly. He knows he should be paying more attention to her, but his mind is on all the shit he has to get done today. He gives her a flimsy, apologetic hug. She has every reason to stand him against a wall and pelt him with oranges.

"Let's get breakfast, then go to the beach."

So they get up, get dressed, and go out. While they wait to be seated, Melissa places her feet on top of his. Her larger feet almost completely cover his. "I always thought what they said about foot size was true," she says. "But in your case, it's not. We fit in so many ways."

Another couple is listening in, and they smile and start up a conversation: *What's good here, we're visiting; we used to live in Sacramento, and before that, Pittsburgh.* Stuff Thomas couldn't care less about. When they ask what he does, he tells them he's in charge of electrically charged prodding sticks, and his job is to help kill cows. "I can't take you anywhere," Melissa frowns as the conversation flounders. To change the subject, she tells the newcomers that where she's from in California, people don't go out for breakfast.

27

"When they do, they say how great it is, but the breakfast places there really suck."

They wind up getting a table together, all four of them. The couple from Sacramento, and before that Pittsburgh, is enormously fat but Melissa is gracious. "Most people eat too fast, that's the problem." She tips her head at Thomas. "Him, definitely."

This is why he hates eating in front of people. She notices a lot about him. After breakfast she says he has "kind, crinkly eyes". Thomas fidgets, she notices too much about him.

When they get back to his house, Thomas sees blood on his sheets. "Are you having your... you know?"

"No, it's part of something I'm going through," she says.

He remembers the last time there was blood on his sheets, it was his—he'd given a beautiful mess of a girl a hard time, and she smacked him good. That blood was thick and red. In life, Thomas thinks, he's either pushing people away or pissing them off. He pisses himself off.

At the beach the waves are tumultuous from a hurricane that hit further south two days ago. They're safe on the shore. The town is broken down, no longer what it used to be, and most of the arcades that hosted the joy of young couples have become abandoned. In peeling paint their signs say "*Madam Psychic: Find out who you are!*" and "*This door for the time of your life!*" Everything seems to be falling apart. Melissa's bony fingers intertwine with his while she says she's going to miss him. She thanks him for seeing her during her visit east, which she calls her "furthest and final booty call." Then she tells him everything, collapses onto the bench in front of Mr. Happy Fried Dough, and breaks bigger than the waves out in the ocean.

Stella: Systematic Knowledge

Stella realized on her honeymoon that her second marriage was just another big mistake. Lying next to her on a beach in Spain, her new husband, Carlton, was dark and handsome; he even wore glasses. Stella found glasses very sexy. She closed her eyes for a second and imagined the man of her dreams, tossing his glasses aside so he could ravage her. Carlton was not that man. So who was? Carlton told her that "sex is something that can't be measured" and is perhaps not very clean. He was too calculated. Stella wanted more than percentages regarding ovulation and the velocity of ejaculation. She wanted emotional attachment. She wanted someone to be involved with her in every way. She wanted fantastic sex. She also wanted more kids, a new house and a different dog. She wanted to be a different person. She felt herself split.

Carlton thought more about wave–particle duality than anything else. "It's a central concept of quantum mechanics," he said as they lounged on their towels facing the crystal blue water. "It addresses the inadequacy of classical concepts like 'particle' and 'wave' in fully describing the behavior of objects." Stella didn't give a shit. She tuned him out, focusing on the sound of the ocean. Her breasts felt warm in her black bathing suit, and the waves *she* cared for, the ones that filled her body during sex, came in at perfect intervals, like the ocean's cool water against her shins.

Stella attempted to reach behind to spread sunscreen on her back, but her left arm only flapped like a seal's fin. Carlton didn't notice as men walked by and stared appreciatively at Stella. There was one muscular young man in particular Stella wanted to imagine walking over to assist her with spreading the lotion, hot and sticky between her shoulder blades; his hands firmly massaging her neck. Carlton stayed covered up in his crisp white shirt and pleated khakis; detached from it all.

Ethan: Bipolar

The moon is full, as the magnet pulls iron-filings from the beach where Ethan threw it into the sand. "I'd like to pull Mama through the keyhole," he says, "but Mama's sick."

"Mama *is* sick," his father says, "and you don't have a big enough magnet."

"Some days she's just a bed," Ethan says. "And other days she's running around like a fucking cartoon."

"Shhhhh, watch your mouth."

"Mama says it's okay to curse if you have something worth cursing about."

"There's always something worth cursing about."

"Look at the waves!" Ethan points. The moonlight dances on the crests, but a million flashlights can't fill a black hole. "I'd like to lie on 'em and ride to heaven," he says. He pulls the fine black sediment off the magnet with his fingers, then drops the magnet, cleans it then drops it again. "It's like growing hair," he says. "Hair that's tough to take care." His own hair is so thick that the ocean wind barely lifts it.

"Tough to take care of," his father corrects.

"Mom is taking her medicine, right?"

"Yeah, so she won't see heaven in some people, hell in others. We were lucky, we were only the earth last time. At least we were grounded."

"I hate when the ambulance comes for her." Ethan tosses the magnet into the ocean. "Someday we can all go together."

"Shit," the father says.

Chapter 2: Thursday, January 12

7:22 AM: Alarm clock
Hit snooze button three times
7:43: Wake up and walk the new dog

8:45 AM: Hanna Sertin

The first thing Hanna asks is if I have any later appointments. This is a less than an ideal opening, but it allows me to place my foot directly on her throat with my own remarks about commitment to therapy and why it is so important. "You in or out?" I want to shout. "This is supposed to be for you. It's filet mignon, so eat it!"

Then my foot is flipped off her throat and her foot landed directly on mine. "How could you not know?"

Should have seen that coming.

"You were his therapist," she goes on. "He had to have said something."

I reach for the box of tissues, but she's not crying; in fact, she knocks the box out of my hand. The bright flowers printed on the cardboard spin to the ground. I buy this brand because the office provides tissues in neutral gray boxes, and I feel that it's the little things like colorful boxes that make the difference in people's lives. "I'm talking to you and you give me tissues!"

"I just thought—"

"Fuck your tissues!"

"My issues?"

"Your tissues! Are you fucking deaf too?"

It's interactions like this that challenge my training and education but also poke holes in the bow of my boat of projected indifference. No, this is not going well.

Hanna keeps raging, her eyes bulging out whenever she says Brad's name. After I found out he killed himself, I could have either given or not given a shit; those were my options. In general, I've learned that if I give a shit, I might have been able to prevent disaster, even though my training teaches me, it's all on the patient and not on me. If I don't give a shit, I'm not bothered by anything. Clearly, I always conclude, it's easier to not give a shit.

Hanna reminds me of a younger version my ex-wife, Stella, especially when I manage to tune in, as Hanna says, "When I fucked his best friend right around this time. I needed to feel something." On and on she goes, and the hour passes slowly. She hasn't been this angry since her father died when she was fourteen. She feels she's been searching for replacements ever since.

"These are some of the things we can work on," I say.

"Later," she says.

10:15 AM: Kate

Kate, on the other hand, never gets mad, even though she had to wait an extra thirty minutes to see me. She says she meditated. She tells me that the Universe has a plan for us, and it's not just about time but it's also about location. I want to ask Kate why she sees me, but I'm just going to let it go. I theorize eventually she'll just get to her happy place and no longer need me. She can take her blue eyes, honey hair, and short denim skirt out of here. Can I help her get to that place? She's doing fine on her own.

Kate tells me she's fine having a sexual relationship with her neighbor. They both have children the same age. She thinks it's not going to work because he is too grounded, a financial advisor. She thinks he needs to think more in another dimension, like some of the more spiritual people she is also seeing. One of them is a Spiritual Advisor named Shami. Kate tells me she's enjoying feeling open and free. Whatever happens, happens. She smiles and looks at me and it's a glance held too long. She is not wearing a bra.

"So, what about the Spiritual Advisor?" I ask. "How is that relationship going?"

"We go to the woods and I cover him with leaves and twigs, and then climb on him wearing only my Buddha bangle necklace, until his beard begins to move and he cries out to the wolves."

"I see."

"It's very powerful. I feel much empowerment."

I nod.

"Perhaps see a woman," she says.

I tell her she seems open to nearly everything, and seeing a woman with similar goals and interests wouldn't be a bad idea. She tells me I misunderstood. She has her hands on the hem of her skirt, and slowly slides them down her thin thighs. She was thinking about *me* seeing a woman. I'm not sure how to respond, except to say that her time is up. She closes her eyes and sits until I have to interrupt it by placing a hand on her shoulder. She is soft. Her eyes seem to erupt when they open again.

10:50 AM: Thomas

Thomas has picked the wrong woman again; turns out she's married. He also dumped the woman he was seeing before when he found out she had cancer. "It's shit like this," he says, "that makes me realize I'm not getting anything from you. You should give me some advice, for Christ's sake."

"I've given you advice," I say, "You just choose not to listen."

He pulls an inhaler out of his plaid button down. "Listen? Fuck it." He takes a puff. "This helps me," he says.

"Therapy doesn't work like that," I say. "It's a longer process."

"I don't believe in longer processes, doctor."

33

"I'm not a doctor."

"Oh, and her husband found out. She fucking told him, so he got the number off her cell and called me. He said he was going to come after me. Well then, come the fuck on."

"What did you do?" I go back to open ended but I still draw the question out with a Dr. Phil accent, purely out of boredom.

"Gave the guy my address."

"Why? Do you feel the need to punish yourself?"

"No, I feel the need to punish others."

"What about the woman from California who has cancer?"

"I don't think I can see her. I can't. She gets too upset. I tapped that and now it's over."

Thomas pushes his stringy hair off his forehead, runs his finger over one of the scars above his eyes. I'd like to add to them.

11:30 AM: Lunch—sandwich, apple, juice box
Think about Kate naked in the woods
Don't think

1:00 PM: Stella/Pearl

While she's in my office she wants to be called Pearl, and she wants to call me Dr. Sloan. I tell her Pearl is not her name and she can call me Bill. She says she was going to use Stella, but since I don't talk to Stella, she has to be Pearl. These are the "terms". I don't like terms.

"If I don't want to talk to Stella, then what makes you think I want to talk to Pearl?" I ask.

"I'm smart, William," she says.

I have her figured out. I know her two leverage points. Leverage Point One: She's not going to pay the bill for our appointment. Fine. She's not paid bills before. She has skipped the oil, cable and internet bills in the past, but still went shopping a-plenty. "When one of our parents die we can be out of debt," she once said when we were married. Great. I hoped it would be hers.

34

Leverage Point Two (when all else fails try guilt): "When was the last time you saw the kids?"

"The kids are young adults, and I expect them to have lives. I don't need to see them all the time. They're happy playing video games, and celebrating free room and board, plus allowance."

"They're always around."

"Kick them out and make them find a job." I know she won't do this, even though having the kids at her house makes her feel crowded and freaked out, because if the kids left she'd be forced to be alone with Carlton.

When her leverage points fail, I know an argument is coming. It's the oncoming storm. When you know someone as well as I do her, you realize before the fight even begins, something powerful is going to happen, it's as obvious as black clouds and thunder.

"Don't expect me to pay for this!" she says loudly.

"If you're not going to pay, then I can no longer see you."

I know everyone in the waiting room can hear her loud parade of language, but I've heard it so many times that it doesn't bother me. In this barrage she mentions I shouldn't have that woman--my "girlfriend" waiting in the waiting room. *Huh?* She leaps and leaves the room, and I hear the cannon shot of a door slam violently, but this time it wasn't even as close to the loudest I've ever heard.

4:00 PM: Ethan

He's the last appointment of the day, and today he is very dramatic. He got scared when one of the girls was dancing at school during recess. He said the dancing was a message, only directed at him. I told him I would call his school and find out about this. The Waysworth School is one of the best private schools in the state, but they feel they should be handling everything on their own, and go on the defensive if parents try getting involved. They have a very good school psychologist, which is an integral part of the program. It was the first thing they ever said to me. The very good school psychologist told his mother that too much information will split

35

the boy's alliances. I'm not sure if I believe what his mother says as she also tells me, the doors of the school are made out of gold. I know the school is trying to manipulate her. His father says Ethan has been doing well despite his mother's hospitalizations. I'm worried about Ethan. He should be on different medication. Waysworth won't return any calls on this.

5:00 PM: Leave office; discover that Kate is sitting on the floor of the waiting room. Ask her why, but she doesn't answer, just smiles
5:10 PM: Commute takes one hour; listen to Kanye
6:10 PM: Home. Fix drink, pat dog. Feed dog (should never have said yes)

Meanwhile, outside the office...

Hanna: What do you do when you're seeing his best friend?

Hanna and Randy's relationship is like a warm breeze across the field of Comealy's Farm on a day so lazy that no one wants to do anything. The heat is overbearing. The hay is baled and there is no escape from it, even in the shade of some of the large blocks of stacked hay placed there. Two hours till sundown. A fly may buzz up and play in your sweat.

Hanna pulls off his cowboy hat, wipes the perspiration from his face with her hand, then combs her fingers through his light brown wavy hair. Hanna repeats again that she and Brad had been unhappy for a while, and even though they had a kid together, they haven't spoken for months. She and Randy are still sneaking around for appearances sake.

At the funeral, Hanna played the part of the widow until it was time to leave. Then they made angry love. She said people wanted to blame her. Randy thinks, *Maybe they should blame me. He was my best friend.* Last time he saw Brad, he was angry, and crying out intermittently, like a traffic light flashing on and off. Randy decided not to feel bad that he was fucking Brad's ex. They'd broken up months ago, so why not?

He kicks one of his boots over the other as he sits on the ground. They're only twenty minutes from Boston via Route 2 West, but this feels like a world away. Young Pete Comealy died here from heat stroke. Hanna often sits here under a bale of hay, twirls the straw in her fingers. Randy comes here and sits in silence.

Kate's Mother: Laurie Lou's food pantry

When Kate ran down the stairs her mother's chanting became louder: *My-T Fine, My-T Fine, My-T Fine, My-T Fine, My-T Fine, My-T Fine, My-T Fine.*

Kate had to leave, she had to leave this house and it was not because of her crazy mother. That was the least of her problems. If a box was out of place in the pantry, her mother straightened it. Not a big deal for Kate. Sometimes her mom would straighten all day if she was really tense. Again, no big deal. Who is a teenager girl to talk to when her father comes into her room during the day or at night, and when her mother is the way she is? Certainly her mother would only rearrange more or chant louder if she knew.

One thing that did happen was Kate's bright blue eyes had been replaced by the flat blank stare; her innocence seemed to no longer exist. *My-T Fine, My-T Fine,...Chef-Boy-R-Deee. My-T Fine, My-T Fine, My-T Fine, My-T Fine, My-T Fine, My-T Fine, My-T Fine. Chef. Chef-Chef Boy-R-Dee.*

Her father was in her room, unbuckling his belt, when Kate made the decision to leave. She had a friend she could stay with, and when her mother realized what had happened, maybe she would go back on her medication. On medication, she'd be able to do something–anything–because when you're sick, you need to do something. Kate felt nauseous all the time, along with the blockage of facts, the mental sickness, which was growing in her from the trauma.

37

What happened? Kate used to love her father and his spontaneity, and could always count on him to do something loving; a tap on the head, reach for her hand, a kiss on the cheek. She was just a little girl then.

Mother stepped out of the pantry when she heard Kate come down the stairs. Kate ran to reach the bottom quickly while her father was still at the top. Kate's hands shook, and her father's were tense, as he pulled hard to tighten his belt. Kate saw the blood rush into her mother's face when her husband looked at her.

Kate slammed the door and heard her mother scream seven times, a number her mother found lucky. By leaving, she had hope but sadly imagined her mother running back into the pantry again and again forever. It was the best and most organized food inventory in the country. *My-T Fine, My-T Fine, My-T Fine, My-T Fine.*

Thomas: Calculating women

The world birth rate at the time of Thomas's birth was one baby every 4.2 seconds. Normally, there are a few more male births than female births, so Thomas concludes that there's about 8.42 seconds every time a female baby is born. If Thomas sleeps with one woman on the average of every three months then there are 7.884 million seconds in that time period. In that three month period, 936,342 female babies will be born. The probability of winning more than 10,000 dollars in Mega Millions is one chance in 689,064.85. Thomas thinks screwing women is much easier than worrying about all those Ping-Pong balls.

Stella: The floundered

After divorcing Bill, Stella found internet dating was like fishing in waters emptied of good or tasty fish. She still tried to catch some rotten ones—just to cut off their heads. The dates were mostly with married men trying to disguise themselves as being available. It was a transparent ruse, but Stella played along; what the hell, she was single.

The phone vibrated on her drive into town. It was one of the pissed-off wives, sounding like an angry slam poetry recitation. Stella didn't know what to tell her. "You really need to figure out how to end it," she finally said.

That same day, Cindy, the woman Bill had an affair with, was stopped half-way in the crosswalk. Stella had a wicked thought of pushing down hard on the accelerator. Her foot tensed and she suddenly realized the car actually was traveling at a high rate of speed. Stella stomped the brake and the car locked up, its rear end moved the same way hers did when men began to pound her from behind. The car stopped short of the crosswalk leaving rubber and harsh smelling plume of blue smoke in its wake.

"I thought we could still be friends!" Cindy shouted at her from between the parallel lines.

Ethan: Toys, music, creativity

When Ethan was five, he made his toy cars smash into one another. He screamed in joy when they hit. Then he'd get up and click on his playlist of mp3 songs that he'd been downloading since age four. He loved Bob Dylan. He loved Springsteen. He loved Rancid. He sat still, attentive to the songs. "What do you think he is saying here, Ethan?" his father asked. Ethan shrugged his shoulders. *He's his mother's child*, his father thought.

When Ethan was eight, he'd run around the house while the music played. He jumped on the couch, flailing hands on air guitar. From the couch he leapt straight onto his play table, where he liked to paint. The table collapsed but Ethan kept playing. "I'm Pete Townsend," he cried, smashing the air guitar to pieces. "I'm Who, I'm Who, and I'm whooooooo?"

"I don't know who you are," said the father, as he wrapped him up in his arms, until Ethan began to settle.

"I'm The Who," Ethan said and laughed. "in Cincinnati."

His father had no idea how Ethan picked up on that reference. The Who in Cincinnati? *Wasn't it thirty years ago when they played there and the people got trampled?* Ethan was a sponge.

Today the school calls but the father is not surprised. Nothing in the world surprises him anymore. There are some pictures Ethan had drawn. "Would you like to have a look, Mr. McGrath?" The father doesn't think he can. His wife is in the hospital. It's been three weeks; she's getting better but Ethan is getting worse. Denial is not working. *What is the school going to do about this? Have a meeting?* He thinks it's wise to solve one thing at a time. First make sure his wife is stabilized, and then work on Ethan. Ethan may need to go somewhere to have special attention. He feels completely on his own, but he took this on when he chose to marry a woman he affectionately described as "fiery" to his friends. Now he has no friends. Now he feels that the hill he is climbing is Mount Everest, and his oxygen tank is empty.

Chapter 3: Thursday, January 19

7:22 AM: Alarm clock interrupts dream about being bitten by a dog
Hit snooze button three times
Feel the hangover
Think about being famous like Dr. Phil
7:53: Get up

8:50 AM: Hanna

Hanna keeps her appointment but yawns through most of it. Her hands are very demure, covering her open mouth. She says she thinks that she thinks too much. She doesn't want to think now because it's too early. I try to get her going. I ask if she had been thinking of Brad. She says she thought about Brad's therapy, but mostly is curious if Brad mentioned her during those times. She wants to know the answer to some questions: Was Brad angry about their split? I answer, honestly: I didn't know there was a split.

She talks quicker and gestures more. She says Brad liked his last psychologist, Dr. Sullivan, better. She made him go to him when there seemed to be issues. I laugh to myself, hope I'm not grinning when I wonder if she meant tissues again. It's moments like these that keep my Thursdays moving.

She doesn't know how Brad ended up with me. She hadn't even heard of me. I'd like to tell her I got the referral, after Dr. Sullivan had a heart attack, and then Brad's case got assigned to me.

I'd like to tell her that during our first meeting Brad sat and talked without stopping. He had attended Dr. Sullivan's funeral after Sullivan's office called to reschedule. Brad found out the details on his own. Sullivan's receptionist told Brad he had to discontinue his services. Brad thought it was his fault. When Brad called back they said Sullivan was on medical leave and asked if he would like an appointment in six weeks with someone else? Six weeks was a long time, he said. He needed to talk now because his girlfriend never wanted to see him again, and six weeks was too long to sit and think. So they asked if he would like someone else in two months. "No thanks," he said, "he wanted someone today."

This, of course, was the split he'd been talking about; the one between him and Hanna. He'd never talked about Hanna, but he had talked a lot about Sullivan, which seemed to be a pain trigger.

Hanna pounds the chair's arm. I don't know who she is mad at, but I don't want to ask any questions to clarify. I haven't been listening very well since it's early for me too. I'm staring at her, though. When I become a TV star they can edit some of the not paying attention shit out, but they will probably leave the eye contact in for the cut away shots.

10:00 AM: Kate

Kate says interesting people are everywhere if you open yourself up to them. The Universe sends them to you. When she lived in San Francisco, she owned a black Labrador and they would beg for money. Having the dog helped her get more money. "That's what it was good for," she says.

She says people get dogs to recreate their childhood. "People either want a dog because their families had one, or they want a dog because they were never allowed to have one." Kate got her dog from a man called Lucky, whose name was not an apt description of him at all. The name odd for a forty-one year-old bearded man with shabby, brown hair, cut-off shirtsleeves, and liver spots covering his arms and hands. Kate remembered Lucky's name was tattooed across the knuckles of his right hand in a dense, childlike block print. It looked to be something Lucky had done himself with a Swiss army knife and ballpoint ink.

Kate then asks me if I was interested in how Lucky was named. "Go on," I say, really not caring about how lucky or unlucky Lucky was. Kate says Lucky arrived three months early from his mother's womb, weighing only forty-nine ounces. His parents were only allowed to touch him with sterile gloves, as he lay in an incubator. Since he'd been born so early, they hadn't been prepared. There was no crib, no freshly painted room, and no name selected. At some point during the first week of his life, his tired father said to his tired mother, "We're just so lucky that he survived".

I ask her if Lucky had been a good friend, and she says, "In a way, yeah, because when you're down and out, it's the street people who accept you the most. Anyway, he died on the street." Kate stayed for a month then hitchhiked back to the East Coast.

Kate says that at yoga class this week she was filled with love, and wanted to give it to everyone. "There are spiritual means to solve everything," she tells me.

"Why is she here if love is everywhere?" I wonder. I ask her if she is working, and she answers, "Work? What's that?"

The receptionist, whose name I don't know, sent me an e-mail explaining that Kate stayed in the waiting room and met all of my patients. When I ask Kate about it, she says people don't understand her. "I was just giving them love. There was this woman who was upset. She asked if you were seeing me." *Stella.* I nod and let her keep talking.

"Another asked me if I was a shaman. I told them I can help people just like Bill does." Kate says she wanted to help the next guy that came in after her but they didn't have a chance to talk. She would take him to yoga.

"Who would you take to yoga? Thomas?"

Kate says, "Namaste."

43

10:55 AM: Thomas

Thomas begins by asking me if I've ever done yoga. I tell him no, but lots of people have derived benefits from the practice of –
"Why does that chick Kate see you, is she crazy?"

I tell him I'm not allowed to discuss other patients with him.

"What if I happen to be interested in her?"

"First tell me what happened to the married woman." I notice he has a black eye. Discreetly, I write on my note pad: *Looks like Thomas got his ass kicked* and draw a smiley next to it.

"The married woman didn't work out because of complications," he says. "One, she was married and two, she didn't want to give up her husband. And she doesn't want to try fixing the marriage with counseling." He goes on to say that he doesn't believe therapy works anyway, and that I'm just happy taking his money.

When I ask Thomas where that leaves him, he shrugs. "Beats me." I hate that. I'd like to *beat him*. Instead I just say, "Hmmmm." He says, "Hmmmm" right back, and snickers.

He needs to try to help himself. I'm not helping him and somehow I'm ok with that. In general, I don't want to help people all that much, and I really don't want to help Thomas.

"Just gimme her phone number, I know you got it."

"You know I can't do that."

"Fine. I'll ask her on my way out." He stands, towers over me. "I can do that, right? That's ok, right?"

"See you next week, when I won't be able to help you," I say.

11:50 AM: Lunch–sandwich, apple, juice box
Tell Kate she can't stay in the waiting room after her appointment is over

3:45 PM: Stella (Still insists on being called Pearl)

Pearl's appointment was at 3:00, but she's late because she wanted Carlton to come, and it took a long time to argue about it. She says during the honeymoon she knew it was over between her and Carlton. I ask what she plans on doing about that, and she says she has no idea.

"You know," I say, "Maybe if Carlton came in also…"

She's silent. I tell her I'm more than willing to speak with Carlton alone, but not with her there, and certainly not with her as Stella. She says that is so typical of me. "Perhaps," I say. I don't even think Dr. Phil would be able to pull this one off even though it would make great television. "How are the kids?" I ask. "They'd like to make an appointment with you as well," she says. "And thanks for taking the dog."

4:00 PM: Ethan

Ethan says a lady touched him outside the office. I ask him if he was in the bathroom and whether his parents around. He tells me it's the same lady that touched him in the office last week, but this time it was outside. I head out to the reception area. There is no sign of Kate but I motion Ethan's mother to come in.

Ethan's mother tells me that it's all right. She tells me the woman has great powers.

I say, "I don't think you should let someone you don't really know touch your child."

Ethan's mom tells me to get off it. She is very protective of her son, and she had allowed the woman to touch her head too.

"What happened?"

"A great sense of calm and love overtook me. It was as if I was sitting in a great big silence. I was very sleepy after."

"What about you, Sport?" I ask Ethan.

"I don't like sports."

I try not to smile, but I can't help it. "Okay, then. How did it make you feel when the lady touched your head?"

"I wanted to take off my clothes."

"Ethan!" his mother shrieks.

"No, this is good," I say. "It's all perfectly normal in boys. It may just be a reflex action, you know when arousal happens."

45

"When's the last time you had your reflexes checked, Bill?" she asks me. "I think you need an overhaul."

"So, how is he doing?" I ask her.

She bursts into tears and I pull a tissue out of the box.

5:13 PM: Dan (last name unknown)

Outside on the sidewalk Kate is waiting with a young man. His arms are tattooed and his lips are covered in scabs. He has a dent in his forehead. "His name is Dan. He's your next patient," she says.

"He doesn't have an appointment," is my response.

5:15 PM: Extra heavy traffic, listen to NPR (sort of not listen)
6:45 PM: Home. Feed dog and take him for a long walk. Fix a drink
Start a Facebook fan page: William Sloan, Therapist
Google "Hanna Sertin" and "Kate Hummingbird Warrior." Find nothing

Meanwhile, outside the office...

Randy: After Hanna left a note

After reading Hanna's note—*I can't see you anymore*—Randy walks around a block, down a street, then across the city until it is dusk. The buildings look wet, lit by a dim yellow tint that contrasts the black shadows covering Randy; their darkness forces him into his car. He goes south; drives two days and doesn't stop anywhere until he hits the warmth of Daytona Beach. The morning brings a dark purple hue to the sky, which slowly fades into sunny brilliant brightness. Dark water is visible beyond the breakers which become bigger upon his approach. Randy feels so overwhelmed by their beauty, he feels he could sink into them, as if they are made of the soft tar his car is now parked on.

He feels limp and hot, the sleepiness like the movement of the tide; or the gulls versus the wind. And his eyes hurt against the bright-colored bikinis on bleached white skin, and the kites, siren red against a crisp blue sky. There is the string leading down to an empty beach chair, where Randy looks for her, just in case. The hot sun is something he can't run from, so he steps into the cool ocean, which clenches his body like he's on a dentist chair, getting a filling without Novocain, from a dentist using a very slow drill.

He lies back on the beach, pushing his thick hair against a sand pillow, and falls asleep immediately, to dream a shallow dream with the only thing keeping him from deeper sleep is the sweat in his eyes. There's a set of gray and silver heels in the corner, followed by a thin-strapped purse, a spread open unbuttoned yellow dress, and a soft cupped black bra. The line of successive items lead all the way to her toes, where she slips out of her silk and lace panties.

His hand moves until she is saturated, the water releases in time to the beat of his fingers. He waits for the sign, careful not to miss it: her lips will quiver slightly, followed by her mouth pulsing open, then closing—quickly, once, maybe twice, this gasping, until her forehead creases and her legs tense against the mattress; twitching and uncoiling in syncopation with her mouth. A stretching sound that leaves her all the way open.

When she starts, he says, "Good girl, you're such a good girl," and that's when she shoots like a sparkler on Independence Day, the clear liquid expels in spasm, like an old school water fountain, and then slowly the streaming fades. He pushes inside her without waiting any longer, but before it happens, she says, "Do anything you want."

Randy jars awake from the dream, the heat and the sweat making him crazy. He tries to return to the Hanna dream, but dreams instead about a brown dog, because when you're stuck, some writer once said, put a dog in there. He's correct—if life's a poem or story, a soft chocolate lab would make a lot of people feel really damn good. But people, in general, never think this way.

47

Kate: Somewhere in New Jersey, Kate's first boyfriend, Johnny, remembers her

Years ago, Kate scooped ice cream at Jersey Licks while Johnny waited outside for her on a concrete step, smoking dope. Ice Cream Scooper was not an occupation Johnny's family would approve of, as they preferred him dating more professional women—teacher, nurse, CEO of a company. Women you wouldn't find workin a summer job on the Jersey Shore. Sometimes Johnny felt the same way, but who was he to talk?

Johnny had failed out of a fine business school, and now worked for a management company providing upkeep on vacation homes: stopping a leaky faucet here and gutting a toilet there. The money was good because he was always needed… immediately. That's how he and Kate met—her washing machine broke and her crazy mother was going away. Johnny came, fixed it, and after her mother left, he came back and stayed.

Everything about her, from her toned ice cream scooping forearms to her silky tanned skin, turned him on. She had the best lips in the world, mostly because of what came out of them. Tonight she said, "Johnny Cakes, I like it when you wait for me, it gives me a purpose." Johnny's frozen heart melted when she ran out from behind the counter with a few scoops of Butter-Crunch. Thawed, he noticed he'd put on quite a few pounds this summer.

So there he was, waiting outside Jersey Licks, when he felt a dull pain in his thigh. It was the midget girl he'd dated once, a few months ago, stabbing him with a plastic knife. They'd met and chatted on a dating site and she'd never mentioned that she was only three feet tall. From the photo on her dating profile, he knew she had a pretty face, but when she pulled up to his house, he was shocked to see her waddle up to the door. The whole scene had freaked him out, everything from him lifting her up into his Jeep, to her falling out when they got to the restaurant. He acted as a gentleman, listened to her talk, drove her back to her car and said he'd call her soon. But he never did. And he ignored all her emails, texts, and calls.

When he told Kate about the stabbing, she acted jealous and possessive of him. He had to joke about hiding the plastic knives before she became herself again. That was when he knew she was in love with him.

That night after work, Kate was sticky, sweaty, and caramel sweet. When she slid into bed, she gently touched the cut on Johnny's leg and he leaned over to kiss her.

She held up her hand. "You haven't brushed your teeth yet. I don't want to get it all mixed up with my clean mouth." Johnny didn't want to wait so he kissed her anyway. Most men would act that way with a girl as beautiful as Kate.

Kate had Friday off, and they walked the boardwalk. Most of the businesses had left—it was like a ghost town. They liked being ghosts. Johnny and Kate held hands and hardly spoke. When they did it was short observations, "Look at the black dog!" or "You know, I don't dream at all anymore," but also "I love you."

Johnny said, "If you don't have dreams, you can disappear completely." The black dog ran back to a man wearing a wide-brimmed fishing hat.

"I could live in a dream," Kate said.

"That dog seems to know something." Johnny said as they approached a shack with a sign that said *Wonderwind's Tarot Readings*. Kate wanted to go in, but Johnny didn't, so he waited until she came out jumping.

"Wonderwind said my life will be new and different and an unexpected situation will enter it," Kate said. "Isn't that exciting?"

"Is this change coming right away?"

"The woman said I should wait for a man…"

"Then what?"

"You'll see Johnnycakes. You'll see."

49

A week later, Kate said the man in a brimmed hat walked into Jersey Licks and told her he was a professional photographer. He told her she had a lot of promise. "People get discovered all the time," Kate told Johnny. "Maybe it's my turn."

"I've heard about people like this."

"Johnny, you don't know. He says he can get me into magazines."

"When are you going?"

"Tuesday."

Johnny felt he had to say something, even a lie. "It may be hard for me to go to New York during the week."

"It's in Secaucus, but he said he was sending a limousine for me. Imagine? Just for me."

"Like Channel 9 Secaucus?"

"Johnny, this could be a huge thing for me."

"Who the fuck goes to Secaucus?"

"Me, and something important will happen. Nothing important has ever happened to me. It's just like Wonderwind predicted!" Kate's chin slouched down, her lips pouted.

They walked down to the beach as the seagulls cried overhead. Johnny tried to talk to her: "At some point we need to figure it all out. I need to get a better job and start making money for us. That is, if you think we have a future?"

Kate pretended to toss food into the air as the seagulls yapped and squawked.

"Did you hear what I said?" Johnny asked but the birds were shrieking and Kate was laughing.

Johnny's original plan was to meet Kate later on Tuesday in Secaucus, but work forced him to leave even later than he wanted. He drove to Secaucus and knocked at the address she'd given him, but there was no answer. He lit a joint and drove around. Maybe Kate would be home. Maybe the interview led to something real. Johnny felt could live with that, and decided to head back. On the way home he had almost convinced himself Kate *was* going to be famous, until he saw her crazy mother's car pulling into the driveway. "Did you put her up to that?" her mother accused Johnny from the porch. Johnny stopped in his tracks, a chill shooting down his spine. Johnny shook his head.

"What are you doing here?" Johnny asked, before realizing how stupid he sounded.

"I got a call Kate had assaulted a police officer," she replied. "And she's also being held on a lewdness charge. Mighty fucking fine." The end of her cigarette glowed intensely, fueled from a long pull. "I want you out of my house."

"Lewdness?" Johnny asked.

"Nude modeling," she said as she exhaled some smoke. "I want you out of my house!"

Johnny got back in his car and drove back to Secaucus, imagining Kate in jail–desperate, sad, and happy to see him, their hands pressed together against the glass. But the police wouldn't let him see her. So he went back to the beach and sat on a bench near the ice cream shop, smoking joint after joint. He saw what looked to be the man's black dog walking all alone, staring at him. The dog pointed his nose in the direction of the boardwalk. Johnny knew dogs couldn't communicate but he decided to sort it all through with Wonderwind.

When Johnny entered, the woman named Wonderwind said, "Wash your hands, they feel sticky."

In the bathroom there were twenty different kinds of fragrant miniature soaps. Johnny assumed each one was for some magical, purpose but noticed the one he washed with said *Holiday Inn* on it.

"You don't have any powers, do you?" he confronted Wonderwind after coming out of her back room.

"Oh, yes I do," she said calmly. "I can tell you what people will do and where they are going."

"Did you know Kate was going to wind up in jail?"

"Kate? Who is Kate?"

"Kate! She came to you about a week ago."

51

"Oh, yes, works in an ice cream shop, very pretty, with a Johnny who fixed things. Very unlucky boy. You are him?"

"I am him," Johnny confirmed grimly.

"Sit, sit," she laughed. "I'll do yours for free." She motioned Johnny to a table and pulled out some cards. "Jail, huh? I told her to be ready because out-of-nowhere her life would change. I didn't think she would end up jail. She must have taken a wrong turn. People tend to view things the way they want to view things. Like here, like what's happening now. Listen carefully. This is what I see for you. She pointed to a card with a picture of five stars glowing in a snowy sky, and a church in the distance. "Yes, the Five of Pentacles...I see something financial going on, perhaps something going on with a relationship..."

"No, things are fine there."

"Financial issues or a spiritual bankruptcy going on? Did Kate rob someone?"

"No, it was assault."

"Yes, yes...I see now. Yes, the Two of Swords. You've reached a time of decision, because of what just happened. You are frozen; you don't know what to do....but you need to make a decision. Kate may not be the woman you envisioned for your future, but quit running back and forth. You need to go to her quickly before she disappears...if you get there in time then everything which has happened will be forgotten. If not, you will not see her again. Where is she now?"

"Secaucus."

"You should move there."

"Does it really say that?"

"Yes."

Johnny sat there as dumb as a pat of butter on steamed rice.

"GO!" Wonderwind commanded.

Johnny stood. On the wall was a photo of the man in the brimmed hat, posing with Wonderwind on their wedding day.

"Holy shit," he yelled as the black dog jumped out from under the table and almost made him fall.

In Secaucus the police told Johnny that Kate's mother had come for her. He never saw her again.

Thomas: At his house

Thomas' lovemaking with the married woman had been savage. They fucked the way a knife sliced through a red bell pepper, finished as the onions caramelized, then burnt. The sides of the road back to work were now ice. One slip from the tire's firm edge onto the bald tread would send them through a guardrail. "We can't do this anymore," she said. He thought, *Tears never freeze*.

Stella: Before their divorce

Stella and Bill's house was overrun with shopping bags full of clothes piled higher than the children's heads.

"Can you do these returns to the Gap?" Stella asked as he came in.

"What? No."

"I do all the shopping, William, you do nothing!" Stella yelled. "Here are the receipts." She held out a shoebox. There were an uncomfortable number of receipts held together by paper clips. Each had multiple staples holes and pen marks.

Bill took the box. He crammed all The Gap bags into his car. It took eight trips to pack the car and another eight from the car to the store, to get all the stuff to the Customer Service desk. It was the first time ever, that Bill thought he could do better than this. He could *be* better too. Bill had something to show the world, and the entire world would find out soon enough, but he had to get out of this.

The manager shook her head. "This stuff is four years old. We can only give you 10% of what you paid."

53

She looked at the piles of clothes; identical outfits in different colors, identical outfits in different sizes, same color hats in different sizes and identical shirts with pictures of different dogs on the front. The dogs all had their tongues hanging out, mocking him. The most ridiculous thing of all was the 20 green children's lumberjack winter hats with ear flaps. All these items had been purchased within a month of one another.

The manager put $1,028.72 back on the credit card. Bill called the company and found out that the balance on the card was ten times that. Driving home, he realized he was about to let things go.

Ethan: Windows

Every day Mrs. McGrath stood by the window and saw a small dog being walked in the afternoon. The Chihuahua was sending messages to their boy. Ethan's father told his wife this was nonsense. Dogs do not send messages to humans.

"A Cocker Spaniel told me you were cheating on me," she said.

"Excuse me?"

"But those dogs are known to lie," she continued. "So I asked a German Sheppard."

"Honey, things are *not right* again."

"THAT dog, the Sheppard, said everything was good. So, I'm not worried."

"I *am* worried. I counted your pills."

"Soon, you won't. The Pit Bull says you are a strong candidate for arthritis in your hands."

The next time Ethan stood by the window, he saw a police car's blue lights flashing outside. His father asked him into his bedroom, and closed the door behind him; told him not to come out until things settled. Ethan heard a lot of things being thrown around the kitchen and the living room. Glass was being smashed. Ethan touched the window pane. Would he be next?

CONFIDENTIAL CLIENT RECORDS

Central Services: 25 Saniford Street, Boston, Ma, 02114

Client Profile: GRADY SIMON

Grady Simon is a forty-one year old gay male, who suffers from a Nervous Disorder and insomnia. In the past he has received treatment for skin infections and rashes caused by a high frequency of scratching. Grady works a high-stress job as a television developer and producer. Upon intake, Grady had a difficult time retaining his focus and kept jumping from his problems to the schedules and ratings of programs. Grady would like to get mentally and physically healthy and lose weight, but he states that his job prevents that, and claims he would do a lot better if he could retire. Grady has no plans to retire, as he is not financially stable. He worries about being fired. Grady's employer, WHDH in Boston, contacted Central Services after Grady told them he was seeking a therapist. WHDH wants Grady to be productive at work, and be able to deal with stressors. Also, they want him to remain in a "decent state of mind" in the event his employment is terminated. They want him to be "less sweaty and blotchy".

Referral Source: Grady was referred to this office by Central Services, by his employer's health plan as a preventative measure, based on his stress and health level. Assigned to Bill Sloan.

Chapter 4: Thursday, January 26

7:22 AM: Alarm clock
Move dog off chest
Hit snooze button three times
Dream about having a TV gig
7:53: Get up

8:56 AM: Hanna

Hanna had a birthday. She celebrated by going for a walk with her son and thinking about all the people she knew who had died. "Happy fucking birthday," she said. Her mom wanted to take her out. She refused. She didn't receive any cards. She wrote a break-up note to Randy instead. That was her card. I tell her someone should have taken her out.

It is a common practice to blow up your life after someone's suicide. Sometimes people schedule themselves to be busy all the time, but in reality it's impossible to stay one hundred percent busy. Hanna wants to discontinue her therapy. She stands, ready to go.

I shake my head and hold up my hand. "I think you should stay."

"I don't know if I want to."

"I want you to."

She tells me she can't commit to this. She may not be back. The last two men in her life didn't like me. Do I care about that?

"No." I don't give a single shit. I thought I had a good rapport with Brad, but only met Randy once–at the funeral when he acted like an asshole. I gave him the benefit of the doubt and chalked it up to grief.

Hanna says she always gets involved with the wrong guys. They're all mean and abusive. I tell her breaking up with Randy was a good move. She nods, and says she can't see me anymore. Not here. I ask if she is breaking up with me too. She laughs, says, "You think someone should take me out?" She'd like to have a drink without all this therapy since it didn't work out for Brad, and nothing seems to be working for her. I ask her if she's positive she is done with therapy. She says, yes. I tell her I'll have a drink with her. She says she still may be mad at me.

10:00 AM: Kate

"We're heeeeere," Kate says. She's brought Thomas with her. She says I should see them in that way. The way I see them is: she's a fruity nutcake and he's a non-committal jerk.

"Okay, but you guys only get an hour and I will charge you both," I say. Kate asks just what I'm up to. I explain why I'm billing that way, but I don't tell her the real reason is because I can. Kate says, no, it's not about the billing; she senses something else. Then she says a woman has entered my life and I should do something like sit in a field with her. I tell Kate we should get down to business, but she says I'm cute and we should all go out together, the four of us. I tell her it's a bad idea. Kate says don't worry, she knows all about it, and also not to worry because she knows all about Thomas too. She has been giving him spiritual treatment and sharing love. I ask her what she knows. Kate says she knows about my dog. "You love your dog," she says, "You looooove him." She shows pure joy when she holds the "o."

I tell Kate she should consider opening her own practice, and if she does, would she please start with Thomas. It would free up some of my day. Just remember to open it far away from my office. Kate says that's a fabulous idea and she's still willing to have therapy with me if that were to happen.

Thomas says Kate should still come here as there would be no reason to stop coming. Kate asks why that would be so. "It could get sticky," Thomas says. "If something were to happen to us," he laughs an evil laugh.

Kate says, "Huh?" Thomas shrugs. "Oh, I knew that," Kate says.

"Is it too late to keep my eleven o'clock?" Thomas asks.

11:01 AM: Thomas

I confront Thomas about seeing my clients, about how it might affect their treatment. Thomas says he started seeing her first in the waiting room, so he thought it was okay. Then he tells me he's no longer seeing her that way, only professionally.

"So," I say, "what gives? You used to be fine once every three months but now you are landing and tossing them like a bunch of underweight fish."

"You're just mad I was with her."

"No, I'm not. I don't see my clients."

"That's not what Kate says. She kind of likes you, you know; says you're different."

"It would be unethical."

Thomas laughs loudly at the word. "Kate taught me a lot of things. A lot of things. In the middle of doing her I asked her what we were doing and do you know what she said?"

"No, what?"

"She said we're just having fun."

I tell Thomas since I saw him earlier, he could leave now or I'd have to bill him twice. "Fuck that," he says.

If I could quit this job, I would.

11:50 AM: Lunch—sandwich, apple, juice box
Wonder what the hell just happened

59

1:00 PM: Pearl

Pearl says things are going better with Carlton. He's doing a lot more around the house. He and the kids went mini-golfing and then to Chuck-E-Cheese's.

"How old are the kids?" I ask.

"They're your fucking kids you should know."

"Okay, Pearl, I'm just playing along. Damned if I do, damned if I don't."

"The kids are 19 and 22."

"Don't you think they're a bit old for Chuck-E-Cheese's?"

"Yes, they wanted to play the games but then they got kicked out. Turns out they were testing Carlton to see what he would do with their bad behavior."

"So, Pearl, you're a therapist now too?"

"I know more than you do about our kids! How old are they? Jesus, Bill!"

"Stella, kids that age shouldn't be testing their mother's new husband!"

"Am I Stella or Pearl?"

"I don't know *who* you are anymore. So tell me what happened at Chuck-E-Cheese's."

"Billy was drunk and pulled Chuck-E's head off. All the kids were screaming. Meanwhile, Ruby was running around, knocking kids over. I don't think she was drunk, though. Poor Carlton was figuring out the probability of which game would produce the most tickets per token." Pearl rolls her eyes. "He never had kids."

"Maybe he needs to come in."

"What about Billy and Ruby? When are you going to see them?"

"Call me and we can schedule."

2:30 PM: Grady Simon, aged 41 (new)

Grady says he lives in the present as he should, but he works too hard and nothing makes him happy anymore. I've been looking forward to meeting him since I reviewed his referral and discovered he's a television producer!

I suggest he produce a new show, one kind of like Dr. Phil, only fresher. Grady scratches his left arm until it's red, then puts his head in his hands. He says he's too burnt out to even think about producing,

"I think it's a good idea. For you, I mean. It would give you something to feel fulfilled about and save your job."

"Maybe. Maybe it could come on late night," he says.

"Any time after five would work."

He tells me he knows an interactive therapist who works with hand puppets. He asks me if I think that would be interesting to people.

Jesus, he's gone. "No," I say. "That's ridiculous. You need a professional. You know, I've worked in community theater."

"So you know where I can find puppets?" he asks. I don't answer. He says he and his boyfriend have signed up for a baseball fantasy camp in Florida. "Do you think it's a good idea?" he asks, scratching his neck. He has not stopped scratching since he's come in.

I tell him it's a bad idea if it's going to put his job in jeopardy. He says it's only two weeks, and he'll meet some old players and managers. He thinks it'll be fun. He's overweight and has a comb over. He wears a thin black belt, but you can't see most of it because of his gut. I question his physical fitness.

"Oh," he says, "I'm not going to be playing; I'm going to be part of the fantasy sports writing camp. It's a side camp to the player's camp, where you write about the fantasy players. It's cheaper."

I ask him if he has ever written, and he says he always wanted to write for a newspaper, but got sucked into television. I tell him it will revive his life to produce the new show. A TV therapy show would be a gold mine.

"It was good you came to see me," I say. "Really, really good." Every visible area of his skin is now raw.

4:00 PM: Ethan

Ethan says that ever since he had that experience with Kate he's felt really happy. I ask him if he's sure it's not because of our appointments. He says, yes he's 100% sure. It's almost as if Kate pulled mud out of the top of his head. Ethan's father agrees. He wants to know if I can help him find Kate, so Ethan can get some additional therapy. I tell him I'll check for Kate on the street later.

5:00 PM: Dan

I run into Dan on the sidewalk outside the liquor store. He says he's here to see me. It looks like he has a fat lip, the redness matches the permanent red dent in his forehead. I tell him only Kate sees people on the sidewalk, and sometimes she sees them in the woods. Dan says he hasn't seen Kate today.

5:15 PM: Moderate traffic

Open a beer in the car
Listen to Dropkick Murphy's
Fantasize about Hanna
Open a nip
Fantasize about Kate

(I DON'T KNOW) PM: Home

Take an Ativan and walk dog
Fix a drink to wash down the Ativan
Open a porn site
Open my Facebook fan page
Suggest Hanna Sertin and Grady Simon like me

Outside the office...

Hanna: Going out with your ex-therapist

Hanna says there was nothing about her, or their son, in Brad's suicide note.

Bill scratches the top of his left hand with his opposite one. "I didn't know there was a note."

"Yes, we were supposed to meet that night about child care and custody issues. That fucking asshole left the door open for me to walk in and find him. I hated him both before and after he died. There's a farm down the road from my house, and sometimes I sit in the field and read and reread the note." She downs her third vodka and signals for the waitress.

"That's very normal."

"What my drinking? We're not in session, are we?" she says sarcastically.

"No, reading the note. Sorry, I don't know what to say or how to act around you."

"Well that's pretty obvious. Why don't we quit talking about Brad, or, for that matter, quit talking about me altogether. Tell me about your dreams. What do you want out of life?"

"You're very interesting. Where's your son tonight?"

"Did you not hear me? Tell me what Bill Sloan wants."

"To be famous," Bill hears himself answer. "To be important."

"How can you be famous doing what you do? Are you writing a book?"

"I could, but I want to be on TV. After that, a book will sell like crazy!"

"Would I be a part of a book?"

"No, I'd never do that. It would violate client confidentiality."

"I wouldn't mind. It would show me all your secret thoughts." She twirls her plastic stirrer between her thumb and pointer. "Fantasies, perhaps..."

"One of my clients is going to a Fantasy Baseball Camp. Isn't that awesome?"

"No," she sighs. The waitress appears and Hanna points to her empty glass.

"He works in television." Bill already has had three drinks at home and is working on this third here. Hanna is about the same age Stella was when they had William Jr. "You're pretty when you laugh."

"I bet you say that to all your ex-clients," she says. "Especially the ones not laughing."

"Just to the ones who are still alive."

There is a silence now; now they're like two strangers sitting across from each other on a bus. "Oh, I'm sorry," he says awkwardly. "I forgot. I was having so much fun."

Hanna's shoulders start to shake but instead of crying, she lets out a long laugh until she rests her head in her hands. "That's the funniest...that you said that..." She continues to howl, "Oh my God, you're the worst person ever. And I liked you, too."

"I'm sorry. Do you not like me now?"

"No, I meant on Facebook, you fucktard, on your public profile. I hit the 'like' button when it suggested I become a fan of yours. You're so bad at figuring things out; maybe you should try acting lessons instead, if your dreams are being in television."

Bill doesn't say anything. Why is she laughing? He wonders if she is crazy. Is this a good thing?

"Do you want to take me home? You don't, do you?" she says.

"I would."

"Would you?"

"Yes."

"You would?"

"Yes."

"Let's go sit in Comealy's Farm first," Hanna says.

Kate's Father: Dad down

Kate's father collapsed at church and never regained consciousness. He was closer to God that way; as if the church could deliver him to Him directly. Maybe God would be able to forgive him faster than Kate could, but Kate guessed he was going to Hell and would never be forgiven. This gave her closure from the abuse, closure from her running away to places like Jersey, then San Francisco, and everywhere in between. Her Hell had no such confirmation, and maybe that's why she stopped believing in Him, and entered a new spiritual world based on loving herself and all other living beings.

Kate wasn't at the church at the time her father collapsed, she'd already moved on. She may have floated over during a meditation, but she wasn't paying attention. She never went to that church anyway, even when she lived there. Her father's sudden decision to go to a church was probably why her mom never threw him out after everything went down. The only credit Kate could give him was he made a decision to go. Chances were her mom, when she had a few moments of clarity forced him. Maybe it was some sort of ultimatum while she was sifting through cans of old tomatoes and tossing expired boxes of pudding into the trash.

Kate learned to love everything in the Universe, but when she thinks of that church, she wishes it would be destroyed by a hurricane. At those times, her energy gets pulled out of her and she feels like an empty shell whose love is covered by a heavy lead curtain.

Her father's funeral was held at the same church. Kate cried when she found out he died. Everyone assumed she was grieving, but she was crying out in relief, joy, and love. She'd become Hummingbird Warrior by then, and she had her closure when she pictured his name on a grave stone.

65

Thomas: College

Thomas left college after a semester and a half. He didn't grasp the concept of leaving on his own, versus being asked to leave, versus being thrown out. Fuck it. The University cited his 0.75 GPA, combined with probation for using a special light to grow pot in his room, combined with sneaking a keg into the dorm, and finally, combined with being arrested for stealing tools out of someone's garage. Truth was he never stole the tools. The owner called the police when he heard Thomas taking a piss near the garage. The case was dropped, as the tools Thomas was carrying actually belonged to him. He had been working to decorate his friend's dorm room with a stolen STOP sign a few hours earlier.

On the positive side, school taught Thomas to make contacts, and to manage a business. He failed Economic Theory 101, but was still able to cultivate an impressive clientele to sell pot to. For a while, he lived with his parents and rented a small office in the next town. He went there every single day. But after two years he had to close, when the man hired to clean the office cleaned him out of five pounds of dope. There was no way to recover that loss, so the office rent went unpaid. On the day of his eviction, Thomas returned the office furniture back to Rent-A-Center, cleaned out all remaining drugs and materials, and then waited after hours in the office for the cleaner. He knocked him unconscious with a metal scale, and planted 2.5 ounces of pot in a baggie hanging out of his pocket. He turned on a flashlight and left it propped up at an angle so it would shine out the window. He then called the police to report a possible break in, and bolted. He let the proper authorities take care of the case. The police arrested the cleaning man for breaking and entering, and according to the crime report in *The Newton Journal*, there was a note pinned to him which was too obscene to print.

Stella: Catching your husband

As far as using a friend, Stella used Cindy often. If Stella needed to shop, their children could have play-dates at Cindy's house. Sometimes Stella would get very busy shopping, and Bill had to come by and pick up the kids. Cindy would offer him a drink, and say that the kids could play some more.

She started seeing Bill in his office on Thursdays; she used the last appointment of the day. Bill would be late getting home.

Stella watched Cindy's kids for her Thursday appointment. Cindy kept quiet about where she was. Cindy told Stella she had no problems. She was attractive, single, and chose not to date because she didn't want her kids to meet a lot of men.

Bill's secretary, Alice called Stella at 4:15 PM one Thursday. Alice was leaving for the day but she thought Stella might be interested in the progress Bill was making with a client named Cindy. Stella packed up the kids and drove away. The next day Alice was fired for breach of confidentiality and Stella joined Match.com under a phony name. On the nights of her dates, she told Bill she was going shopping.

Grady: Someone wanted you

Someone wanted you: A Marriage

Grady was an up and coming television executive; thin, with a full head of dark hair, and headed straight to the top when Camille met him. New York, Hollywood, nothing was out of the question. Camille found him sweet, hardworking, a little neurotic, but exuding confidence and success. He was a breath of fresh air, not someone obsessed with her and her body—the things of long-term unimportance. Most of all he was her best friend. They had a huge wedding in

67

Manhattan hosted by her family. They both smiled the entire day.

Someone doesn't want you: A Divorce

Grady agreed to meet Camille in a hotel bar; a fancy place with marble floors and maroon oriental carpets. The tables and desks were edged with gold. He could never stay at a place like this now, as he slept on a cot at his office—one his now large body barely fit on. He hoped she was going to invite him back into her life.

The bar was a dark place, lit with candles. Grady was at a table, rubbing his neck red, when she walked in. Her perfect skin was the color of light cocoa, she'd straightened her short brown hair, and her white buttoned top complimented her. It disappointed him. There were never enough candles in the world to make him see her as something sexual, or perhaps there were always too many. He continued rubbing his face and neck after they embraced and pecked each other on the mouth.

"You will be served soon," she said.

He gulped a gin and tonic. "Is this how it's going to be, Camille? We can try to keep things as they are?"

"That would just be for appearance sake, right? Your precious job might object to your new life choices, and you might be at risk. That's how it works, isn't it?"

"I should have told you…"

"Told me what? That you didn't want children? That you didn't like sex, or women in general? ONE of those things would have been fine five years ago."

"I'm sorry," he said. "I knew I preferred men, but I was too embarrassed and afraid of what everyone would think."

"*You're* embarrassed?" she said. "What do you think people think of me now that everyone knows my important television producing husband is gay?"

"I'm surprised you'd be worried about that. Friends have been telling me about you. I got a call from the parents of that boy you've been having the affair with. The sixteen year old…"

"The Mahones are good parents and they think highly of me, if that's what you were wondering. They signed a consent for me and their son to be in a relationship, and they wanted to make sure you and I were no longer involved. It was all very responsible, if you ask me."

"Camille, he's sixteen! Is this some sort of sick thing about your need for nurturing?"

"He wants me," Camille calmly added. "It suits my needs at this time, and Lord knows I've not had those met in years. You're the one who had me convinced you didn't like sex, but apparently you do."

"Yes, but there's a difference in embracing my sexuality with men and doing what you're doing with a boy."

"What's the difference? Look, I don't know why we're going here. It's actually none of your business. Grady, you are a sweet man and a good guy. Besides loving you as a person, I still like you as a friend, even now. I just met you to wrap things up, to tell you face to face you're being served for divorce."

"I still love you as a person too, Camille. I accept whatever you want to do, but tell me, how do things get so messed up?"

"Love is not good enough without honesty. I can't live the rest of my life the way we were." Camille checked her watch. "I gotta go. Benny's waiting for me."

"The boy?"

69

"Yes, he doesn't drive so I'm going to pick him up. And Grady…"

"What?"

"When you settle down and quit doing what you're doing with a bunch of different guys, pick a nice guy; one who will be loyal and dedicated and that gives you everything that you deserve."

Someone wanted you: Lots of Men

Grady needed to be wanted. After a relationship ends, people sometimes do what Grady did, which was go out and have sex with lots of men. He went to bars and dance clubs; places he generally didn't like. He wanted happiness, but instead found emptiness. He wanted to be wanted. He succeeded, but didn't like himself.

Someone doesn't want you: Not a Singular Man

When a lot of people desire you, you have a lot going for you. When no one picks you, when you are not the one, then you are not wanted. Grady thought there was an irony in being wanted and not wanted at the same time.

Someone wanted you: Joe

Grady met Joe at a small market on Newbury Street. They felt they had a connection, which seemed so natural when they started talking in the produce aisle. Outwardly, neither man appeared gay, which is something they still like to talk about, but obviously there was something there, enough to comfortably exchange numbers and meet for coffee the next day. They were both in down periods of their lives. They had a lot in common in this regard, and they were both nice people; Joe a bit less serious, less mature than Grady, but in a fun way, which made Grady laugh. Grady had waited for perfection of this kind his entire life. "Joe wants you, all of you," Grady thought, "And I deserve that joy and there actually is joy. There is joy."

Ethan: Before private school

What is it like to fly? To fly in the air; to fly in the air like a bird; to fly in the air like a bird without wings; to fly in the air like a bird without wings spiraling down; to fly in the air like a bird without wings spiraling down increasing speed; to fly in the air like a bird without wings spiraling down increasing speed as your face is pushed by the pressure; to fly in the air like a bird without wings spiraling down increasing speed as your face is pushed by the pressure-tears pouring from your eyes; to fly in the air like a bird without wings spiraling down increasing speed as your face is pushed by the pressure-tears pouring from your eyes until you taste them; to fly in the air like a bird without wings spiraling down increasing speed as your face is pushed by the pressure- tears pouring from your eyes until you taste them and the air pushes back your face; to fly in the air like a bird without wings spiraling down increasing speed as your face is pushed by the pressure-tears pouring from your eyes until you taste them and the air pushes back your face and it captures your scream; to fly in the air like a bird without wings spiraling down increasing speed as your face is pushed by the pressure-tears pouring from your eyes until you taste them and the air pushes back your face and it captures your scream that bounces off; to fly in the air like a bird without wings spiraling down increasing speed as your face is pushed by the pressure-tears pouring from your eyes until you taste them and the air pushes back your face and it captures your scream that bounces off the quickly approaching ground; to fly in the air like a bird without wings spiraling down increasing speed as your face is pushed by the pressure-tears pouring from your eyes until you taste them and the air pushes back your face and it captures your scream that bounces off the quickly approaching ground which you will die on.

Chapter 5: Thursday, February 2

7:22 AM: Alarm clock
Hit snooze button once
Get up
Kiss an angel good morning
Give dog some extra attention

9:00 AM: No one

This morning I gave Hanna the chance to come in at her regularly scheduled appointment, but she asked if I'm fucking kidding her. What I'd rather know is: if she's kidding fucking me.

I feel it isn't unethical, since she discontinued therapy with me. Maybe it's not ethical to ask her if she wanted the 9 o'clock slot. I suspect it's because of Brad that we threw ourselves at each other. Her stare, her anger was attractive. How would Dr. Phil handle this? He'd say, *I think you've had a loss and your way of dealing with it is not healthy.* I think that's what he'd say to her. I don't think she would fuck Dr. Phil. I don't know.

If I could go over this scenario with Grady, as an audition, perhaps do a little role play with him. He may see how interesting a television show could be. He'll be back from Florida in a couple of weeks.

My phone rings. The secretary wants to know if I could schedule, blah, at some time, and blah, at another. I say fine. I tell her to leave a voicemail with Grady to remind him of his next appointment, and then I tell her not to bill Hanna. "It seems something must have happened," I explain, and that seems to satisfy her. Then, from my cell, I call Hanna. Four rings, then to voicemail. "I think everything's okay. You've had a loss and you're dealing with it the best way you possibly can." I am not Dr. Phil.

Grady has left me a voicemail and says he's been doing well. He's watching a lot of reality television. *Intervention*, he says, depresses him. It's too real. *Bridezillas* makes him happy for his own life. *Kitchen Nightmares* makes him happy to not work in a kitchen. He says you can always find anger with kitchen work but making a good Risotto? He knows nothing about that, but any show which involves ghosts is a golden ticket. "I need to think about ghosts," he says.

10:00 AM: Kate

Kate tells me she is taking my advice about officially going into practice. "Look, Bill," she says. "I have a gift. It's something I can share for the good of everyone. I can increase the use of my Love Sharer abilities." She's going to call her business, Sunny and Share.

I feel everything Kate says is crazy, but even if I understand only a quarter of it, there's something about it that sort of makes sense. I need something like this today. It's like watching television. "Go, on," I say.

She says I'll have no more problems with Thomas or that girl I'm attempting to treat. I ask her what about that girl? Kate tells me she might see her once a week or so, maybe less, if she's not seeing me, but she's *obviously* seeing me, so Kate says she will wait. "Oh, and that little boy?" Kate says. "If he would see me regularly, he would not need you either."

I ask Kate how she gets her information. Is it healthy for her to sit outside my office or on the sidewalk and take everything in? She tells me, no, it's not like that; she puts her hands on people, and the information is transported to her, a process that's physically

74

exhausting and a little like dying. I tell her nothing she has said to me, so far, makes any sense.

"Oh yes it does," she says. "You'll find out."

11:06 AM: Thomas

I ask Thomas how he is. He says, "No, how are you?"

I say, "Do you care?"

He says, "No, not really." Then he laughs. It's not a mean laugh, but a laugh. "I'm happy," he says.

"What's on your mind?" I ask.

"I don't know. I've had 'I Got You Babe' stuck in my head for days."

"Are you still seeing Kate? Is that why you're so happy?"

"I'm happy because I feel I don't need anyone. I don't need people, and Kate's the one who taught me that."

"Really? If you want, you can stop coming to see me."

"Really?" he mocks. "Nice try. I think the court would find out."

"I honestly think you've gotten all that you can out of me."

"I want to get more outta you. It's like the fairy tale where the gold coins come out of the cow."

I have to think for a minute. Thomas always makes me think, because he is so ridiculous. "No," I say, "it's a goose that laid the golden egg. A man and his wife own a *goose* which lays a golden egg every day. Then they get greedy and imagine the bird must be made of gold inside, so they kill it. But inside it's just like any other goose."

"Fuck the goose. Kate tells me you want to fight me?"

"I never said THAT."

"It would be good therapy if I killed you, the goose, and pulled the golden coins out your sorry ass."

"Are you about done, Thomas?"

"Hey, time's up? Good. See ya, Doc!"

Damn, if he's not a bigger jerk when he's happy.

75

11:35 AM: Lunch—egg salad sandwich, apple, juice box
Watch TV in the break room

12:45 PM: Pearl, Billy, aged 22, Ruby, aged 19 (my children)

"The kids look good. Don't they look good, Pearl?"

She looks at me blankly. "I see them all the time."

"Who's Pearl?" my daughter asks.

"I don't know," Pearl says, and leaves.

"What the fuck?" Billy says.

"Language," I say.

"Dad?"

"Pearl is someone Mom invented, so I can talk to her."

"That's crazy," Ruby says.

"Sick," adds Billy.

"Well, speaking of crazy, I heard about the Chuck-E-Cheese's adventure you took Carlton on."

"Ha!" says Billy. "What a dork!"

"Listen, kids. Your mom could send you on your way, to a land where you have to pay rent, so it may be best to get along with Carlton."

"She'd never!" Ruby says. "What a joke. She'd send him away first."

"That's right," Billy adds. "She doesn't get along with him, either. Plus, what's he going to do? I already told him I was gonna shove his bowtie up his ass and he better hope the clips don't pop open, because it would be tough to explain that in the ER."

"Did you really?"

"Yeah," Ruby nods. "Mom says Billy is getting more and more like you each day."

"So Dad," says Billy, "how's my dog, which you stole from me?"

"Bullshit. He's my dog, and we have a solid bond."

"Language, Dad," he says.

76

Stella suddenly barges in and asks if we've all had enough quality time together. I tell her we have. She asks about next week. I ask if Carlton is coming. She doesn't know but I know her too well and the translation is that she won't let me know until that day. I should just take whatever she gives me. I know Stella way too well.

"Come on, *Pearl*," Billy says.

2:30 PM: Grady

Open hour. Grady at Fantasy Sports Writer camp. I'd never join a Fantasy TV Therapist camp. I'd just do the real thing and reach my goals. Loser. Hope he comes back soon!

4:00 PM: Ethan

Ethan doesn't cry when he says he has no friends and that kids make fun of him. He wants them to be his friends, but he doesn't know why they won't be. I assume if they're at Waysworth, then they have problems too. I ask Ethan if he knows why those kids are in Waysworth, and if they take medicine? Perhaps they have the same things going on that he does, or other problems.

Ethan says he doesn't know what he has going on. He's not like his mother, who has things going on. If he realized how much like his mother he was, then he would understand why he has no friends. I ask him about his father, and he tells me his dad wants to play catch with him, but Ethan doesn't like sports. He wishes his dad would learn music, so they could be in a rock band together. Ethan just wants to be normal. He wants that more than anything.

I look away so he doesn't see my face. He reminds me of my brother, who died. My father blamed himself for his death, and blamed my mother for being on valium and not reacting to anything. My brother didn't have any friends either. One day a bully pulverized a rabbit with the edge of a skateboard, and told my brother to smash the rabbit's skull in, or else the same thing would happen to him.

My brother…my friendless, sensitive brother's life was a nightmare.

I wish I was Ethan's older brother. That's when it hits me, and I feel myself getting too emotional. I tell Ethan to go out and get his parents.

Even though I have great fear of becoming soft, I'm fine that I cried. Feeling your deepest emotions is a good thing. Plus, crying would make good television. In the movie, *Broadcast News*, William Hurt cries fake tears during a news report he's doing. If fake tears would work on television, than real tears totally would. Audiences are dumb. I also made sure Ethan didn't notice.

5:11 PM: Dan

Outside I can hear Dan yelling. When I leave the office, he stops. I ask if he'd like to set up an appointment with me. He pops his palm against his head and starts yelling again, something about making time for a variety hour of love sharing. Walk on.

5:22 PM: Sit in car for five minutes before turning the key
Listen to 70's station on satellite radio
Turn up volume when "I Got You Babe" comes on
Drive with the cruise control

6:09 PM: Home
Smile at dog lying on disheveled bed
Turn on On-Demand
Take some Klonopin for my nerves
Watch back to back episodes of Bridezilla

Outside the office...

Hanna: Nightmare

Hanna lies in Bill's bed and she thinks she is awake. Of course she is not awake, but she still feels a layer of sweat on her. It's the type of cold misty sweat you can squeegee off, rather than the large beady droplets that form on the hood of a shiny waxed car after it rains.

Brad is in front of her, seemingly alive. He reaches into a pack of cigarettes. The pack has a green circle with the brand name *The Truth* on it. "You want one?" he asks. Hanna shakes her head. She is naked under a tree at Comealy Farm, but at the same time, it's not Comealy Farm. The field is not full of hay, but green sod, and it's as plush as a garden.

"You don't want...?" Brad laughs.

Hanna reaches for the cigarette and Brad starts to kiss her. Then it's Randy's kiss and Randy's hand between her legs. This is followed by Bill Sloan's scratchy beard; thorns against her thighs. Hanna imagines he's munching one of those pulpy apples he keeps at his house. "Stop!" Then it's back to Brad and her sitting against a bale of hay. "I'm glad you were the one that found me after. It's all okay now. You're going to be ok," Brad assures her.

Hanna feels relaxed. She feels the truth, and the truth is that Brad is okay for the first time ever. They sit with big smiles, which burst into laughter. Brad lies down on the grass. "You did this to me," he said. "You made me into this. You were created for me, but look what happened."

Hanna smiles at him, loves him, surprised at her calm in the smile, so frozen it hurts.

"I'm not mad, I'm dead, and you were a puzzle piece to make this happen," he repeats. She reaches to touch his face but she can't reach far enough. She struggles until she gets there and comes out of there with a fistful of beard. Suddenly, she is jarred by the ring of her phone.

It's 9:22 AM, and Sloan's name pops up on the caller ID. Hanna gets up, stands sweaty and naked. In a downward motion, she pushes the thin film of cool salve from her upper chest and her breasts. "Now, I've done *this*," she says.

Kate: When she learned how to be spiritual

Kate recovered from her breakdown without medication. She used martial arts. She kicked the crap out of her training partners and she studied everything having to do with The Eastern World, it's philosophies and meditations. She learned to breathe. She quit her job and the Universe paid her bills. She stopped drinking. She got wasted on spirituality. She found less and less importance in the day-to-day world. It felt like she was waking from a dream.

Kate fell in love with her sensei, Kumiko. His name translated to "long time." She learned to love Kumiko without having sensei sex. Her sensei had unconditional love for her. Her head was clear for the first time since she was a little girl. She learned how to heal people by practicing on her sensei. She would tell him, "Me love you, Kumiko." He laid on the table while she placed her hands on him. He wanted her to be happy. She was strong now. She had worked hard, and she had healed herself. She learned the opposite power for a breakdown, was a break up. She stopped seeing her sensei.

Thomas, who is to blame for a shitty life?

We've all had them and we learn to adjust. Perhaps something happened. Some days Thomas wakes up and he loves his life. He loves it so much that he never has the urge to leave. How dare he try to find a well to pitch a penny in? One day, however, he'll actually wish for something.

Last night he had a dream he was very old. He picked up Kate and they went to yoga. It's a long drive. Ten miles in, she said, "I can heal you, old man." So there on the side of the road, by a cornfield, she placed her hands on his forehead. She pulled some sludge, green mold, and crusty grits out of him. Thomas had never liked grits, but they were there, inside his soul. The car was a mess when she finished, but inside Thomas was clean.

Kate motioned Thomas to follow her deep into the cornfield. Thomas followed, because Kate had made him well. "Help me pull this down," she said, yanking a scarecrow off a cross-post. She handed Thomas a hammer and said, "This is the only way that you can understand."

Thomas pounded a nail in each of her hands and another one into both of her feet.

Stella: The recital

They sat next to each other at their daughter's high school string concert. It was their first public appearance together since the separation.

Beforehand, Stella had drank with her friend Leonard. Leonard would never cheat on his wife.

The music was anxious and jagged; the tension built but nothing snapped–all strings were attached. Stella wanted a hacksaw, to bow through Bill's pale white neck the same way the cellist was hacking away at her instrument. Stella leapt up and screamed during the standing ovation.

Grady: Fantasy Camp, Fort Meyers, FL

The grass is green, as green as it should be, and at the same time, more colorful than can be digested within the brain. The dirt is glowing; red burnt clay. The balls seem bleached and white, arching across an endless blue sky. The uniforms are flaming red;

bright enough to make one not want to look directly at them without squinting. Still, there is something wrong with this picture. Missed throws bounce across the field. The crack of the bat is more like a splat, than the thunderclap of a professional. The team is old, lumpy, wearing the numbers of David Ortiz, Curt Schilling, Carlton Fisk, and Ted Williams, but looking more like Paul Williams than Ted. They've all paid top dollar for this dream of re-living their youths, experiencing the big "*what if?*" even if a "*what if?*" was never even close.

The group is broken into several squads, each led by an ex-ballplayer. Grady recognizes Jim Willoughby working with the pitchers; Jim Rice at the batting cage, Manny Alexander at shortstop, and Bill Buckner around the bag at first. When a ground ball goes through the legs of one of the campers, no one wants to look at Buckner, except Grady, who notices Buckner rolling his eyes. He glares right at Grady, more flushed than the team's red jerseys. "Hey," he barks, "Mr. Reporter."

"Me?" Grady asks.

"No, the other hundred Fantasy Reporters." The squad laughs. "Mac wants to see you. Be at the bar at 2:30."

"Thanks," Grady says.

"Now catch the damn thing," Buckner yells to the camper. "Christ, how can you miss something like that?"

Grady arrives late. John McNamara is more grey and wrinkled than Grady remembers, but 1986 was a long time ago. The manager's plaid button-down shirt is neat, pressed, but still in colors popular twenty years ago. Grady sticks out his hand. "Thanks for the invitation," Grady says.

"Well, there should always be a good drinking relationship between the press and the coaches," McNamara states.

"Speaking of which, where are your coaches? Don't you usually have a few hires to hang out with in the lobby bar?"

McNamara scratches his head. "Well, it's been harder since '86. Must be a guilt-by-association thing. I spend lots of evenings exactly like this." He sips from a white creamy drink with ice.

Grady had pictured him as a bourbon man. "White Russian?"

"Fuck no. It's Ensure. It's all I drink now. It has vitamins and food products all in one. Try some."

Grady notices boxes of his belongings sitting ten feet behind his barstool.

"Can you believe this shit?" McNamara asks. His face is slow and sad. "It was the damnedest thing." He points to a box with pens, pencils, sunflower seeds, and handfuls of other snacks. "I get called into Dan Duquette's office. Now, I've never met the man, but he introduces me to another guy...some early-twenties kid, and they're in some Fantasy General Manager's Camp." McNamara shakes his head, his face beginning to turn red. "And this kid says, 'Mr. Kennedy...' Can you imagine? This kid thought I was Kevin Kennedy. Imagine that? So anyway, Duquette corrects him, and he's all embarrassed, and apologizes to me. Then the kid says he's a big fan and what a great manager I am, and then he says, 'What I meant was, Mr. McNamara, you're fired.'"

"Fired?"

"Yes, fired! Then this kid turns to Duquette and says, 'So, how did I do?' Duquette's giving him feedback and shit, and then he wants the kid to do it again with a firmer voice. 'No wavering,' Duquette says. Then he asks me if I could turn around and re-enter the office. They wanted to do it again!"

"Jesus."

"I've been fired many times, but I never thought I'd ever have to deal with it again...and then have to go through a goddamned do-over for that matter." He starts to sniffle, wipes his nose with the back of his hand.

"Really sorry to hear it, John." Grady sees all the years of managerial disappointments on his face. "You're a good man, a good baseball man. Something will come along, it always does."

"Well, there are always the Padres and the Cubs. They have camps too; they may want to give me another chance."

"I hope so. Thanks for the time you've given the press. Even if it was only a few days, I appreciate it." Behind his desk, cases of Ensure are stacked up on a metal dolly.

"Good luck," McNamara says, dumping the contents of the center desk drawer into another box. "I'm sure something will come along. It always does."

Ethan: Before private school, Part II

The McGraths take Ethan to the doctor and videotape the session. Ethan says, "I am failing. I am failing school." The doctor says, "So, how are you?" Then there's silence. Ethan wants to scream, but it seems so silly. So, he says nothing. The camera follows Ethan as he walks to the back of the office wall to squeeze the black bulb of the blood pressure cuff. "Ethan, how are you?" the doctor asks again.

"I'm fine!" Ethan yells; then he can't stop yelling, "*I'M FINE! I'M FINE! I'M FINE!*" So, they put him in an ambulance and he spends the next week in the hospital. His dad is there most of the time. His mother says she can't bring herself to visit. By the time he gets out, he's medicated, calm, just like his mother. For a while, anyway.

CONFIDENTIAL CLIENT RECORDS

From: The office of William Sloan

Client Profile: *DAN O'SHAY*

Dan O'Shay is a young man of unknown age, who suffers from a head injury, caused by an automobile accident. He also has anger issues, caused by the frustration of his memory loss. Because of his high frustration level, he may only be seen in the office, or in passing (for less than fifteen minutes). However, he should be billed for one hour, as treatment is based on his psychological and medical condition, not the short-sightedness of his therapist.

Dan talks loudly to himself, and will shout at strangers while in the community. At times, he is incoherent. He is unable to remember a chain of four words, five minutes after they are given to him.

Referral Source: Dan was referred to this office by *Sunny and Share*, who also stated that we referred Dan to them. *Sunny and Share* has no record of Dan, as they do not believe in the keeping of client records. This documentation was produced from the office of Bill Sloan, as a referral, to be seen by Bill Sloan.

Chapter 6: Thursday, February 9

7:22 AM: Alarm clock
Hit snooze button once
Get up
Oh, no, not again

8:42 AM: Hanna

I tell Hanna she's early, and she says she's been up getting ready. Hanna has applied her make-up perfectly; eye shadow, which makes her eyes look as blue as a summer sky.

I ask her why she needs to see me. It's been two weeks. She says maybe she kind of missed me—but she says everything has to be on her terms. When she looks as good as this, I want to agree, to shout, *Name the terms, I'll agree with them!* I tell her missing me is bad for her treatment. She says, "But it's good for my therapist."

Hanna needs to work on her issues while she is here. She's having bad dreams. Most involve Brad, but there was one where their son was walking down the aisles of a Toys"R"Us, looking for a new father, but there weren't any. And there was a sign that said, *Everything Dead On Sale.*

"Do you see the meaning, and also how dreams are impossible? Especially with so many Toys R Us stores going out of business."

Hanna says, straight faced, "Yes, especially that. Death tends to directly affect capitalism." Then she smiles.

"Would you want to keep seeing me?" I ask.

She says she's ready to d/c again, in order to date. I tell her I'm concerned it might affect her well-being, but on the way out, she plants a soft kiss on my mouth. "I'll call you tonight," I say.

"I'm planning to take you to the top of the globe, and spin you around and around, so let's go." Hanna's terms are very sarcastic.

10:00 AM: Kate

Kate tells me not to worry about her past. It's something not to dwell on. She tells me she only lives in "the now", and at this moment, right now, she's doing fine. She's happy healing others. She's also healing herself.

"In what way?" I ask.

She answers that she has a lot of work to do, and not to worry. She frustrates me. I would like to push her limits until she breaks; until I can create a reason for her to come here.

I tell her that things in her past are very important to bring up here, so that we can work on them and resolve her inner-conflicts. She asks why I would need to worry about that. I tell her, because I'm a very important person in the process of all this, and I'm all about succeeding.

She looks at me for a long time, then announces that there's something I'm not telling her. She says I need love from a lot of people in the Universe. She says to be careful with success.

I ask about Sunny and Share. Kate says she has a street team, but it's only one person, and he needs some healing himself. She thinks a free clinic would be a great accelerant for her business. I ask her if she has a space in mind, and she tells me she was thinking about using some of the space in my office.

"Here?"

"When it becomes available. But right now, a booth on the sidewalk could work."

88

"There's not going to be… you can't use my office for…"

"Well, if not here…" she gestures at the room, then points to her heart, "here." She tells me she reveals all this because of my love for her. I tell Kate I'm fond of my patients, I don't love them.

Kate says, "Ha! You'll find out." She then tells me to lie down and she'll do some free hands-on healing. I refuse.

"I've done wonderful things for Thomas, but you're the one full of blockages."

"I'm fine with that."

"Just wait till it's time to blow. Your life is going to be a mess."

She stands–her hour is up. "Love is more than kissing, you know. It's about opening up to a vast area, which you can fill. Try to open up before I see you next week."

"Wait," I say, "just hold on a minute. Kate, let's get this straight: *You* see *ME!*"

"If you say so," she says.

11:03 AM: Thomas

Thomas is having a conversation with Kate in the waiting room. I tell him to come in. "Oh no," he says and then, "Really?" to Kate, then, "Thank you." I tell him to let me know when he's ready, and I go back into my office.

At 11:25 my secretary pages me. I still don't know her name. I make Thomas wait an additional ten minutes, then I have her tell him to come in.

"Her name is Aimee," Thomas says.

"Who?"

"Your secretary. Only you don't call them secretaries now, you know. She's your Administrative Assistant."

"Oh. Thanks."

"I'm going to work with Kate," he says, "and Aimee may be part of the crew."

"As you know, Kate is a patient of mine. How well have you thought this out?"

"You'll find out soon enough. Always up for a fight, aren't you, Sloan?"

"I think you want to resolve conflicts of your feelings by trying to provoke me."

Thomas cups his left bicep in his right hand and gives a little flex. "Kate says she sees you because something in the Universe tells her to."

"Jesus, does she know I'm a part of the Universe too?"

"She respects that. She told me if she can't respect that, her whole perspective is wacked."

"I know that song! Jay Z, right?"

"Song?" Thomas is like a fish, open-gilled and flapping on a dock. I like having him laid-out and gasping this way. Thomas repeats the lyrics in a flat monotone, then gains some steam and says them again. By the third time, he's positively rapping: "If you can't respect that / maybe your perspective is whack / maybe you'll love me when I fade to black. December 4th."

"December 4th is my birthday," I tell him.

"I won't remember."

12:15 PM: Lunch—slimy turkey sandwich, apple, damn, no juice box
Need to food shop

1:10 PM: Carlton, 35, (ex-wife's new husband)

"Stella is shopping," is how he greets me. Then he doesn't say anything for a little while. I ask him what he's thinking, since he's not talking, and he tells me he's calculating. Even when he talks to his friends, internally he's working on something mentally.

"Ugh," I say.

"I don't know what you take me as," he says.

"Lyrics? I know that song, Jay Z."

"No," Carlton tells me. He's been calculating how someone like Stella could marry someone like me. Now that he's met me, he thinks that I don't seem like I've done half the things she claims.

"Don't take all she says at face value," I tell him. "It's all about data you can measure." I also tell him, the kids never messed with me at all, and they are, in fact, not kids at all anymore.

"Precisely. When is the last time you saw them?" he asks.

"Precisely and unequivocally, last week. And it can be measured."

"Stella says it's been longer."

"Who the fuck are you to be coming in here and…"

"I'm a client," he says.

"No, Pearl is the client. Now get out!"

Carlton stands to leave, and I walk a few feet behind him. When the door opens I give him an extra shove past the desk and into the reception area. Aimee and Kate see this and stare. I put my hand deep into my pocket (find a dog treat) and walk back to my desk.

2:00 PM: Grady

Open hour. Grady leaves me a voice mail saying the fantasy camp is going well. In fact, there is someone who knows me from the office, who is also attending the Fantasy General Manager's Camp. He wants to call a meeting when he gets back. I mutter, "Fabulous;" but at the same time I think, *Grady will be back soon!* I'm thrilled when he concludes, "I have some things to discuss with you."

4:00 PM: Ethan

Ethan is drawing a picture at the art table where I sometimes meet with children. I sit across from him and say, "Ethan, there are things you should know about life. Sometimes things are not your fault. They are no one's fault. You have something inside you that balances your brain. It's called your chemical makeup. It's like a seesaw. Certain chemicals on one side, balance certain chemicals on the other."

I pause. He keeps drawing. I go on, "Say that Happy and Sad are sitting on the seesaw together. If Happy is on the ground then Sad is way up there, and it's very sad in the seesaw world. If Sad is on the ground, then Happy is way up there, and you can be very, very happy. You can be so happy that you might not sleep for days, maybe an entire weekend. Has this happened to you? I know it has. Pay attention Ethan."

Still no response. I press forward: "Certain chemicals are mixed up in your brain. The seesaw may get out of control. Sad might suddenly stand up, while Happy is up there, and suddenly Happy comes crashing down. Do you understand?"

Ethan is filling in his drawing, using the edge of his pencil.

"Ethan, THIS is what happens with you. It is also what happens with your mom. Now, both of you take pills that prevent Happy and Sad from standing up. In fact, they prevent them from even being waaaaaaay up in the air, while the other is on the ground. It's completely normal to feel happy and sad, but the medication you take keeps the seesaw balanced, so no one crashes. Ethan? Did you hear me?"

At last, he nods. I go out and get his mother, and ask her to sit. We make eye contact, and she smiles as I tell her we've been talking about bi-polar disorder. "Well, Ethan," she says. "What do you think?"

"I want to go to a playground."

"Okay," she says. "Life is for living not living uptight."

I'm about to say, "Jay Z?" but this time I don't even bother. After they leave, I look at Ethan's drawing: it's Da Vinci's *Design for a Flying Machine,* drawn to perfection.

5:21PM: Dan

Dan is not outside my building today, but I see him two blocks away, walking toward me. We're going to intersect. At a distance of twenty feet he says, "Do you know where the antelope roam?"

"Beat it," I say. "I'm done for the day."

5:32 PM: Commute in bad traffic
More bad fucking traffic
Pop in Jay-Z
Sing along

6:59 PM: Home
Take out treat from pants pocket
Give to dog

Outside the office...

Hanna: When will she reveal this? On a date or in therapy?

When Hanna found out she was pregnant, Brad asked her if they were going to get married. She said, "As a prerequisite, don't you have to love someone first? I'm not sure if I even like you."

When the baby was born, she moved in with her mother, and Brad purchased a two-bedroom condominium. It was where he shot himself. Neither the baby, nor Hanna, ever stayed there.

Sometimes the baby stayed with Brad's parents, but only if Hanna stayed there too. They lived in Boston, so Hanna had to be dropped off and picked up. Neither Brad, nor his parents, trusted her driving or the reliability of her piece-of-crap car which was old enough to vote. She was stuck.

When she bought a brand new car she had been saving up for— a shiny red Cooper Mini, Brad was furious. He called it non-practical and irresponsible. His exact quote was, "Could you not be a stupid moron, for once in your life?" Of course Hanna returned the car, and bought a Honda that met with Brad's approval. The return cost over $5,000, and since she was in debt, Brad put the Honda under his name.

At some point during a pick-up and drop-off of the kid, Brad ended up with the Honda, and Hanna got stuck with his old Chrysler. She had pretty much stopped talking to him anyway so it was like....okay, fine. His car was six years old and had bad ball joints. She was amused: A guy really bad at balling, had a car with bad ball joints. Brad told her he knew a lot about cars, but as it turned out, he didn't.

On the contrary, when Randy balled her, he knew what he was doing. Randy was Brad's best friend before he was her supervisor; but not that she minded him being her boss, in the bedroom first and foremost. One day the Chrysler blew up. She and Brad didn't know to check the oil.

When Brad died, his parents talked about selling the Honda and the condo; they needed money to pay for the funeral. But the funeral and wake were on the cheap. Where had the money gone? Hanna didn't know, but she didn't care either–she didn't want her kid to ever see Brad's family again.

Hanna's current car is the worst one yet. The brakes feel like they barely come together, as if they are a CD spinning in the player at every stop-point. The frame is almost completely rusted out, and the doors creak when they close. Hanna takes the kid in it all the time now. No one tells her what to do.

Kate: I Got *Who* Babe?

Kate used to love Sonny and Cher; the way they used to kid one another, then sing together. They were toast with butter, pancakes with syrup, and pie with ice cream. Cher would launch into height jokes and Sonny would counter with banana nose ones. There was no violence, but they would fight on the show, and the best part for Kate was that Sonny wasn't her abusive father and Cher wasn't hiding in a safe area counting pudding boxes. Later, when Cher's relationship with Greg Allman became public, Sonny's

Fuck you, bitch, for fucking Greg Allman vibe was noticeable on TV, and could never be erased with a joke, and a just-kidding smile.

Kate never understood why someone so damaged and evil could move in on her dear friend, Sonny. Greg Allman was like a dark cloud. He caused the divorce. It was his fault. There would be no Greg and Cher show. Didn't Cher sing duets with Carol Burnett? Steve and Eydie? There was no possible way she would be the type to hang out with a dope-smoking southern rocker. And what about Chastity? What kind of environment would she be brought into? The whole thing was heartbreaking.

Sonny first died for Kate when he did *The Sonny Comedy Revue*. It was a bomb. Kate thought it was because he couldn't look in the mirror and properly tell jokes on his own about height or bad singing. It was hard when Kate looked in a mirror and didn't find love.

When you grow up, life gets even weirder. Sonny became a Congressman and married a woman in a suit. Cher sat on a gunboat for a video and showed her butt (which was real) as she sang using auto-tune (which wasn't). Her nose looked to be perfect.

In 1998, when Sonny tagged a tree with his skull skiing, Kate remembered exactly what she was doing when she heard the news. She was about to look up her father to confront him. Instead she called her mother. "Who's Sonny?" her mother asked.

Thomas: Business appointment

Thomas gives Aimee a call to discuss business. He suggests maybe they could have coffee or a drink. He tells her he knows someone has been hired to build Kate's booth, so they really need to start planning. Aimee would like to know if this meeting is his, or Kate's idea. Thomas says, "Why does it matter?"

"Because I've read both of your case files, Numb Nut!" she says. "Plus, I told Bill I wasn't going to get involved in anything

95

outside, with any of his patients. He's kind of pissed Kate was healing me the other day, during work time."

"Is Sloan discussing my case with you?"

"I'm not going to talk about this anymore." Aimee hangs up.

Stella and the visit to the Dr. Pooch, the Dog Therapist

Before Stella gave up and gave the dog to Bill, she took it first to Dr. Pooch.

"Can you fix my dog?" she asked.

"Does it need to be spayed?"

"No, fix it. You know, make it better. Make it stop doing things."

"What things?"

"It eats shoes, and towels, and furniture, and anything that's on the floor. And sometimes it knocks itself out by running into the wall."

"Greyhounds will do that?"

"I saved this dog!"

"You *think* you saved it. I really should ask the dog." Dr. Pooch leaned close and whispered, "Hmmm, hmmmm, uh-huh…I see."

"Well?"

"It's not getting enough attention."

"You can't be serious. The kids love that animal."

"You don't understand. You've never chased a rabbit in front of thousands of people. She knows the rabbit is fake, but everyone's cheering. A dog can really get off on that."

"The dog wants us to cheer for her?"

"No, but the dog certainly didn't want to be adopted."

"Listen Doc, this dog is splitting us. She has Borderline Personality Disorder."

"How would you know?"

"My ex-husband is a therapist. He used to say I had it."

"Oh great, the two of you living in the same house with a Borderline diagnosis. No wonder the dog is having trouble. Hold on…hmmmm, okay, okay…yes, she says she wishes the TV remote was made out of beef."

"Come on."

"The components are crunchy enough for her teeth and gums, but it's flavorless. She's having trouble passing the batteries."

Stella leaned in and pulled the dog by the collar, and spun her around so they were face to face. "Tell me what you think," she said to the dog, who clamped down on her nose. "You, sonofabitch!"

"She says she actually is a son-of-a, I mean, daughter-of-a-bitch. She also said she doesn't like you very much."

Grady: Goddamn job

Grady knows that every day you take off from work means you've got twice as much work the next day. It's written on his boss' coffee mug. So after taking two weeks off, Grady has ten times the normal work today.

WHDH-TV says, "Welcome back," and "Get to work," the second Grady walks in the door. Before logging onto his computer WHDH-TV shouts "Did you read my e-mails?" and a machine gun shoots a rapid round of further instructions "Bot-dot-dot, bot-dot-dot-, bot-dot-dot, BA!"

Grady needs to get cracking, or WHDH-TV is going to replace him with a new Head of Programming from a survey company. WHDH-TV has indicated that all late-night programming could be determined by focus groups, comprised of workers from third shifts and insomniacs. WHDH-TV said this in the e-mail that Grady has just returned to, and he needs to produce immediately. Even without buying the survey information, WHDH-TV thinks Grady should work on a ghost program, or a local reality television show dealing with bizarre and addictive characters. WHDH-TV states that there is great interest for people in these types of shows.

WHDH-TV suggests developing a show called *Ghost Intervention* where ghosts confront individuals dealing with serious addictions, but trick them by saying they are shooting a documentary on ghosts. Then they do a séance/intervention. Another suggestion by WHDH-TV is a show called *OCD Ghost,* where a team of ghost hunters find spirits with obsessive compulsive behaviors manifesting symptomatically by needing to scare people a certain number of times, or having to repeat a haunting word over and over again. Grady stares at the e-mail on the screen for almost an hour. He'd call Joe, but Joe will tell him he is ruining the momentum of their just-finished vacation. He wishes he could talk to Bill Sloan today. Grady begins to scratch.

Ethan: At the playground

Ethan and his mother sit on the seesaw. "Aren't you a bit old for this?" she asks. When he jumps off, she thinks she has broken her tail bone. "Dr. Sloan told me to do that," he explains.

Dan: The volunteer

In his dusty old basement, Dan pulls a handsaw back and forth across the grain of a 2X4. Kate says to make it look like a kissing booth, but better yet, it should be more of a total love booth since she is a Love Sharer. Dan has an image of himself and Kate making love on the polished board in the back of the booth. "It needs to be humble and inviting at the same time. I should be able to work on people in there," Kate said, "and make sure to paint the sign with polyurethane before you finish." Dan feels calm when Kate is around, and doing work like this is very therapeutic.

Dan works a little bit at a time, so that he won't forget all the steps of the job. He's never been much of a carpenter, but somehow, having someone believe in him is making the project turn out pretty decent. Kate is the only one who has shown any faith in him in a long time. Kate says if he does this well he may be able to start building caskets or something. "It's a good living," she says.

She tells him that people believe in caskets and will buy them, but she personally does not share that belief. He agrees, as they have cremation in common. Dan likes the idea of producing something for sale he would never buy. He thinks he will live longer if he starts building caskets. Even if he made urns for his own cremated ashes, he would make sure his ashes got dumped somewhere that meant something to someone, and not end up in an urn. Anyone who might want them could take them, if his life had meaning to them. Dan thinks maybe a good business would be building white boned driveways out of people's bones, to look like the ones made of bleached seashells in ocean-towns. That would involve convincing an entire family to donate their ashes and non-pulverized bones to his company. He knows he could charge them for this. He thinks it's a great idea, and then suddenly, he can't remember why he's smiling.

Chapter 7: Thursday, February 16

7:22 AM: Alarm clock
Hit snooze button two times
Get up
Admire Hanna sleeping and at peace

9:16 AM: Hanna

Hanna calls me. Aimee patches her through without asking. Aimee knows.

Hanna says that after leaving my house this morning she was stopped by the police. It's the third time this month, and it's because of the big red "R" the scarlet letter of car inspections on her windshield. She was on her way to see me. In Massachusetts, you'd better fix your ball joints. "Fuck me," Hanna says she told the police officer.

I interrupt to remind Hanna that she can't see me as a patient and see me in a personal relationship. "Would you like to see another person?" I ask her. She tells me she is having a good time with me. "That's not what I meant. Would you like to see another therapist?"

She says she'll tell me what she wants later in the week.

I say she really needs to do something about her car.

"Oh, really, I need to do something? Thanks for that piece of information, Bill. You take to the older man, father-figure role well."

"You said you're okay with…" I then understand she's being sarcastic. "Sorry, I won't tell you what to do."

"So, I got the ticket and said fuck me. The lady cop walks back to my car and says, 'What did you say?' I'm like, hey, I didn't say fuck *you*, I said fuck me."

"You should…I mean, be careful."

"You know, jail wouldn't be bad. Three squares and free room and board. I could sit and figure out what has happened the past six months."

When Hanna is upset, her eyes don't shine, they glow. I wish I was seeing them, I wish she was here. I would like to know when I can see her again. Hanna pauses and says, "I have an appointment with you next Thursday." She hangs up.

"Fuck me," I say.

10:00 AM: Kate

Kate is excited. Dan is building her a booth, directly on the street, to use as an office for her new clients. It seems very Lucy Van Pelt to me. I tell Kate I don't know if it's the best way to do business. "Well," she says, "it's a start."

Kate tells me Dan is doing a fine job. I tell her Dan appears to be a crackpot. She looks at me, so I add I wasn't making a clinical assessment. Kate says she enjoys working with him, and that a lot of healing has begun. Dan will soon be in a very good place, plus he is a hawk.

"How so?"

"His totem is the hawk. Hawk's piercing shrieks tear through the air. In its shrill cry lies an important message which represents illumination. The hawk teaches us to scope out the situation and focus on our talents, trying to draw them out. The hawk learns to see the big picture, in order to understand the past, present, and future. The hawk asks us to be observant of our surroundings, so we won't get distracted from our path by others. It also reminds us not to get caught up in minor annoyances, so that we may maintain our inner balance."

I tell Kate that Dan is a major annoyance, and possibly a danger to others.

"Yes, that is why it was great you referred him to me."

"I didn't give you any referrals. In fact, you tried to pawn him off on me."

Kate lets out a *humph,* then says, "So, Bill, what about me? Do you want to guess?"

"Well, my guess is, I think you need to be grounded so that's why you keep coming."

"No, not that. Guess what animal totem I am?"

"I don't know. You remind me of that t-shirt with the wolf on it."

"Exactly," Kate says. "Wolves are known to run 35 miles a day in pursuit of their prey. They are highly misunderstood animals who have gained the reputation of being cold-blooded. In reality, wolves are friendly and social creatures. Because the wolf is a teacher and pathfinder, he comes when we need guidance in our lives. Those who have a wolf totem will move on to teach others about sacredness and spirituality."

"You're kind of strange," I say. "That's not a clinical assessment either."

"I know," she says. "Oh, and by the way, you're a snake."

"My totem?"

"Oh no. Not that."

11:03 AM: Thomas

Thomas doesn't want to talk about much today. I say, "How about those Celtics?" and he says he's not a fan. I ask him what he wants to talk about. He says, "Nothing." I think, fine, this will be an easy hour, and then he reveals something to me I never thought I'd hear from him.

"I cooked dinner for some people last night. Tuscan steaks with garlic mashed potatoes, served with a tossed pear, walnut, and gorgonzola salad."

"Wow, that sounds delicious."

"Damn right."

"Is this something you do often?"

"Well, when I was a kid, we weren't allowed to speak during meals. My mom was a great cook, so I loved eating, but I would just sit and chew and not saying a word. We all did. Hey…"

"What?"

"I was wondering about Aimee."

"What about her? You want to know her status, like is she single?"

"No. I want to know her availability. I'm sure you know we are all working together: me, Kate, and Aimee. I need to know her schedule, so we can arrange to have our meetings. Otherwise, we'll have to hunker down and meet in the reception area, the way Kate and Aimee do now."

I hate that he said *hunker down* and try to sound calm. "I can't give you Aimee's schedule, and I usually tell Kate to get the hell out of here."

"Well, don't get terse," he smiles. "Can you tell me if she's single, then?"

"Time's up," I say. I really hate his fucking guts.

11:53 AM: Lunch—sandwich, apple, juice box
Speak to Aimee

1:20 PM: Stella/Pearl

Stella slams the door behind her.

"Please don't do that, Stella," I say. "What's the problem? I just saw you in the waiting room and you looked fine."

She walks around the office, picks up the framed photo of the kids, lays it face down and then picks it up again. "Just what are you doing?" she asks.

I don't know what this means. I've never understood anything out of her mouth, which is open ended, so I don't answer.

"Are we going to talk or not?" she asks.

"Stella, I…"

"Pearl."

"Okay, Pearl, how was your week?"

"Carlton doesn't like me either. What the fuck did you say to him?"

"Confidential," I say.

"Well, he said to not take me at face value, and now he wants me to say things that only are scientifically measureable…. and the kids! They're pissed at you, so they're pissed at me! Plus, you told them to get along with Carlton, so they're all ganging up on me! All of them! Him, them, and probably the dog, if he was still with us!"

When Stella talks, her focus and words spin round and round like a laundry dryer. When she opens the door, the words fall out. She also seems to be twirling around randomly within her two characters.

"Pearl, I think you should…"

"I'm not here for advice. Give Stella a call, I'm here to talk. I'm Pearl! You! You're here to listen, so listen!"

"Okay."

Pearl paces around the office some more, bouncing like a tornado, then stops to read *The Oath of Hippocrates,* I have framed on my wall. It includes the promise, "Whatever, in connection with my professional service, or not in connection with it, I see or hear, in the life of men, which ought not to be spoken of abroad, I will not divulge, as reckoning that all such should be kept secret." Stella pulls it off the wall and smashes it.

105

3:00 PM: Grady

Grady was supposed to be here at 2:00, but when he didn't show, I was disappointed as I've been thinking about my show, and I'm ready to pitch him the idea. Just before 3:00, I go into the waiting room and he's sitting there with a well-groomed man in his twenties. Aimee is nowhere to be found. Grady tells me she's been fired.

This makes no sense. Who would fire her, why, and how would Grady even know? I just gesture that he and his young executive friend should come into the office.

"Sit down," says the young exec to Grady, and Grady sits. He's smiling. I've never seen him smile so much; he looks like a hungry man with a knife and fork about to cut into a big slice of pot roast. He looks like he wants more gravy.

"The vacation seems to have agreed with you," I tell him.

The young exec speaks up. "It was a difficult decision, but you had to fire Annie."

"Fire who?"

"Annie. She had to be fired, so I took it upon myself…"

"I don't know what you're talking about. I don't know who Annie is, and I don't know who you are either."

"I'm Robbie," he says. "I've been away for two weeks, at the same camp as Grady, as part of the Employee Career Enhancement Incentive. As fantasy General Manager, I learned the in's and out's of Human Resources. I learned to fire people!"

"But…"

"You may recognize me—I've been providing janitorial services for your office for the past two years. You sent me Christmas cards with pictures of your kids on them."

"Oh, my ex-wife takes care of Christmas cards. Who exactly did you fire?"

"Your current secretary…I told her she was fired."

"Administrative Assistant."

"Whatever. It was exciting."

106

"Okay, fine, what you did was consistent to my firing practices." I look at Robbie and his white shirt is sticking to his chest. He is mumbling something, as if he's practicing to say it louder, then I hear, "Now about you... "

I interrupt swiftly, "Hey, Grady, it's nice that you met Robbie at the camp, but we need to talk about the show you need to come up with... I mean, your things, issues... that you want to talk about." I turn to Robbie. "So, if you would excuse us... "

"I will not be excused right now. I'm here using the skills I learned at Fantasy Camp. Human Resources asked me to tell you: William Shore, you are suspended without pay for one week." Robbie gives a long exhale and breaks into a wide grin.

"What? I'm not taking this from a janitor!" I say. I dial the number for Human Resources and ask to be connected to the supervisor. Robbie's cell phone rings immediately.

"Ah, see that," Robbie says, clicking off his phone. "Mr. Shore, I'm suspending you for not following the code of ethics pertaining to being a psychologist. Specifically, for dating and fighting with the various clients of your practice, and for in general, not caring very much for ethics at all. So, Mr. Shore—"

"Sloan."

"What?"

"My name is Sloan, like on the Christmas cards."

"Sorry." Robbie turns to Grady and says, "So, how'd I do?"

"The demeanor you used just now in suspending Bill was better than when you fired Aimee and McNamara," Grady replies. "You're learning but you still blew the name."

"Yeah, oh well," Robbie shrugs.

"I refuse to accept this!" I yell, then feel the dry hand of Grady's on my forearm.

"So, Bill," Grady says, "I think the television idea is something I'd like to try. That is, if you can do something with ghosts in therapy or something. Let's talk soon... say in a few days?"

"I want that in writing," I say. Both Robbie and Grady simultaneously say, "Sure."

4:00 PM: Ethan

On my way out I tell Ethan and his parents I have an emergency and can't meet with him. I have no idea how he'll react, perhaps a tantrum; perhaps laughter. He says, "Oh fuck, really?"

"Ethan." his mom says, then to me, "Oh fuck, really?" She looks like she might cry, but I have to go. I can't interact with them while I'm suspended. I'd much rather kick something. "See you next week, kiddo?" I say.

Ethan kicks the magazine table. "Really?" his mom says. "Fuck, really?" She stands behind him ready to wrap him up with both arms. Kate comes out from behind the desk and says, "I'm able to see him today." I walk out.

4:11 PM: Dan

Dan is painting the words, Sunny and Share on a wooden panel, mounted over the wooden booth, on the street outside the office. I do need a week off.

4:32 PM: Earlier than usual, so traffic not bad
Listen to "Working for the Weekend" by Loverboy
Sing along

5:13 PM: Home
Take out prescription bottles
Stare at them

Outside the office...

Hanna: The things you wish for

Hanna wishes she could be thirteen again. She wishes she could go back in time and play with her best friend. She wishes for do-overs. She wishes she'd never met Brad. She wishes Brad had been a better person. She wishes her child still had a father. She wishes she didn't have to leave him for Randy. She wishes Randy was never Brad's best friend. She wishes they were both dead; wishes for that easiness. She wishes she didn't have to go to funerals. She wishes she didn't have to be the one to find Brad's body. She wishes when she sees stars shoot across the sky, at Comealy's Farm, that the Comealy family could have had a wish too. She wishes she knew *their* son. She wishes her son knew his father. She wishes to never cry again. She wishes for a different life.

Hanna never wished to be a parent, never wished to live with her mother, never, never wished to sleep with her therapist. Hanna never wished she'd have to pretend to get through each day. Hanna never wished to walk through a sea of shit.

Hanna wishes she weren't so attractive. She wishes sex didn't fill her empty soul. She wishes Randy was still her friend. She wishes she never had to see Bill again. She wishes she could see him right now. She wishes people would stop teaching her about life. She wishes she hadn't learned so much about it on her own. She wishes all those people she's thinking about lived in her hand. She wishes she didn't have the urge to clap.

Hanna wishes to stop wishing. She wishes it were all that easy.

Kate: Shocking her heart without paddles

Kate used to think her panic attacks were heart attacks, and tried to control them by reaching a state of catatonia; not to be

109

confused with the meditation she learned later on. Her meditation was peaceful, relaxed breathing. Not at all comparable to the catatonic state of panic, focused on the thought she was not dying.

Kate had run from her father's abuse and mother's OCD to New Jersey, only to find herself in another toxic situation. From there she ran across the country, accompanied by her desperation and talent for making the worst choices in any set of circumstances. She ran and ran, and when she got to the coast, her heart finally gave out. Yes, she died of a heart attack, and then opened herself up to a rebirth, except this time she raised herself in an atmosphere of love and support. How? She met a Master who studied directly under Hawayo Hiromi Takata, the Japanese-American woman who introduced the western world to the ancient science of Reiki.

At last something good had happened to Kate. Under spiritual tutelage, she learned about healing and meditating and being "One with It All". One evening, she was in the woods, sitting in silence, sending out beams of love, and when she opened her eyes, she was surrounded by foxes, deer, rabbits, and even the shyest of hummingbirds. They were all attracted and drawn to her.

She went to Bill Sloan because she knew it was time to deal with her father-issues. She could continue to practice peace and love and healing, but that was just a way of avoiding her past. Yes, it was time to work out the nuts and bolts of it, in order to forgive her father.

But still, she's avoiding. Why does she see Sloan? She knows there's a reason, but she can't put her finger on it. Wolves do not haunt ghosts, they howl at them. Sloan can help her if she can pull out of him all the selfishness her dad showed her. She needs to understand Sloan, why he falters from lack of morality or ethics much like her father did. Healing him, will heal her. That's it. That's why she came.

She doesn't like how he called her strange and then told her he wasn't available. But she takes a deep breath and deals. In the past, having a man like Sloan tell her she was strange, followed by him not being available for her, would have sent her to the ER. Now, she will use all her energy to jump start her dying heart. She will not repeat a mantra. She's had her fill of those.

Thomas: Thanksgiving break from college

Tammy ran for her cat every morning, five minutes after she let it out. She ran, retrieved it; under cars, across the lot, arms wrapped around it, hauling it home.

Today she was late for her first class. She was late too, with other things. Damn cat couldn't be found. It was nine o'clock and she had decided to get rid of it. That decision upset Thomas, but mistakes happen–like the time they made love under a blanket at Ocean City, plush towel in Tammy's mouth so the beach couldn't hear her.

Now she was late and she ran for the cat. Who would take care of it when she needed to go with Thomas to his parent's house for Thanksgiving? It was the only thing to do, the only way she could avoid breaking down in front of her own parents.

At Thomas's house, the family took her to see the sites of Boston. When Tammy took the elevator up to the top of the Prudential she almost threw up. Thomas, his mom and his dad watched her turn green. She had been able to hold it down the entire visit to Boston. Thomas's parents never knew. They never knew his grades at the time either. By January they would, but they never found out the secret Thomas and Tammy kept to themselves.

Later, his parents thought she was the reason he never studied, and she caused his grades to go south. "She is too important to him," the mother said.

When Thomas finally did fail out of school, he left on a bus. Tammy stayed at college; sad, but not wanting any part of Thomas, a kid who couldn't hack it.

111

Stella: S is for Cookie

Stella was not named after the character Marlon Brando yells for in *A Street Car Named Desire*. Stella was named after Stella D'Oro cookies. Her father was eating them during her delivery. It was apropos, as metaphorically her parents allowed her to eat any cookie she wanted, anytime she wanted it. If she wanted a toy, she got it. A certain item of clothing, it was a yes. A car? A man? Kids? She had it all. It was only after she realized that having it all wasn't making her happy that she finally gave in and suggested counseling for her failing marriage.

Bill would not go. Therapists don't see other therapists, much in the same way McDonald's workers don't go to Burger King. It was an unwritten law. So, Stella was not getting what she wanted. She didn't understand, because she went to both McDonald's and Burger King a lot. She bought a vibrator. She named it Vinnie the Vibrator. Vinnie was more useful than Bill.

Grady: Planning the 2 AM slot.

Grady pulls the knot of his tie up and down, then up and down again. He failed to sell former Red Sox manager, John McNamara on the idea of appearing in *Boston Ghost Stories*: McNamara slammed the phone down, confused, thinking he was being asked to appear on some kind of *Ghost of the Bambino* program. Grady knows he's stuck; his one lead—off the clipboard.

He pulls the hair by his right ear all the way over his balding head. He needs another idea… a show that features real people with real problems. His last idea, *Food Stamp Office*, had not gone over well, because no way would "those" people agree to be filmed. Wait… what about a reality show based on the production team at WHDH? Maybe starring one of the news anchors or featuring their wife? One of their newsman has just come off a messy divorce with a field reporter. The station tried to minimize the damage of that by running a "reporter gets the hard facts" public relations campaign. Grady thinks that viewers might enjoy an entire show escaping into the life of such a person.

There isn't much time to do this. The vacation feels so far away already. Joe tells him not to let the pressure get to him. Grady reminds himself, "Tell Bill your stuff so you won't explode."

Ethan: The dreams of his mother

Ethan's mother is having dreams of death, which manifested last week with her lying in bed thinking about her own death and suffering. She knows it's not going to be her, but she feels something coming; something so horrible she's afraid to think it, afraid to say any of it out loud to anyone. Damn. It's going to be someone else. Damn. She feels it the way she feels wet when it rains. It's something she knows, doesn't question.

This death will come like a train, and she'll be standing on the platform. It will be devastating, but she won't be able to control anything–like the train being on schedule and her odd justifying thoughts of jumping in front of it so someone else can be saved.

But when the train comes, she's stands paralyzed. The conductor takes her ticket and looks around, shakes his head. "Where's your son, Mrs. McGrath?"

She knows it'll all happen quickly, and then the train will pull away.

Dan: The heat

The booth smells like burnt sage. Kate's hands feel hot on Dan's arms. Kate moves down to his legs, and he feels loose and free. Dan feels like he's been riding a bicycle, that's been slowed by heavy mud, ever since his accident. Her hands pull the mud away, and now it feels as if his legs are peddling faster and faster; his brain

113

synopses firing and connecting. He imagines chasing down wild animals on foot.

Kate circles him. The warm breezes of the street blow through the booth. The bench he built is comfortable; the wood shellacked to a gloss so smooth that it doesn't feel hard at all.

"This is going to work just fine," Kate says when they are done. Dan sits up, light-headed and feels like he wants to kiss her. "No, Danny," she says, "I'm off to the woods right now. I hope you will continue on your path of hope, help, and love. This is what I share."

Chapter 8: Thursday, February 23

9:22 AM: Phone rings
Hit snooze button by mistake
Phone continues to ring
Wake up, answer

9:22 AM: Hanna

"Hello?"

"Bill?"

"Yes?"

"Where are you?"

"Who is this?"

"It's Hanna. I'm at your office. We have an appointment. Where are you?"

I sit, rub my eyes for a moment, can't understand why I'm not in my office. Then, remember, "I got suspended."

"Because of us?"

"I'm not supposed to talk about it."

"The secretary is gone, too."

"Administrative Assistant, yeah, she got fired."

"Why?"

"I think she's the one who ratted us out."

"So they fired her?"

"Well, it was a breach of confidentiality."

115

"But then they used the information and suspended you?"

"Look, Hanna, I really can't talk about it." I'm touched by her concern; also getting a little turned on. "Why don't you come over?"

"I don't think I want to. I still have issues. I'll have to talk to someone else about it."

"Screwed up dependency issues?"

"No, I'm not dependent on anything,"

"Neither am I."

I hear her sigh. Then, "I'll be there in twenty-five minutes."

"I'll be in bed, waiting for you."

9:40 AM: Kate

Kate's answering machine apologizes for not being able to take my call, but gives me an alternate number, which I recognize as my own office phone. I call it and she answers in a crisp warm voice, "Thank you for calling Mental Health Solutions of Sunny and Share, Inc. May I help you?"

"Are you looking for a secretarial job?" I ask.

"Bill!" she exclaims, "I'm just trying this out this week while you're away. Isn't it exciting?"

"No, it's *not*. It's not going to happen, Kate."

"It's just for the week, for now. Some of my people wanted to get off the street, and Robbie thinks having a space will bring in the new clientele I'm looking for. Oh, I've talked to Hanna and Thomas today too!"

"Who the hell told you to talk to?..."

"I cleared it with Robbie. He's so great; head held high, with so much newly-found confidence."

"That little shit!"

"Careful, your anger is being released into the Universe."

"Kate!"

"Oh, and speaking of anger, I saw Hanna today, and she was having a nutty."

"How bad of a nutty?"

"Don't you worry, Bill. I diagnosed her as having dependency issues. I suggested she do a quick breath meditation, but she was on the phone. She should be there soon."

I hear Hanna turning the key to my front door. "I have to go now," I say.

"See?" Kate says smugly.

10:25 AM: Thomas

I reach Thomas's voicemail as Hanna begins to touch me. "Thomas, mmmmm, ahhhhhh, I hope you get this in time... this is Bill Sloan, ooooooh, and I'm calling to tell you I won't be in today... so... umm... we'll have to pick up with everything next week. Sorry for the inconven...mmmm..."

"Hello?" Thomas picks up and I wave my hand at Hanna, so she quits tugging and slows it down to a very light touch.

"Yes, did you hear what I said?"

"Oh, I already knew. Kate told me."

"She did?"

"Yes, she's right here."

"You're at the office too?"

"Yes, Kate needed some help. Dan's here too, if you want to cancel his appointment."

"I don't see Daaaaaaa, ahhhh." I remove Hanna's hand from me, as she has started pulling again.

"That's not what Dan says. Dan says he's been paying for his appointments for two weeks now and that Kate referred him to you. He's getting kind of pissed."

"No. That's not right. There's no way he would remember, plus I referred Dan to Kate not the other way around. Wait a minute! I didn't even do that!"

Hanna stops again to give me a *"don't worry things, will feel great in a few minutes"* glance and then nuzzles up to my neck to kiss it.

"Bill, you're getting angry," Thomas laughs.

117

"No, no things are fine. Everything's okay."

"That's not what Kate says. She says you were suspended for unprofessional conduct. Ha!"

"Ummm. Mmmmm,"

"Is that what's going on?"

Hanna pulls the phone out of my hand and presses it to disconnect the call. "Shut the fuck up," she says after it's hung up. "Bill, you're off this week."

11:03 AM: Lunch—cherries, bacon, cheddar and Swiss cheese omelets, freshly-squeezed orange juice
11:44: AM: Back to bed

1:55 PM: Voicemail from Stella:
"I'm here and you aren't. To think you would ever be here when I need something! This is so typical of you Bill, and so totally you! The next time you're not going to show, why don't you let me know!! Fuck you!"
2:05 Second Voicemail from Stella:
"I don't know why you canceled. Are we on for next week? I hope so. Bye. Everything's fine."

3:00 PM: Grady

When I check in with Grady, he tells me he's going to explode, and I can hear him scratching over the phone. When will I be coming back to the office is the burning conflict he's facing? I have to make restaurant reservations at the moment is what I tell him, because it's hard to think. Grady asks if it's better to talk when I get back to my office. "Yes," I say.

He's voice raises to near panic, "When? When?"

"Listen, Grady," I tell him. "I'm just checking in. You knew I'm out for a week. If you need emergency psychiatric services you should go to the local ER."

He tells me he doesn't need the ER, he needs a ratings hit, something for late night after 2 AM. I tell him I can't talk about his problem now, but I can talk general television with him. He wants to know what the hell the difference is. I tell him to relax, fix his tie, and comb his hair over. "Have you ever considered producing a local self-help or a moderated help show?" I ask.

"Hmmm, can there be ghosts involved?"

"It's possible, depending on the patients, I mean the guests. Currently, no one I'm treating has issues with ghosts."

"Will very weak people that viewers might relate to, but will never meet in real life be included?"

"Absolutely."

"Okay. Good. I feel better."

I tell him that when my suspension is over, I'll have to bill him retroactively.

"Just save my job," he says.

4:00 PM: Ethan

Mr. McGrath says on the phone there have been fewer tantrums from Ethan, and that he's been dealing with things in a better way since the medication switch. I tell him that's good and I'm very fond of Ethan. Actually, the way I put it is that we are making great progress in his therapy. Mr. McGrath wishes the same thing would be true with his wife. "Sometimes it's good, sometimes it's bad," he says. Seems like when Ethan is doing better, the wife is doing worse. Lately she's been accusing him of being away from the house too much, but he says he's just working his regular hours. He doesn't know what to do. "You know what?" I say, "I think we can work on this when I see you next Thursday. It's really not okay to be doing all this by phone."

5:11 PM: Dan

I don't call Dan. Why would I call Dan? Kate says I should.

5:12 PM: Still home

Outside the office...

Hanna: Questions

The kid wants to know where his father is. Hanna no longer wants to say that he's in heaven, or that he went to a better place. She could tell him his father is not in pain anymore, but the kid's too young to understand. She used to tell him, "Daddy's gone." but then he would ask where, and she couldn't think of what to tell him. Now when he asks, she just says, "Dead." or "Go watch TV." Eventually he'll put it together. He'll know that death is forever; and his dad is in heaven, or in some place better than here. At the moment, he is learning he is alone in the world, and that his father and mother are both not around.

Hanna hopes that once the kid understands this "better place" concept, she will be able to explain to him what the worse place–pain and depression–is. She prays that she hasn't screwed him up the rest of his life with this plan of hers, because Brad screwed the kid up enough. The guilt alone is tough to deal with, but her mother, when she babysits, is far enough away from the situation to explain things much better to him than she ever could. Hanna knows her mother can't tell him the truth to when he asks, "What's wrong with momma?" When the kid asks where his momma is, Hanna's mother only says, "She's at a friend's house."

Thomas: Television

Growing up, Thomas' babysitter was the television. He wasn't allowed to leave the house very often. Maybe it was because he didn't play well with other kids, or maybe it was because his parents also would never leave the house. He watched sit-coms, dramas,

After School Specials, game shows, and every day, the 4:00 movie on Channel 38.

It was here that Thomas learned from Archie Bunker that racism was stupid, and that wives were ding-bats. He learned how to fantasize while watching *I Dream of Jeannie* (if he had any wishes, he would wish for her!). Ann Meara taught him in the movie, *Lovers and Other Strangers,* that when your husband's hair stopped smelling like raisins, love was gone–so he rubbed raisins in his hair. He learned about minorities, that they worked in odd junk lots, or as cleaning people. The projects weren't all bad, if Jimmie Walker was around. If you had a dream, you could "move on up", and live with the white people on East Side of New York.

Thomas learned role play and routine from *The Match Game.* A lesser-known character occupied the spot in the top left, Brett Sommers was top middle, Charles Nelson Reilly was top right, the hot chick was bottom left, Richard Dawson was bottom middle, and the awkward female comedian was bottom right. He also learned the show's contestants always picked Richard in the Super Match, so *Match Game* had to rig it with a wheel of chance, so that every celebrity had even odds to play.

Thomas thought John Belushi was funny, and Chevy Chase was not. He thought Larraine Newman, coked up and anorexic, was the sexiest of the three SNL women. Late on Saturday night was the only time he could touch himself; it wasn't a very big house. He loved a lot of women that way. Thomas thought Burt Convy was a goofy pot head, and everyone on the *Gong Show* did cocaine. Thomas learned to clap his hands like Chuck Barris when he spoke. He wanted more wishes from Jeannie (Barbara Eden, bottom left on the *Match Game*). Thomas wanted to go crazy.

Stella: What Bill does in the basement

Right before their marriage tanked, Bill started slipping out of bed in the middle of the night. He didn't go out–he went

121

downstairs and turned on his DVD player. Porn? No, Stella caught him in the act of watching Dr. Phil. The first time she walked in on him, she heard Dr. Phil introduce today's show as being about sex, divorce, relationships, infidelity, mid-life crisis, domestic violence, children, breast cancer, fashion, "and much more." Without revealing her presence, Stella watched too. It was worse than porn, and when that show ended, Bill put in another DVD, in which Dr. Phil had a heart to heart with Pat O'Brien. Stella went back upstairs and locked the bedroom door.

Grady and Joe: Their new beginning

Grady tried religion, because he thought he needed to try something. At first, he watched The Christian Cable Network, for enlightenment, but when his cable network's early morning broadcast of a Good Friday service at the Vatican abruptly changed to a 30-second *Girls Gone Wild* ad, he knew he needed a more direct approach to salvation. A year to the day after his wife kicked him out of the house, he and Joe stood in the ocean to be baptized.

During that year, Grady had slept on a cot in his office at WHDH. *This is where people sleep when they're dishonest*, he thought. *This is where they cry.*

Joe said that ever since he'd met Grady, he too was a changed man. Grady was his moral compass, and he was going to do everything differently; no more cheating, lying, or drinking. He was going to be serious. Joe got drunk twice more: the first night that they were together, and today; the day of their baptism. Both times were for damn good reasons, as far as Grady was concerned.

Grady and Joe stood in the shallow water, while Reverend Standish loomed above them on a rock. Grady's ex-wife stood alone, on the shore to bear witness. It was hard for Grady, not being of strong faith, to listen to Standish, especially with Joe whispering, "Prepare to Baptize," or "Captain, we're taking in water!" into Grady's ear. Joe suddenly snickered and Father

Standish was forced to pause. Joe pulled his beard for pain, which kept him from laughing even louder. Then, Standish went into the Prayer for Baptism Day:

Living and Loving Father,

I praise and thank You with my heart for the liberation You have given me from the clutches of sin and Satan. By Your death on the Cross of Calvary, You have put my old life with its sin and judgment to death forever, and endowed me with a new life that is abounding with joy.

Father, I commit this Baptism Day into Your most precious and loving hands. I believe that by Your crucifixion on the Cross, my old self was rendered powerless and I was freed from all sin. You were raised from the dead that I too may live a life victorious and overcoming all evil.

Father, this day, I rededicate myself to live in You and live a life for Your glory. I remember the day when I was baptized and washed off all my sins. Lord, it is Your grace that I must be counted worthy to be called Your child. Help me to keep Your commandments. Renew my strength this day that I may be strong in faith and increase in zeal. Preserve me for the glorious day of Your coming. I believe Your Word which says, "He who has begun a good work in you will complete it until the day of Jesus Christ". Let this day be the beginning. Lead me into greater spiritual depths even in the coming days. In Jesus' precious name I pray.

Amen.

Reverend Standish poured water over Joe's head.
"Honey, I have soap in my eyes," Joe shouted.

Father Standish steadied himself, so he wouldn't fall off his rock. "Are you all right?"

"Not until you say it," Joe demanded.

"Say what?"

"I now pronounce you man and husband," Joe yelled. This time, Standish slipped off the rock and splashed into the water. Joe jumped into Grady's arms. "I'm cleansed," he said. "It proves we are not terrible people."

Reverend Standish wouldn't even look at them. He'd had enough blasphemy for an entire lifetime.

Ethan: His mother's previous boyfriend

Jesus and Mrs. McGrath broke up twenty years back, but they're still friends. It had started to unravel when she asked Him to make a small fish dinner, then invited hundreds of her friends.

Mrs. McGrath tried to save it, by taking Him to the beach for a little getaway. She learned you should NEVER take Jesus to the beach; the lifeguards all hate Him. They get pissed when He walks on water, because then all the kids try it. A few times they kicked sand in His face. Then the clouds got dark, and the thunder boomed, and they had to go home.

At home, He was grumpy, as if He needed a miracle for her to see Him the way she used to. "Jesus Christ, it's not all about miracles," she told him. "I'm not asking you to save the world."

"See, that's just it. Whether I'm a hero or a martyr, I always come up short."

"No, you come up short when you want to know who's e-mailing me and how much money I have in my Goddamn bank account...oh sorry."

"Which reminds me, when we're in bed and you keep saying, *oh God, oh God, oh God.* How do you think it makes me feel when you cry out the name of my Father!" Jesus frowned.

"You had to go there, didn't you?" countered Mrs. McGrath.

"You remember what they said in Sunday School? That you can't invite Jesus into your house, and then not let him see what's in the closet?"

"Are we seriously back on this fucking closet thing?"

"I want you to tell me. Tell ME in all honesty about that. I AM part of the Trinity."

"Jesus, baby, you're part of more than one Trinity."

Then Jesus placed his scratchy straw hat on his thorn-scarred head and walked out.

Sometimes Jesus still gives Mrs. McGrath wine for her birthday. "Really Jesus?" she said. "You could have just made me a card."

Dan: The things you *do* remember

A nurse walked Dan back to a bed. "Where's my ice cream?" he asked. He saw the pillow and then he disappeared again. Being in a sleep-like state was the only time he remembered things, but when he woke it was all forgotten. Often, when he was asleep he saw images of concrete breaking and flaking into course, and then fine sand. His inner-consciousness would be jolted and some memory would come back to him. Then he yelled whatever was in his head.

Dan clicked the button for the pain medication. He didn't remember the last time he'd clicked. His lips were a bloody pulp, as once more, he had gnawed at them. His forehead and left arm were covered by thick bandages. His entire world was about clicking. It angered him. The television mini-speaker was in his bed. It was Chuck Woolery, "Two and Two" —too loud. *Click-click* again.

The ice cream here was terrible. The hospital had the kind in thin cardboard cups. The vanilla-chocolate mixture reminded him of the Yin-Yang symbol, and he yelled the word "Hoodsie!" at the top of his lungs. The nurse arrived, and asked if he had anything going on, and placed her warm hands on his head. She said she had unusual healing powers and asked about his car. He envisioned the

Chevy. He'd forgotten, until right that moment, that the car was blue. "Don't expect anything in return," she said.

There was a crystal clear blue sky, as if God had spread water color over a pane of glass.

There was a note Dan must have read for the tenth time today, stating that a van would take him to a Rehabilitation Center. "You know where you're going?" Dan asked the driver. "There's this place after you make a left called, *Bart's Homemade Ice Cream.*"

"No, not here. You're in Montana now," the driver said. It was one of the first days a large amount of Dan's mental concrete broke into sand. A day he'd always remember.

Chapter 9: Thursday, March 2

6:52 AM: Alarm clock
Hit snooze button once
7:02: Get up, shower
7:15: Take dog for half-assed walk

8:00 AM: Call from Robbie

Robbie tells me I'm reinstated. He says suspending me has gotten him promoted.

"How does *that* feel to you?" I ask; knee jerk reaction, because I automatically ask that in session, when I don't give a shit how people are feeling.

He says it feels good, and he's overcome his fear of confronting people with suspensions and firings. He tells me to come to the office.

"By then, I'll have figured out the Guidelines for Reinstatement," he says.

"Okay, I'll be there soon."

"Welcome back, Mr. Shore!"

"Sloan," I say.

"What?"

"Never mind."

9:00 AM: Hanna

I tell it's good to see her, but when I stand to hug her, she holds up her hand. "Not here," she says.

"What difference does it make? We've already broken the rule."

"I might only want to see you here." She holds up what looks to be the corner of a small plastic bag. "I found this at your house."

"How does finding the corner of a plastic bag at my house change things? Every household, I've ever been in, has plastic bags."

"I thought seeing you was going to help me through things, but it's not. It's turning out to be as bad as the last few guys, except you're not dead."

I tell Hanna it's not what it looks like, and that it's part of a treatment plan for someone else, and I'm using it as a kind of method acting. She says that I'm only fooling myself. I tell her if she is here to work things out, she'd better start bringing up some of her issues. "OK," she says. "I have an issue with this— you and me. I don't think it's working out too well."

I tell Hanna it might be good to keep coming, and I tell her I'm not using drugs. Hanna says she liked me better when I didn't care, and when I wasn't her therapist. I tell her I'm starting to care about her. "Go fuck yourself," she says.

9:45 AM: Kate

I see Kate a little early, because she's been in the reception area since 7 AM. "Isn't it exciting?" She throws her head back to laugh.

"I'm not comfortable with this, Kate. You can't see people here. What was wrong with seeing people on the street?"

"Oh, I do that too." She's dressed professionally today, but when she sees people on the street, she's casual. She says it's fear which paralyzes people, and it's what gets them get stuck in personal ruts. She says to "just let go". I tell her I didn't approve of this, and it's affecting my practice. Kate says Robbie has given her the okay.

"In any event," I say, in an effort to regain my status as her therapist, "I've noticed an improvement in regards to your own well-being. You're not as provocative, and you've embraced your therapeutic role. It's really commendable."

"You're funny. You don't mind me being provocative at all." When I don't answer, she says that the world is loosening me up a bit, but I'm still uptight. I swear, I have never understood why she comes here, and now I can't figure out how she figured out my façade. "Relax and close your eyes," she says. Then, she places her right hand on my forehead, and says that she can sense the tenseness from my last appointment.

I feel her warmth, a few inches from me, and it's intoxicating. "Open your eyes," she says, and when I do, I see that she has opened her shirt, and her small breasts are inches from my mouth; her nipples pointed and erect. She tugs on one of them lightly and places it in my mouth.

"There, there," she says, as her breathing gets heavier. She pulls her panties down beneath her skirt, unzips, and slides down on me. When she starts to orgasm, her legs tense and clamp, and I release myself into her.

10:45 AM: Thomas

He's talking about the voids in his life, and I'm thinking about Kate and Hanna. Hanna on-the-out, Kate on-the-in; both of them really great partners on the in and out, in and out, in and out. Am I using my position of power to be putting my patients in risky situations? Hanna, yes. Kate... I think she can handle it. Thomas doesn't know what to do. I can't focus on all of this at once. I make myself tune in.

"The Universe is fucking with me. Bad luck seems to happen, if I masturbate to porn. Better luck happens, when I use what's in my head. I put it out in the Universe, because of my Catholic upbringing, that porn is bad, and it causes the Universe to frown upon me. Then, bad things actually happen. I know that it's a bunch of shit."

"I see."

"Plus, too much mouse-clicking kills the mood, plus there's too many choices of different film clips."

"What about Kate?"

"She's more like my boss now. We don't fuck anymore, because she says she's saving it for one person. Jesus, I really liked her. In the beginning, I put up with the healing stuff just to have sex with her, and I think the sex opened me up to the healing. You know what I mean? But I'm still not completely open, and I'm not that healed. I wasn't doing any work on myself before her."

"Uh huh." I think about Kate's short skirt, her hard nipples. When she told me to close my eyes, I pictured her on the day she wore the tight t-shirt with no bra. Can Kate do whatever she wants to people? She must have produced that image purposefully. Oh, nipples.

"Ummm, Doc?"

"I'm not a doctor."

"You just said 'Oh, nipples.'"

"What? I did not!"

"You sighed and said, 'Oh, nipples', almost as if you were reading my mind, as I was thinking about..." He gets a funny look on his face, as if something has shaken him. He stands, and takes a step towards me, but I'm still on a state of relaxed bliss, so I don't react when he punches me in the side of my head, knocking me off my chair. "Fuck you, you asshole!" He opens the door to step out.

Robbie's anxious face appears. "Everything okay in here?"

"I'm fine," I say, getting up rubbing my head.

"Not you, HIM! You want to file a report?"

"No," I say, "I'm okay."

"Not you, HIM!"

Thomas has left the office, but I hear him shout back, "You bet your ass I do!"

In the waiting room, Kate is sitting crossed legged on the floor.

11:30 AM: Sandwich, apple, juice box
Toss it in trash

2:00 PM: Stella/Pearl

Stella tells me she's sorry that she yelled at me last week; she just gets frustrated. Stella is always frustrated. I ask if she can be Pearl now. I can't deal with Stella right now, because I'll just yell right back at her, if she stops being sorry.

Pearl wonders if I have to be this way, since I wasn't available to her last week. She's pissed.

"Let me get this straight," I say. "Stella is sorry but Pearl is mad?"

"What happened to you? The side of your face is all red."

"One of my clients got aggressive. It happens." *When you fuck the woman he loves.*

Pearl studies me, then asks if I've been drinking. She says I don't seem too lucid. I tell her that I've had an interesting day. She tells me to imagine her "interesting day" (using curled fingers in the air to indicate quotation marks) last week, when she went to see her therapist and he wasn't there.

"How *is* Carlton?" I ask.

"Wrapped up in permutations and self-preservation."

"Wrapped up in permutations and self-preservation," I repeat, because I like the sound of it, but she glares and says that she's going to be the next client to get "aggressive" (more fingers in the air for quotation marks). "How's that anger management thing working out?"

"Fuck you," she says.

131

I don't respond. Pearl asks if I'm okay. I tell her I'm fine. Stella says that I have a screw loose. I tell her there's a bunch of us, on the inside, that have a lot of screws loose.

2:55 PM: Grady

I tell Grady I've been thinking about the self-help television show some more, and if his station would like to produce it, I think it would really be good. I tell him I'm going to be direct with him, because I'm his therapist, and he's been a little thick, by not picking up on things.

He says he's been thinking about the show too, and here is his idea—a celebrity gossip show with dogs, providing the commentary using computer technology.

"What the fuck!" I say.

"No, just listen. I'm thinking Mel Gibson. He can have two dogs—a male and a female—with voiceovers, acting out the parts of him and his ex-girlfriend's famous fight. We can use the transcripts from their actual phone call. We can do it with all the celebrities, using animals, you know what I mean? If some movie star punches someone in the paparazzi, we could have a pit-bull acting out his part."

"Call *Animal Planet*," I say sarcastically.

"You don't think it's a good idea?"

"No, I think you'll get laughed out of your job."

"Oh. Oh, my," he says sadly. "I thought it was such a good idea. Maybe cats? That's it, cats!"

I tell Grady this is why he comes here. His ability to think clearly has been compromised, because of extreme stress. It's not going to take cats, dogs, pigs, or squirrels to save his career. Not even fish. I tell him to close his eyes, then tell him to open them, after I've moved my face right in front of his. "Look! What do you see?"

He eyes scan my face. "A red spot on your head and the beginning of a black eye."

132

"No, not that."

"Are you trying to say I should produce a regular guy's ultimate fighting show?"

"No! We've talked about this! Don't you remember? A live self-help show. Look at me," I smile. "I can do this. All my clients will agree to appear."

"They'll need to sign consent forms."

"Of course, it's perfect, live interviews and maybe some footage of their day to day lives. I'm volunteering to star in this! I won't ask for too much money, maybe $500,000?"

"Let me think about it."

"You think you can pitch this?"

"Maybe," he sighs. "You don't think the pet gossip show would be better? Or maybe ghosts of pets?"

I step away. "Jesus."

4:00 PM: Ethan

"Ethan, my boy," I say as he enters. "Today we're going to color." I've spread a large piece of paper on the floor along with a box of 64 crayons. He looks doubtful, and says he does this at school, with the school doctor. I tell him, today's coloring will be different. It won't mean anything. "It's just for fun. Don't you need some fun?"

He nods, then wants to know if the lady, on the floor by the magazines can color too. I tell him she's busy, doing something else.

He pulls out a red crayon and pushes a pattern out of wide, red arcs. "It's blood. It's blood," he says. He doesn't sound happy.

"It's nothing. It's fun. Let's try something together," I say. "Here's a story. Once upon a time, there was a boy, that nothing bad would ever happen to, for the rest of his life."

"That won't happen," Ethan says.

"Now, now go with it." I continue. "The boy is protected, by guided spirits, who watch over him. There is nothing bad, nothing painful, nothing at all, which causes him to be unhappy. Now, draw that."

He takes his fingernail, and tries to scratch the color away. "I can't get the blood off the paper," he says.

5:00 PM: Dan

Dan is sitting on the floor, next to Kate. "She's worried about you," he says to me. I tell him she's been very helpful, but he's not listening.

"Ever been on drugs?" I ask him. He has the blankest look on his face, as if he's a frozen frame of a movie. "Medication?" I ask.

5:22 PM: Commute, traffic very heavy
Call Hanna
Weave a bit
6:59 PM: Home
Go straight to bed

Outside the office...

Hanna: An early Randy encounter

"You can help heal my sadness, if you're still here, when the sun rises," Hanna says.

Randy tosses this around in his head, then laughs. "Oh, is that how it works?"

"I'm serious."

"I know you are. I don't know what to do with it."

"It is like this: We are here. We go THERE. When we wake up, we have breakfast."

"I've thought about it," Randy admits.

"That was fast."

"No, I've thought about it recently."

"And…"

"What about Brad?"

"What about him?"

"It's just a thought."

"Forget him. I want to devour you."

"Slow down. You see, that's just it. I don't want to be devoured, and I don't want to be a healer. I don't have it in me to heal anyone."

"I need to be healed. You can do it."

"No, I can't."

"I'm serious. It's not bullshit, what I said," Hanna frowns.

"Oh no? Your *how 'bout dinner* turned to *how 'bout breakfast…If I said you had a beautiful body…*"

She interrupts fretfully, "It's not a line; my heart IS sad."

"It struck me as odd, Hanna, given our track record. We both know breakfast would be impossible. I don't want Brad to find out what we've been up to."

"What would you rather I say? Would you rather hear I'm sorry for what I've done, and that I won't do it again? Do you want to hear, I'm trying to become a better person, and that we should stop doing this? Would you rather hear that? Because, I'm not there now. I'm not sorry."

"No, I don't want you to say that. I don't want to hear you say anything. What I want you to do, is take off your clothes. Then, I want you to go home, to your kid. I don't want you to say anything, Hanna, okay?

"Okay."

"Now… please stop talking."

Kate: Being in the Here and Now (after Kumiko)

It's not supposed to be like this. It's not supposed to hurt, and you're not supposed to cry. You are not supposed to make up ways to get over him. You should just be. Work, breathe, you are Zen and love, with great power over things like this.

It's not working.

You are supposed to want to grant forgiveness, not be stuck in the past. Today is now. Your past is not forgiving, and he doesn't know how upset you are, doesn't want to know, and doesn't care. You want to forgive the world, shout out this forgiveness, but whatever it is, it gets returned to you as faint as an echo.

You are also not supposed to miss him, but you do. In theory, you release him, and say, "There, go now, be happy, there is someone out there different than me; someone wonderful who deserves you too." You thought it was you, but there was an important difference of opinion on this.

You are here, and this is now. You deserve someone too. Remember how easy it is—a simple, transparent kind of easy; like air, like water.

When you grab someone new, you do it with love, but without feeling, and you spend the day in bed. You grant love to someone you hardly know, who doesn't deserve you. It was the first since Kumiko, and you wonder, *which now, what then* and *how did I get here?*

Thomas: You've got to take care of yourself

Thomas's father taught him about life with a pair of boxing gloves. Thomas was eight, and his father boxed him from his knees. *Thwack.* "Keep your hands up," he yelled. *Thwack, Thwack, Thwack.* Thomas was eight. *Thwack.* "Get outta the corner!" *Thwack, Thwack, Left, Right, combination.* The basement had a brick wall on one side, laid out in a semi-circle. *Thwack.* Thomas went down, banging his head on the bricks. He didn't cry. "Get up, get up," his father

136

yelled. "I didn't even hit you. You've got to be tough. Don't be a pussy!" Thomas was eight.

Thomas's father rarely spent time with him, so life's lessons occurred in this way. "Get up," he said "and make something of yourself." Thomas got up, and in a fury, threw lefts and rights, as fast as he could, grunting loudly, and screaming out with savage sounds, and still didn't cry. His father pretended to cover up, pretended the punches were knocking his head to the left, and to right, back and forth, like a pendulum on a grandfather clock. He waited for Thomas to slow down and tire out, which took longer and longer. That made his father happy. Thomas stayed in a rage until he was completely sucking in the fumes. Then he stood there, arms down, too weak to throw another punch, as his father peered at him over his boxing gloves, smirking before tossing out a heavy right jab; the hardest one all day. Thomas went down again. He wanted to cry, but he twisted his face and didn't.

"Son, you've got to take care of yourself," his father said, slipping out of his gloves. "Everyone you meet, is going to think they're better than you." Thomas wanted to swear, but he was only eight, and didn't know a word that was strong enough.

Stella: A good man never left (or even entered) the building

When Stella was six, her parents lived in a house with Elvis-patterned wallpaper in the bathroom. It was gold and white striped, with stenciled Elvis portraits, from various points of his career. The Elvises ranged from the early greaser years, to the big bell-bottomed, over-sized glasses, and shaggy-haired ones, toward the end of his life. Stella loved all of them. She thought when she grew up, she'd marry a man who would be flexible enough to be able to meet the needs of his career and life; a man who could be wonderful in many different ways for over a span of twenty years. When he stopped being wonderful, he could die, she thought, just like Elvis. Of course, Elvis would love her in such a way that he'd

137

never take drugs, never get fat, never lose it, and laugh while singing, "Are You Lonesome Tonight". She would keep him happy as long as he lived.

Bill was a handsome man when they met. In her mind, he had near-Elvis potential. His dreams to become famous were something she latched onto. As the years passed, she realized he was only a small therapist in the big treatment pond—nothing special; not really empathetic, and worst of all, he was unhappy. She eventually stopped caring. She grew tired of the bare trees that bloomed every spring with leaves that changed, and fell until another cold winter gripped their lives, without love or joy. Bill did his best to keep up with the snow; to keep the driveway clear. He was happy to be out of the house, even if the snow built up and buried everything else.

Has she totally given up the ideal? She'd done a check list on Carlton. He didn't like rock 'n' roll, but he would listen to Rush. Rush Limbaugh, that is. Is this what it had all become? How do you save your life when it felt as if, first, Elvis had left her alone in a vacant building for years, followed by, Carlton, who was as simple as white bread, as safe as never leaving the house? Being with Carlton was like looking at plain, white painted walls. But Elvis was out in the world somewhere, just like the old wallpaper: Elvis, guitar slung over his shoulder, and hips skewed, pushed out at an angle.

Grady: Insomnia

Grady tosses and turns, lies on one side, then the other. He can't stop scratching. He moves to his stomach and rests his forehead on the back of his hand. He lies on his back and looks at the ceiling. Grady doesn't count sheep. He never counts sheep, because it occupies his brain. Joe is in the guest room, because he can't sleep with Grady when he's thrashing around.

Grady wonders if he were to suddenly die, who would feel sorry for him. He thinks about getting a gun and shooting himself in the head. He thinks about getting angry at his boss and having a fistfight with him. He has never had a fistfight in his life.

Grady took an Ambien two hours ago, but obviously it didn't work, and the window of opportunity for sleep has closed. Wide awake, he lies there helpless, as the bad ideas blow in the breeze.

When he was a teenager, he masturbated to sleep every night, thinking about a boy he knew. After, he felt angry and alone. He always knew he was gay, but also always identified with his masculinity. Joe was the same way. That's why, after years of being alone, Grady was ready to settle down with Joe. Before Joe, Grady felt friendless and impenetrable. With Joe, he had someone to sit down and talk with.

Except moments like this, when Joe was asleep in the other room, and Grady was wide awake. Grady thinks he's messing up the relationship. He has the sudden urge to run into the other room and wake Joe up.

There is nothing to help this feeling of pressure and void when you're stuck in the middle of the night. Bill Sloan is a once-a-week visit, but somehow Grady feels that after the appointments, his problems are about other things, other problems, and even other worlds. It's not about him, he thinks, it's about television. Grady's never had therapy before. It's supposed to fix things, right?

Grady thinks that if there was someone, or something, in the middle of the night to take care of all of these thoughts, life would be easier. Then he thinks, Wait a minute! What if Bill were available in the middle of the night—on television? *I'd watch it right now*, Grady thinks. *What a brilliant idea! His best ever!* He no longer feels an itch.

Ethan: Parental anger

"Ethan doesn't know what he's doing!" she said.

"We can't help him!" he said.

"You're the one who wanted to send him away!"

"Why won't he stop sometimes?"

139

"It's my fault he was born this way!"

"It's your fault he was born this way!"

"It takes him hours to calm down!"

"He'll never get married. He'll never be a normal kid!"

"He's no good at sports!"

"He laughs too much!"

"He's always angry!"

"I wish he would eat more!"

"Why won't he sleep?"

"I'm not seeing the things he is seeing!"

"You're causing this!"

"He's causing us to do this!"

"I hate him sometimes!"

"I hate this!"

"I wish I could grab him and make all of this go away!

"I love him too much, it's impossible!"

"I'm not sorry for any of this."

"We do the best we can."

Dan: The pursuit of something

On January 1, 2000, Dan got in his car and drove across the country with twenty cassettes to listen to. It was the first in a series of driving back and forth, (every three months), back and forth, and back and forth.

Dan found great comfort in accomplishing this drive, accomplishing something, yet doing nothing at the same time. Dan thought he felt like most people; people find comfort in their unique pain. It belongs to them and it's a familiar place to go. It can even be healthy, when it's not totally debilitating.

On September 19, 2002, Dan's car hit an antelope in Montana. The beast's horn pierced his windshield, surged into his forehead, and caused a dent in his brain. The accident also opened a ten inch gash on his left forearm. The large wound ruined the inked tattooed sleeve, he'd paid to have drawn on, by his ex-girlfriend. They'd broken up on New Year's Eve, 1999.

The antelope's horn is prized by many cultures, for medicinal and magical powers, but this was not a prize, as the horn totaled both the Chevy, and his brain.

After the accident, Dan's unique pain was replaced by a more basic anger, and short term memory loss. At first, he could only remember flavors of ice cream. The doctors said that there would be frustration, from the loss of brain functioning. Dan thought it was the inability to find a release from his place of unique pain, which caused this frustration. He was mad at these doctors for misdiagnosing him, but he had no understanding of any of it. They were, in fact, agreeing with him.

Dan is too scared to drive. He doesn't remember the accident, or the antelope, but he has dreams of antelopes chasing him across the grasslands and attacking him. Equally alarming, are his dreams about lions and tigers attacking antelopes. He dips his hands into the bloody hole, punched out of the animals' torsos, and pulls out the bloody raw meat, and eats it. Then, he wakes, and his lips are sore. Every night, his teeth break through them.

Chapter 10: Thursday, March 9

7:22 AM: Alarm clock
Turn it off, oversleep
9:00: Get up
Feel pretty good
Oh, shit

9:42 AM: Hanna

When I arrive, Hanna is not here.

Aimee gives me a note. "It's from Hanna, I read it."

"Didn't you get fired?" I ask, but she doesn't answer right away.

"You should view the passing of information as a favor from one office to another. I work for Kate now."

"Bullshit! Hanna doesn't see Kate."

"Just a matter of time."

I'm glad she was fired. She was offered to re-join my team by Robbie, but she didn't take the offer. Hanna's note is written on the back of two yellow pamphlets from the waiting room, *An Improper Diagnosis will Ruin Your Day.*

> *Dear Bill,*
> *Going back and forth as your lover and patient has thrown*
> *me for a loop. I wasn't expecting that. I wanted someone safe*
> *to go to, someone who might help me, someone who could be*

both those things. I view you as selfish, but I too am lost. I'm the one doing all the work. I come to your office to work on me and to your house to work some more (on you). You told me at one of our appointments that commitment was something difficult for me and I think I've shown something toward you. I don't think I care enough to carry your baggage with you but I do care enough to need therapy. Can we do that?

Hanna.

P.S. I think you're too old.

It takes me a few minutes to read, so I think I'll bill her for it. I grab a pamphlet from the waiting room, write, *"Yes, we can do that"* on it, and tell Aimee to mail it out. She says, she no longer works for me.

10:00 AM: Kate

Kate and Aimee come in. Kate says that I'm creating an uncomfortable, non-loving work environment, because of our dual practices, and the harassment of her employees. I tell her Robbie is the one confusing all of these lines.

"It's Aimee's report, of your behavior, that's damaging."

"Oh, so, how do you feel about that?" I ask.

"I feel that everything about it is really fucked up."

"Hmmm, it is?" I ask. "Can Aimee leave, so we can talk about this?"

Aimee clears her throat. She says she feels I've overstepped my bounds.

"Really?" I ask. "And reading personal notes, between a patient and their therapist, isn't overstepping yours?"

"I don't mean *that*," Aimee says. "You told Thomas I was available."

"Thomas is a liar. That's why I treat him! I told him, I couldn't give him your number, or your schedule."

144

"The client information you are giving me right now, that Thomas is a liar, is overstepping your bounds as well!"

"How is this happening?" I ask.

Kate says that everyone should center themselves now and take a deep breath. There is nothing we can do with the external things in our lives. Robbie is there to deal with all of that.

"Excuse me?"

"Oh," Kate says, "Robbie is my new HR person too. He says he can handle two jobs."

Again, I'm left wondering why Kate should see me. Redirection is in order. "How is Sunny and Share going, since you brought it up?"

"Oh, this is going to surprise you. We are getting some new clients very soon. Aimee, you can be excused, to work on some of those referrals and transfers."

Aimee shoots me daggers as she smiles. I can see why Thomas was interested.

"Why would that surprise me?" I ask.

"Well, you're my therapist, and you might think I'm flawed, but let me tell you, the street team, plus the people I treat in the booth, are getting to be almost too much…"

"I don't view my patients as flawed, but if what you're doing is getting to be overwhelming, you should think about not doing it."

"Ha! Nice try, and yes, you do think I'm flawed. I know for a fact. I get this information in meditation. Don't you know that about me by now?"

"Yes, and you get it from reading notes from Hanna."

"I didn't read it, but I knew what it said. Let me tell you about you, Bill. You need love… pure love, and that's what I give back to you. Everyone needs love, but the world is not a very loving place. The Universe offers much more than that. This is what I am offering, and you will need it later, believe me."

"Kate why do you come here?"

"I come here for you, of course."

145

10:56 AM: Thomas

"Well," I say to Thomas.

Thomas says, "Well, what?"

I'm attempting a technique, which gets clients to talk without giving them a topic. It's also a good method when you don't want to deal with someone. "Well?" I say.

"Well, what?"

It's 10:59 now. I'm willing to wait this out.

"You're crazy!" Thomas blurts out.

"Well…"

"Well, *what!* Quit fucking with me!" He looks like he might hit me again, so I switch up, "Well…how are things with Aimee?"

"You can ask her yourself, but she doesn't like you very much. I really don't talk to her. We're co-workers."

"That doesn't make much sense."

"Anything I tell you," Thomas says, "is a breach of trust."

"You mean a breach of confidentiality, don't you?"

"No. I don't. That would indicate some sort of confidential relationship."

"So," I say, "let me get this straight. You don't talk to her, you only work with her, but you only have a professional relationship. Still, you know she doesn't like me, because you and Aimee talk? Do you see where I'm going with this?"

"She was fired by you, dumb ass. Can't you connect the dots?"

"I am working on you, Thomas, and I can't connect dots unless I ask questions."

"Try."

"What?"

"Try to connect them."

"All right, Thomas. I'll play."

"You're taking a long time."

"Quiet! I'm thinking."

"Well?" Thomas asks.

146

"What."

"Well?" he grins.

"What."

"Well?"

"I think you'd make a great person for television," I say. "What do you say?"

"Ha!"

It's the first time I've seen him laugh.

11:55 AM: Lunch
Check my desk
Check the fridge
Avoid Aimee
Check my car
Listen to Beyoncé
Run to Taco Bell

1:35 PM: Stella/Pearl

Pearl says that it's good to see me.

"Really?"

"No, not really. I'm just saying that because I felt sorry for you, Bill. Your life is in shambles. Even your reception area is in total chaos."

"No, it's not. It's just no longer my reception area. Any chaos out there, you can blame on Sunny and Share."

"Cher? Didn't she just break up with someone?"

"No. Sunny and Share. She spells them both with an "s"."

"Oh, cute," she says.

"Well, everyone says she's cute, and that she has talent."

"Is she a threat to you? You wouldn't talk to any of your own clients, if your job didn't force you to. She's offering them something different."

"Well, Stell...I mean Pearl, she also offers her services to them on the street."

"Like a whore? I'm surprised you haven't acted on that."

"No, she offers them free healing, if they're not official clients yet. In fact, she offers everyone free healing."

"Oh," she says, "so that's what she was up to. I thought she was collecting for some cause that needed money for the Universe. Kind of like Greenpeace with a wider scale."

"So, how's Carlton?"

"He's fine. He thought you were boring."

"Boring? I threw him out. How boring could that have been?"

"Look, I think he's boring too, but I've been re-evaluating, and I've decided that he's good for me. You're not supposed to feel exhilarated through your life—when you're doing the dishes, when you're cleaning the house. Normal day-to-day life is boring."

"Stella, that's profound. I've never seen you do the dishes."

"Look, Bill, I think I'm making progress, at least I'm doing that."

"You're not here to make progress, are you? You're here to catch up and monitor me, as if I can still be the pawn in your life that I used to be!"

"Bill, you're getting upset. Can you state any of this without anger?"

"Sorry, I'm having a bad day."

"Would you like to wrap this up?"

"Yes," I say. "See you next week."

3:00 PM: Grady

Grady walks in and says he's ready for our "meeting". He's practically vibrating. He says that he's solved the main problem of his anxiety, and it had everything to do with me. His skin looks clear and untouched, almost as if air-brushed.

"That's what I get paid to do," I say. I almost say, "Shucks."

"No, it's what *I* get paid to do," he counters. "It has nothing to do with your therapy. It has to do with an idea I had, and it's wonderful!"

"What is it?"

"I'm going to pitch a late-night television show, which will be self-help or therapy oriented. A late night show, that'll be on after the network news, which will be more intimate than any other talk show. It will involve actual people, who need help with actual problems. We plan to syndicate it nationally when it starts to catch on."

"You thought of this? How did you come up with it?"

"I was awake all night, and it just came to me."

I don't remind Grady this is my idea, because I know by taking the wind out of his sail it might mean him losing enthusiasm about the project, plus he says, it involves me, so I sit quietly. "So you're going to pitch it? Would you like me to come?"

"Yes, but we need to discuss the idea first, so we're on the same page. I don't want you to blow this. This is my idea: half the show will be live couch-therapist segments from your office, and the other half will be filmed pieces, little flashes of the patient's daily lives during the week. There is nothing out there today with a therapy aspect. I mean there are plenty of reality shows that follow messed-up people around day to day, but there is nothing like this happening right now on TV."

"It's brilliant," I say. "I'm so behind this project. I think it may save your life."

"I think all your problems will be over," Grady says.

I don't know why he thinks I have any problems.

4:13 PM: Ethan

Ethan's father tells me Ethan's been agitated. I'm tuning out, thinking: *I'm excited I'm going to be on TV! I'm going to have my own show! Like Dr. Phil!* Ethan is having an easier time at his school, his father says, but when he's home, he's all over the road. *This may be a tough sell to the father to have Ethan on the program.* He's starting to throw objects when he's alone in his room, and then he lies about it. *This show may pay us all pretty handsomely.* He's never thrown stuff before.

149

Hmm, I'll be in People Magazine...Entertainment Weekly. When we confront him, he gets mad; and when we don't mention it, he does it again. *Bill Sloan and Jennifer Aniston pictured in Rome.* So what should we be doing? *Roma!* Bill, what should we be doing? *"Bill, I never knew therapists could be so sexy," Jennifer purrs...* Bill? *Please Jennifer, let's have another glass of wine first.* Bill? *Oh, Jennifer, I'm going to make love to you again and again.* Bill! Goddamn it!

"Oh," I say, the room feeling bright and buzzing. "Where's Ethan? Do you think he'd like to be on television?"

"No, he's not here now. He's in the waiting room. I asked to speak to you first. There are some problems. Television?"

"Well he's doing well in school, which indicates he's thriving with structure."

"Structure? That's a good one. You kept us waiting for nearly twenty minutes today."

"What about if he shows up regularly at 2 AM for filming, then we structure other times during the week, to film some short segments from his life. As far as punctual goes, from now on, on-the-dot will mean on-the-dot."

"Hmm, I don't know."

"Of course, I'll need consent signed by one of his parents."

"I'd have to think about it."

"He *is* doing well in school, right?"

"That's what they say."

"So let's bring him in to talk about it."

Ethan walks in wearing a winter knit baseball hat. "Hey buddy, would you like to be a television star?" I ask.

He throws his hands in the air and jumps around the office as if he were a contestant who just won a huge prize from *The Price is Right*. I get out of my chair to jump too, but his father is trying to restrain him. I wait until they leave to let out a shout.

5:11 PM: Dan

I give in. I do it for Kate. I decide to see Dan, with the memory problem. Dan says that he loved someone a long time ago, but he can't remember her face anymore. He shows me his tattooed arm, the picture ruined by scars from the stitches, but all I see is a ruined life. He says he's that remembering more and more. I ask him if I tell him something, will he remember it? He tells me probably not. I tell him there's not much I can do for him.

5:20 PM: Commute in heavy traffic
Radio on but volume too low to hear
6:45 PM: Home
Fix a drink
Google "reality television live taped therapist"
Find nothing

Outside the office...

Hanna: What do you do with men?

The Original Brad Breakup Plan

Tell Brad you've been thinking about how you live separately, and don't spend any time with each other. Tell him. Tell him you've created a Ben Franklin two-column list, with the pros and cons of staying together. The cons formed a list completely down the page, but the only pro was the child you had together. The cons included various control issues, being told to sell your car, living separately, arguments, and his mental illness. Tell him slowly and logically, so he understands and is able to empathize with you about what a jerk he is.

If things go well, map out the conditions of custody and visitation for your child. You want to be free to date, that's obvious, so individual time away from the child will be healthy and helpful for everyone. Don't say anything about Randy. Nothing specific, just discuss the nights and weekends. Tell Brad, it's really good for the child if we get along, and how it won't be hard. Tell him, it's what everybody wants.

The Actual Brad Move

Run in; take some of the kid's belongings when Brad is not home. Avoid future contact with Brad and his relatives.

The Brad Outcome

Continue to date his best friend, Randy. Struggle with rent and money. Struggle with guilt and doubt regarding *The Actual Brad Move* after the suicide.

The Original Randy Breakup Plan

Tell Randy, that you can't think of him, without thinking of Brad. When you kiss him now, you feel Brad's lips on you. Tell Randy, the sudden turn of events makes everything too serious between you and him. Tell him, you really only wanted a safe out and a fun time with him. Tell him he made you feel loved. Tell him, you love him, but you need a little space, that it's all too intense after the suicide. *It's so intense*, say that twice.

The Actual Randy Move

Avoid Randy on your birthday, when he'll want to take you out. Write him a note that says, *I can't see you anymore*, and put it in his mailbox the next day while he's at work. Let him be angry all he wants and then feel bad, because you like the guy.

The Randy Outcome

Randy gets angry and takes a two-day drive. Date your therapist.

The Original Bill Breakup Plan

Tell Bill, you'd like to see him in his office. Tell him, you rushed into things. Tell him, it's not ethical and you feel guilty. Tell him, it doesn't matter that you discontinued his services, it still makes you an accomplice to his unethical behavior. Tell him, it all happened too fast and it's way too complicated.

Scratch that. The plan is too complicated. Tell Bill, going back and forth isn't working. And that he's too old.

The Actual Bill Move

Don't go to your appointment, but send a note to his office, which ends with you noting his being too old. Also, make it state that you wish to continue therapy. When he objects, stick to not seeing him outside of the office.

The Bill Outcome

Wonder if Randy will take you back.

Kate: What is making love?

Kate thinks *fucking* is a great word. When there is great love, then fucking is also always making love–but fucking is real! *Fucking* is also pure erotic and graphic...physical, release, and then resolving back to baseline, entwined on the mattress. *Fucking* is legs and elbows locking, mouths hinging and unhinging, lips big round and oval, covering each other like soft masks of oxygen; bodies jaunty and sharp, vulnerable, yet dissolved with encouragement, keys found, minds expanded to warped states, a bullet piercing a target, the next bullet passing through the initial hole, a bulls eye again and again, and when there are words for this, you do not hear them. You cannot hear each other's words, which vibrate in such a way.

On the other hand, Kate despises the word *sex*–the phrase *to have sex*–sounds cold. It sounds like some predetermined act. *Sex* is clinical, an assignment with boundaries. You must have *sex* every Friday and Sunday, and then you must shower. You are required to participate in *sex,* and then be clean. If you have a successful position, then only have *sex* in that proven one. Don't forget God watching you from a point, at a known elevation. *Sex* requires instruction for your man: Insert once per second, and then after you manage to feel something, move the speed up to twice that. Last more than five minutes, but no longer than thirty. Define your self-worth in relationships, by all of these numbers. Kate hears it's important to have a "*sex life*", as society defines it. *Sex* is not driving over the speed limit and coming to a full stop, at a stop sign. Never read *Cosmo* and don't think about smells. *Sex* comes with an instruction manual.

Kate feels the best term for "it" is *making love*. *Making love* is the completion of a day; relaxed exhaustion, the sun setting over the water. It's plotted like a good story; a slow insightful beginning, a buildup of excitement to a climax, and then a resolve. *Making love* is pure and slow. It invites each and every sensual and emotional nerve to the same party. *Making love* is like a small rabbit in your lap, wrapped in a blanket. It's the swirl of all the senses, of two people, while the event happens. *Making love* is being the spectator and the participant, at the same time. It's having an orgasm, because you see his hair shake with each movement he makes, and God knows you love when his hair does that. It's giving and clear vision, as if we can see the details of the leaves on the trees from five miles away.

So, let's summarize. *Fucking* is engineering and driving a rocket to the moon, then returning from the moon without the rocket. *Sex* is fulfilling a contract and signing off on it. *Making love* is healing personal incompleteness and completing. We love, we heal. We feed ourselves, we nourish others. Be in the game to love, heal, feed, and nourish, but remember; it's as simple as it is now. Simple as the glorious shape of a laughing round mouth, lips stretched, yet still soft, identical in shape to when you laugh, to when you moan, released, and enraptured. We love. We heal. We love.

Thomas: What is a forced life change?

As bones stuck out of skin so slashed, Tammy waited outside the bus in the rain. The mist was cold, and the feeling on her arm turned from a cold, wet cobweb, to a dripping faucet. Thomas worked to catch her eye, inside this silver-framed monster, for a wave, a sad smile, or a hint of a goodbye, but the windows were fogged and it was impossible to see. Thomas had an opaque view of the world, and the ride would be rough and uncomfortable.

He'd sent more prayers straight to God's open ears than he could ever count. *Please, let this not be happening, please let this go the way I want. Please God, I'll leave it up to You, and I expect something, anything, because nothing has gone my way.* He said the prayers, humbly at first, then each day with growing anger. Finally, he screamed God's name and waited to hear something back. But there was nothing, not even an echo.

His teeth were not as straight as they should be, and his hair reached and twisted like corn up to the sky; his lips always seem cracked, and formed a crooked expression; a crookedness that Tammy loved once, but now found common. His sleeve was torn today, like the new life he already dreaded. It was awful to dread the race, while still in the starting blocks. He anticipated this moment for weeks, and felt a cold, large, wet stone weighing heavy upon his heart; crushing and squeezing the warm blood, the blood beating within, warm and still in love. If his blood were a lake, and the lake were his life, it felt like a hand forced his head under the water, and would not let him up for air.

For the past few months, Tammy had been looking at him as if she were looking through a crystal ball. She saw his future: *It was unfortunate. The road ahead for him will be closed. Still, he wants to ride, broken as an axe, torn off from driving too fast through rough patches, pot holes, and mud.* Tammy was the one driving straight on a smooth surface, speeding past him, with the words he called out left hanging in the air.

Thomas did not tell her where he was headed, and she didn't care until now that she was not able to see him inside the bus. At this moment, Tammy's mind was busy capturing thoughts of the bus heading past farms of cattle grazing, clothes lines with blinding white sheets, children running through meadows, and finally ending in a sunny land of palm trees. Her thoughts were not interrupted by his unanswered prayers. She hadn't heard them either, but she wanted the best for him, and she wanted him far away.

The engine growled to a start. Thomas's palm made a sudden circle on the bus window. A hole in the fog appeared, and for a split second they saw each other, and she was not able to stop it.

Stella: What are the things we deserve?

We give ourselves sheets with high thread counts and carpets we don't dare step on. We give ourselves things we can pay for later, with a credit card, or when forced to by a collection agency; always third or fourth party involvement.

We give ourselves parties. We are there to look good; we marry so we don't give the appearance of being alone. That looks good. We marry the wrong people so we have things to talk about to our girlfriends. We deserve a cleaning person and a personal chef. We shouldn't have to do anything if our mate is an asshole, except divorce him.

When we have kids and they screw up their lives, we don't deserve that. We have given them everything. We have mortgaged our future for happiness. People who die young, don't deserve to die, and their loved ones, do not deserve to be devastated by that.

No one deserves the things in life that people talk to your ex-husband, Bill Sloan, about. When you and he see each other, you think you don't deserve the things in life that *you* talk to him about. When you were married you wondered how Bill could listen to all the bullshit from his patients. You wondered if the patients, or Bill, deserved the hour each week. Was it a good hour? Was it helpful to him? It seemed Bill hated them all and they all hated him. Still, it paid for all the stuff. He says that he deserves to be appointed to Sainthood, or be famous, for all he does. You say, he deserves what he gets.

We deserve new marriages and we deserve having them work. Dammit, what we go through! We deserve someone who is attractive and smart, able express his feelings, has money, and is there for us. We are bitter and resentful when people are who they are, and they are not better, or as good as what we think we deserve. We deserve better, not worse, and we also deserve, "for better or worse".

Grady: What makes a hit show?

Grady knows viewers with little or no intelligence will make a hit show. Funny how hits are measured in a collective *we*, by an industry striving for quality, which measures success purely in the total quantity of mass viewers. Grady has no respect toward what people watch these days, but he needs the job. To attract viewers, a hook is necessary; but these hooks delve into the deepest darkest and most embarrassing depths of the inner soul.

At a staff meeting, Grady says, "When we were growing up, we were taught to respect and treat people with differences as if everyone was all the same. Television teaches you to view the train wreck; to point and laugh at the 'Real Housewives' or the victims of 'Interventions'. Television asks the viewer to extend their disbelief in such matters. Do the addicts really believe they're being filmed for a documentary on addiction? If only viewers knew the stars in these shows were actually paid participants, and the money helps them to purchase their destruction of choice. Talk about a deal with the devil!" When Grady works, it's side by side with the Devil, seven days a week.

The speech is well received by staff members of WHDH. The hook the station used for years, was the local news lead in. If the news yielded bad ratings, the network's late night talk show was doomed. If WHDH's anchor showed less cleavage than Channel 4's anchor did, then Letterman would beat Leno in that market. Part of Grady's job was to suggest attractive actors who were good readers and easy on the eyes. They must have longevity in order to earn the public's trust, because the public is dumb enough to believe the anchors "deliver the news to their homes," at a time when no one invites a stranger into their house.

Grady's department also develops shows for night owls: the 2:00-5:00 AM time slots, where insomniacs intercept with the early risers. WHDH doesn't care about hits during this time, but they do care about profit and cost. Infomercials are preferred as they are paid programming; no cost, even if there aren't any viewers. Research reveals that televisions are on, but no one can say whether the viewers' eyes are open. WHDH doesn't care, and because of this, they don't need Grady's services the way they used to. It used to be, Grady produced all-night shows, which featured interviews of local celebrities, along with common B-list celebrities. His shows back then were never as interesting, or as slick looking as a sixty minute Magic Bullet commercial. People bought into "Six Minute Eggs", "Lickity-Split Deviled Ham", and "Before You Know It Bean Dip."

Grady thinks he'll be out of a job soon. He's not much of a gambler, and tends to like to check all bets at work, but the blinds are getting higher, and his chip pile is getting smaller and smaller. Grady feels he has to go all-in with all he has left; otherwise it'll be him and his husband struggling, through the last years of their lives.

Grady is spending nights without sleep, working on the pitch for *The Dr. Bill Sloan Show*. It's a huge gamble, but it's all he has.

Ethan: What do I want to be when I grow up?

Ethan's bipolar disorder is cycling. He's wide awake, wondering if he will ever grow old. *I'd like to be normal. I'd like to do something important, and get famous or something, maybe. I know I'm messed up. I go to a special school, but it's not "special" as in retarded; it's a special arts and thinking school.*

He thinks about Bill Sloan and how Bill likes to help him. The other day Bill told him he would be on television. Ethan thinks it's a huge opportunity, as finally, people will be able to see him the way he really is, and the way he really wants to be. He wants to walk down the street and be recognized.

Ethan wants to thank Bill, but he won't see him for another three days. When Bill told him about the TV show, Ethan started jumping around. His dad made him stop, but he couldn't, for about fifteen minutes. Sometimes things feel out of his control. When he's tired during the day, they change his medicine, and then it feels like everything else is jumping around. So when Ethan jumps around, they change it back again. He has a hard time trusting his parents because they always agree with the changes. *Can't I ever be right?*

When he sees Bill, he doesn't want to say anything, but he trusts him. Bill tells him he understands, and he'll try to fix things. Ethan wants to get fixed and to do better. His teachers say, that he's smart, but he doesn't think so, and if he tries to sit still, the next thing he knows, he's running around the room, screaming. Later, the doctor at Waysworth just sits there watching him without saying anything. It makes Ethan feel like a jerk.

It's 3:00 AM, and Ethan wishes he could talk to Bill; thank him for what he's doing. Ethan feels like he can flap his arms and fly to Boston, right to Bill's office. *If I concentrate, I know I can do it. I just can't tell anyone.*

Dan: What does Dan do today?

Dan pulls out a piece of paper from the front pocket of his work shirt. It says Thursday, an address, and the name Bill Sloan.

He calls a cab. He doesn't remember the bus number, but he knows he needs to transfer at Harvard Square, and that the bus route begins with a seven. Did Bill Sloan decide to see, or not see him? Does he stop at Kate's first? Today is Thursday, and Thursday's schedule is written down on the piece of paper. If Dan can get there, somehow Kate is connected to that. Dan's brain connects Bill with Kate, and Kate helps him a lot. Dan, now remembers more things. He remembers the word *Reiki* and *antelope*. Somehow, that helps. Kate and Reiki are connected, and she helps in the Universe. Kate tells him, when he does not know what to do, to just do. It's a key and it makes life better. Dan can remember that.

Chapter 11: Thursday, March 16

7:22 AM: Alarm clock
Get up
Coffee and a donut
7:45: Not much traffic
Arrive early

8:17 AM: Robbie

When I walk into the office area, I smell something burning and yell for Robbie, who runs in. "It's just Kate working with Hanna," he explains. "She's burning sage."

"Hanna doesn't see Kate," I say.

"She does now."

"I'm surprised the smoke alarm doesn't go off."

"If it did, we'd have to evacuate in two and a half minutes, otherwise OSHA would make us run monthly fire drills for a year, two during the overnight shift."

"Who's here at that time?"

"I can't say anything, but those are the regulations." Robbie stands in a spot for three seconds at a time, then he moves to another spot five feet away. His jittery behavior is bothersome.

"Boy, haven't *we* taken the job seriously. Are you nervous about something?"

"Bill, we should plan a time to meet."

"Oh, and you got my name right. Look Robbie, I get a little booked up on Thursdays. I can refer you to someone I think is really good. He works well with adults in their early twenties."

"I'm asking you to make an appointment to speak with me at Human Resources."

"Is this about the Rules for Reinstatement? Honestly, I haven't had the time to look at them. I'll get on that and catch up to you sometime."

"I'll be in to get you at your lunch break."

8:50 AM: Hanna

I let Hanna in early. I'm curious about what she's doing with Kate. She charges in, her dark brown hair shines, appearing almost dark black, with blue highlights.

"I'm so glad you decided to see me," she says.

"I didn't decide to do anything. You kept your appointment, so it's something you did for yourself. What were you doing with Kate?"

"Well, Kate and I are doing some beginners healing. Very basic stuff, but I'm not sure about it. Maybe it's for you, you know, maybe use the energy to work on your own issues."

"And what would those be?"

"I don't know, but I don't want to talk about it here. I'll discuss it during my sessions with Kate. She seems to know everything. Perhaps I'm done with men for a while."

"So, the work we did, you and I, didn't help you to see any of that? I'm not sure if I agree with what you just said."

"Maybe you helped scratch the surface, but I don't know. There's some sort of clarity when Kate works on me. I can't put my finger on it."

"Are you thinking of seeing her?"

"NO! And to be straight, you and I are in a professional relationship now. I'm retaining you, because I still think you can help me. I feel I'm getting better dealing with things. I want you to

162

know though, that if I want to see people in a different way, I have every right to see them. I think I've earned that."

"I have something to ask you, as long as you're being open…"

"Lately, I'd like to shout everything out to the Universe; being a single mom, the death of Brad, the relationship with Randy, what I had with you… how I'm a survivor and how I'm succeeding."

"You interested in shouting your view of death and dating to the Universe? If you really want to shout it out, I'm prepared to give you something you could use as a platform for this. What do you think?"

"I want to shout it out."

"Good, sign this." I hand Hanna the television permission form.

10:00 AM: Kate

Kate says she burns sage to clear the negative energy fields in an area, and apparently she burned a lot today. When she comes in I ask her if the fire is in control. Kate tilts her head as if something has struck her funny. "I mean that in a very non-literal way," I say.

"It burns very hot," she tells me.

"I've been hearing your business is going well, and you're picking up new clients left and right."

"Yes, it's very exciting. Ever since Robbie let me move into the reception area, new patients seem to fall right in my lap."

"Yes, but as you know, those are *my* patients."

"I don't think we're supposed to talk about your patients. Aren't there professional limitations there?"

It funny that Kate is suddenly speaking about limits. "It's fine, as long as I don't start to lose my clients. With everything going on, I don't want to stretch them too thin as I need them… er, I mean, they need to deal with their issues. Are you still making love to any of them?"

163

"Bill," she says, sweeping her hair over her shoulders, "you're so funny. You know I can offer them something you can't. I'm very specialized."

"Is that what you call it? What exactly are you offering?"

"Help," she says. "They get it from me. I no longer want to make love to any of them. It felt good and it helped them, but somehow, it left me feeling empty. I'm only going to go with one person at this point, is what I think."

"Then what do you get from them?"

"I don't know what you mean."

I look at her and she appears lost in the world. I'm amazed someone as strong in their convictions can look as lost as the deer in headlights. No one wants to think of what happens next when the deer gets hit, but I do. "Does helping others, help you?"

"Yes, it does. The same way seeing you, helps both of us."

"Do you think you might be projecting there?"

"Of course, we all project things all the time. We all want things to be positive in the end, and in the future, so I think that's what we all project. We put out, into the Universe, things we want."

I see her sitting on the chair, crossed legged, what do they call that, lotus position? I project her in the woods, sitting there for hours, at peace, and at one with her surroundings, white light around her, and she beams of love. I would like to go there, but I shake my head quickly, as if to clear the cobwebs out. "I have a tough time believing that crap Kate, but if it's helping you get better, I don't have a problem with it."

10:25 AM: Thomas

"Tell me about the show again," Thomas says. His t-shirt rides just over the waist of his pants, and I can see the hair on his lower stomach. I'd forgotten that he was the first one I'd told.

"I'd like to fight someone on the show. Not real tough street fighter types, but people my age, who might be out of shape. You

164

told me last week, I'd be good on television. Did you think of that after I knocked you in the face?"

"No. It's not going to be a show about you, and only you. It's mostly going to be about the people I treat, and my perspectives on them. Like now, I observed you smile, when you used the word *knocked*. That's very indicative of something."

"Don't you think Kate is the one who should have a show?" he asks. "She seems to be an up-and-coming player in what you would call, the help department. She could do a show like that, but without the violence."

"Do you ever watch Dr. Phil?" I ask, trying to change the subject, but immediately realize I'd made a mistake.

"*That* fucktard?"

"Well, he may be that," I say, "but he's entertaining, and TV is an entertainment business." I'm making another mistake by trying to reason with him.

"Maybe the two of *you* could fight." He contemplates, or it's close enough to contemplation, that I imagine it within the realm of possibility for him. "It IS an entertaining business, and two psych doctors fighting it out would be very interesting. It would kind of be like a chick-fight. Everyone likes a good chick-fight."

"Look, the last time there was aggression in here, I was the one who got hurt, both physically and professionally. You're lucky I continue to treat you, and also lucky I didn't report you to the court."

"Lucky? I would have sued you, if you refused to treat me," Thomas laughs. "I still might."

"What grounds?"

"Did you ever read your personnel file? There's plenty in there. You should ask Robbie to take a look. It's quite interesting."

"You read my personnel file? How could you possibly?"

"Well, Robbie and I both work with Kate. You really should take a look, doctor."

"I'm not a doctor," I say.

165

"Oh, it says that in there too."

11:30 AM: Lunch
Shit, dammit, forgot to bring lunch
Eat two (2) packages of individually-wrapped saltines from the break room
Forget to meet Robbie

11:40 AM: Stella/Pearl

I tell Stella that I think she might really be developing a Multiple Personality Disorder, based on how she goes from Stella to Pearl with such ease. "I'm feeling you really don't remember the person you come here as, the one you booked the initial appointments as, and the fact of the matter is, you *are* Stella, period! Stella, what are you doing here?"

"I'm visiting you. Where's your sandwich, apple, and juice box?"

"Never mind," I say. "Do you understand that visiting me for lunch is not a wanted visit, and I charge you for that time? Perhaps, you should be visiting Carlton."

"No, that would be an unwanted visit, too. Hey, don't you worry, you can charge Pearl for the time."

"Ah-ha! So you know who she is!" I'm always victorious over her missteps.

"No, Bill. They bill her at my address."

"Oh, course."

"I also have a release which Pearl signed, allowing your show to film her." Stella passes the paper to me. It is signed in a way, which doesn't approximate Stella's signature, one I would recognize in a second from all the checks, which came back in our bank statements, and the signatures on our divorce papers. "Your *show*?" she cackles.

"They will be following you, too," I say.

"No they won't! I didn't sign anything."

"But if Pearl signed for it, I think the show is all set. We're clear, legal and segmented for your time slot, but do me a favor anyway. When the camera suddenly appears in front of you, don't punch it, or get angry, because it's there for Pearl. Can you remember that?"

Stella is a short woman, but now she suddenly appears three to six inches taller. "I don't know."

"Maybe write something on your hand."

"Why would I want to do that?"

"If you suddenly see you're surrounded by cameras, you can't blame me, as you must realize it's Pearl's doing, and those cameras are there for Pearl, and not for you, Stella."

"Stella?" she asks.

2:04 PM: Grady

Grady says that before he tries his pitch to WHDH, he has to make sure all the ducks are in a row. "That's industry talk," he says.

"I'm familiar with the term," I say.

"So, are all the stars of the show ready? Do we have them all signed?"

"Yes, I'd say almost all of them, and half of one."

"What?"

"It's mental illness. It's complicated."

"Television is my field, Bill. I know how complicated things get, especially at the last minute. You'll see how amazing it is when everything comes together and we have a show. It will be thrilling. But let me guess…some of them want more money?"

"I didn't offer anyone anything. The permission form states in the fine print, that this is part of their treatment, but they won't be charged any extra money for any of it. That would be the offset."

"Oh, that's marvelous," Grady says. "Cheap will help so much, when I'm pitching the show. Free is good, but potentially, the station could bill their insurance carrier extra, for their promotional appearance. Plus, the permission form clearly states that they can't sue us, right?"

"Yes, it does, but let's not push it with the extra billing part."

"Good idea," he beams.

"I've never seen you as happy as during these past few weeks."

"Happy about the potential of this," he says, "but it feels more like delirium. I'm hardly sleeping."

I could refer him to the office psychiatrist, for perhaps some medication, but I don't. What if he gets nailed down with a diagnoses requiring Lithium? It could flatten him out emotionally, and then it's goodbye TV show. "A little sleeplessness is normal, and never hurt anyone," I say. "You're fine."

4:00 PM: Ethan

Ethan's father walks in alone. "You got to help us," he says. "Ethan is manic and out of control. I can't get him to settle down."

"Sometimes the medication change will work temporarily, but when it all balances out, it may still need to be fine-tuned."

"He was getting better, and he was starting to focus a few weeks ago. Then things started to slowly head on the upswing, and then when he found out about the TV show, he's up all night watching. He says that he's checking to see how the show is going to do, compared to the competition."

"It's healthy to be competitive," I say.

"He's nine! He has no fucking idea or reason for why that's important, and when he is manic I can't stand it! I'm thinking of pulling the plug on him being on the show."

"You can't!" I quickly scream but then use my calmer voice. "I mean, he *is* looking forward to it."

"It's live, and it's going to be in the late-late slot, right?"

"At first, but I have confidence it'll be daytime, then primetime before you know it. Look, he's awake anyway, and it's something positive for him to be a part of."

"He's more anxious than excited," Ethan's father says. "He says he's off the seesaw, and needs to power himself back up, because if he doesn't, 'mom will break.' What does that mean?"

"I'm not sure. But in terms of his mania, we can treat that. The viewing audience will see the improvement, and Ethan will see it too. His confidence will grow. It will happen live and on tape! Nothing bad will happen. I promise that, and we can edit out anything, if something does!"

"I don't want you to edit, I want you to help him. I know Ethan trusts you, so that's good. But I don't know…"

"Do you think if he stops seeing me, Waysworth will be able to make any progress with him? I've seen cases like this before; in fact, my brother was just like this. It's why I went into this field, so nothing bad will happen to my brother."

"Your brother?"

"I mean your son. I will do whatever it takes to set him up to deal with what he goes through, and to have a happy, healthy, normal life."

"So this TV show…"

"It'll make him a household name. He'll thrive, like one of those plants you see expanding and opening in a time-lapsed film."

"Huh?"

"He's a flower growing. Give him a little time, and he'll be vibrant and alive. He'll be a normal kid. I'll challenge him, but he'll succeed. You watch…

"I'm usually not up at that hour, but I'll watch. You make it sound like a slam dunk."

"Nothing is guaranteed, but I believe in the show. See you next week, and make sure Ethan is ready. I want him to have some creative control over his own segment."

"But aren't you concerned, at all, about that?"

"He'll be fine."

4:55 PM: Dan

I forgot that Dan was coming in. He said he paid me, but I don't think he did. I don't remember if we billed him. It's something I can ask Robbie, but I'm trying to forget to run into Robbie, so that way not running into him, would not seem like I'm intentionally avoiding him. Dan has a slip of paper with him. "Number one," he says, "I have a job."

"Let me see that," I say. He hands the paper over to me. "That's number two on the list. Number one, is to see me at 4:45 today, which you did."

"Yes."

"What would you do if you didn't write it down? Where would you be right now?"

"Oh, I'd probably be right on this street, doing something related to my job."

"What is your job?"

"I'm doing whatever Kate wants me to do. I'm helping her help others, the same way, she's helping me."

"How come you remember that?"

"Kate does Reiki on my brain and it helps me remember things related to what she needs. I remember to contact her every day. It's all pretty good. Whenever I think of an antelope, I get an instant message in my brain about what Kate wants me to do."

"Antelope?"

"Yes. Sometimes it's just a message to call her."

"What, exactly, do you do for her?"

"At first I was just helping promote her business, but now I'm involved in the construction of her new office. You should see the blueprints!" He waves his arms around my office area. "This place is going to be amazing; perfect for meditation and sharing."

"No, no, no. She should be setting up somewhere else, Dan. Perhaps your wires got crossed, inside that head of yours."

"No, I don't think so," he laughs. "It's almost as if there's a direct access from her brain, right into mine. When she knows

170

things, I know things. The blue rug and grey chairs—we're getting rid of those."

"Dan, I'm worried about these delusions. First of all, Kate may or may not be talented, but she doesn't have ESP, or the ability to project herself into your brain or my office space for that matter. It's not going to happen—it's a boundary. This is MY office, and she works somewhere else. She shouldn't even be here; she should be on the street doing what she does. She's projecting these delusions upon you, and they're now your delusions."

"Wow, that sounded pretty good, but these thoughts are clear as a bell."

"Dan, do you know what schizophrenia is?"

"Yes, but I have a head injury. I don't have a psychosis."

"Would you like to see a psychiatrist?"

"I see you, and I see Kate, and I'll continue to see Kate here, and you on the show. I can't see any more people."

5:34 PM: Leave office
Shit, run into Robbie

Robbie is standing by a large black Lincoln, with a man in a blue suit and matching tie, waiting for me. "This is Dan Dossette," Robbie says, "the former General Manager of the Red Sox."

"Step inside Mr. Dossette's office." Robbie points to the Lincoln.

"Good job, Robbie. You're really taking control, but things would be a lot more effective if you got the names right," Duquette says.

"Oh, right. Duquette."

Duquette sits in the driver's seat, and Robbie and I slide into the back. The seats are soft, puffy, as soft leather clouds.

"Mr. McNamara," Robbie says to me, but Duquette turns around in his seat and interrupts, "Sloan."

"What?"

"This isn't McNamara, Robbie, it's Bill Sloan."

"Oh geeze. Sorry, Bill!"

"It's okay. So, what's this about?"

"Mr. Sloan, you're fired.'"

"Excellent!" Duquette says. "Now kick him out."

Robbie reaches over me to open the door. He settles back, rests the soles of his shoe firmly against my thighs, and shoves me hard out the door and onto the asphalt. From the ground, I watch the Lincoln arc around the remaining parked cars and head out the exit. The trees are green, the sky is blue, the clouds are white; I'm fired, and the world seems as quiet as a womb.

5:42 PM: Final commute
Silence
6:25 PM: Home
Leave a voicemail for Robbie to schedule picking up my files
Leave a voicemail for Grady

Part 3: The Show

Chapter 12: Sunny and Share's Fantastic Thursday Appointments

Very late morning
Wake from the sun shining in window
Smell spring breeze
Feel freedom and love

Glorious morning: Bill

It is absolute joy to see Bill walk in with his dog, the first living things to enter my new office. It's so fitting. Bill will see I've eliminated all the dull grey and blue colors of his old office, and replaced them with fabulous reds, oranges, yellows, and greens; the color of leaves. Black Reiki symbols, outlined in white, are painted on the back wall. The sofa and chairs have been replaced by a massage table. A new light-colored plush carpet has been installed, in case people want to meditate on the floor. The side wall has bright lights, attached to orange brackets; the color of a sunburst. This makes the room appear bathed in light, even when it's raining. My heart leaps with gladness to see Bill, standing here over me. I'm sitting on the carpet, legs folded under me. The dog licks my face.

"Come sit with me," I say.

"What did you do with my files?" he asks. He sounds angry.

"They're in storage. I didn't want all that negativity around."

"You can't not keep files!"

"Bill, I would like you to come to me with love."

"Love? I've been fired!"

"Yes," I say, "but isn't it wonderful? Getting fired opens up so many more opportunities. When one door closes, another opens wide!"

"A door sure seems to have opened for you!"

Bill is having a negative energy flow. His Sacral Chakra is beautiful, and I wish he'd go back to the orange energy of his sensual side, so he could deal better with life. It would also help him be more in touch with sensual love-making, not primal and forceful love-making. That is what I wish for him, and for both of us. "Bill," I say, "this is an opportunity for you to go out into the world in a healing and helpful way, and in doing so, you will find your success. You will not find it with sex, money, and power. It is with love. Just remember, I love you, Bill."

"I want my files, and all the permission sheets, for *The Dr. Bill Sloan Show*. I'm going to need them all, as soon as possible."

"Please lie down. I'm going to do some healing."

"No! I'm not one of your patients! And we've had sex!"

"And wasn't that wonderful? So joyful, especially when you opened up, just as I opened my pelvic chakra to you."

"I can't do this here," Bill says. "This is not an appointment."

"Correct. My healing has nothing to do with appointments, time, or place. It's about love and sharing. Please remember my love for you. You can get your files through Robbie. Aimee will have you fill out a form. Oh, I hate forms."

"A form? Those are MY notes! I own them! Just tell everyone that I will be contacting them about the show...err, about that, and their future treatments."

Maybe Bill should pat the dog more. Waves of calm wash over him when he's caring for that animal. "Surround yourself in light, and within that light, you'll find opportunity. Namaste." I hold my hands open, palms up to him. It is very peaceful, and I am unthreatened, even when he storms out, and I'm left sitting there with my hands out.

Glorious morning: Hanna (Age is not important)

"Hello, you!" I say as she walks in. She has quite a stride on her, I love her stride. "You're beautiful," I tell her. "Head to foot, dark dress, a golden necklace. You could be a spiritual goddess, Hanna."

Hanna stops, tilts her head. I like it when people tilt their heads; it's so vulnerable, yet so wise. I wait a few seconds, silently, until she says, "You know, at first, I thought you were a crackpot."

"Aren't we all?"

"I'm feeling a little lost, coming to see you here. Everything seems different, even the office seems different. I'm used to seeing Bill here."

"Sunny and Share, which is me, has officially taken over Bill's practice. Come, sit across from me, and we can get started by holding hands." I reach up from the floor and extend my arms to her, but she backs off.

"I've decided, I'd rather talk about relationships today."

"Okay, then, go ahead. You may sit or stand."

"May I lie down on the...where's the couch?"

"You can lie on the massage table."

Hanna hesitates, then sits on it. Smoothing her dress down, she lies out flat. "Sunny and Share, my life is really going..."

"Wait, is that what you'd like to call me? I want you to know, I'm open to it. You may call me anything you wish. Sunny and Share is not my name. You've referred to me by my first name before."

Hanna breaths out hard. "I know."

"Good, good, breathe."

"May I speak? The men in my..."

I begin to meditate on her problem. "Hmmmmmmmmmmmm, yoooooooooooo."

177

She speaks louder, "The men in my…can you stop doing that while I'm talking?" She doesn't seem as open as she's been in the past. "Are you listening?" she yells.

The yelling disrupts my concentration, but I can get it back: "Hmmmmmmmmmmmm, yoooooooooooo."

"Kate! STOP THAT!"

I breathe out…then in…taking in the air around us. It is wonderful and sweet. I'm not crazy about her perfume, or perfume in general. "I'm helping you. It doesn't matter what you say, I'm surrounding you with love."

"I don't get it."

"You don't have to get it, it still works. Progress doesn't involve talking. It only involves love. In fact, we don't have to talk at all, ever again, the rest of our lives. The world is so easy, when it is lovely, beautiful, peaceful, and open. Would you like to try this? It's a beautiful meditative prayer to heal you and your loved ones."

Hanna sits up, scowling. "No. I'm more of a talker, a processor in general, but now, being here in your new office, Bill's old office, I don't know."

"You must look in the mirror a lot." I say, keeping my eyes closed.

"What the hell is that supposed to mean?"

"It's what you do, but in the big picture, none of it is important. You don't have to get defensive, because you've trusted me in the past. You didn't even think. Try this: surround yourself in a circle of white mirrors, with the reflective side facing away from you. This will allow the positive, 'white' energy in, and deflect any dark energy."

"I have no idea what you're talking about. I only look at a mirror when I'm putting on makeup, or to see if my ass looks okay."

"Oh, that's wonderful. Hanna, you are remarkable. You're going to make such a big splash on television. The show may not help you one bit in fixing the suffering from your relationships, but you'll have a new place to see Bill, not here, but on television. Now before you go, I want to give you a gift." I reach into my bag and pull out a plastic card. It repels me, because I hate plastic and I've tried to remove all plastic from my life. I hand it to her. "It's a gift card for White Light Books, in Cranston, Rhode Island."

"That's an hour from here."

"I know, but there's a lot of credit on this. It's worth the trip."

"Thanks," Hanna says, putting it in her purse. "There are a lot of shoe stores there."

Glorious morning: Me

Yes, it is a glorious morning, and I give myself love and joy. I didn't schedule anyone, or plan to help anyone, during this hour. This is my hour, and it's sunshine. It's love and light on wonderful, beautiful me, me, me. Remember, I am humble, and I've been sent down into the Universe, to help others, rather than myself. I have no material possessions to speak of. I have this office, with new massage tables, walls, and carpeting, but I don't own these. I would be happy with bare, wood floors and nothing on the walls, equally as well.

I will block out all, which has chained me. I am not my mother, I am not ill; I am not my father, I am not ill. My father is dead, but I forgive and remember, only, how wonderful people are. Of her, the pudding is yellow. It is like sunshine. Of him, I remember nothing.

I am helping all. Everyone I see has been getting, or will be getting better. I must eliminate the negative mud that weighs down their souls. I must open them up to the Universe. They all must relate to themselves, in their smallness. They all must love animals and trees.

I will make minds clearer and more lucid. I will prevent minds from becoming sluggish and sleepy. I will demonstrate just how busy my client's minds are. Distracting thoughts will subside, and experiences of inner peace, and relaxation will conquer. Conquer? That's a funny word. When the sea is rough, sediment is churned

179

up, and the water becomes murky, but when the wind dies down the mud gradually settles, and the water becomes clear. This feeling of contentment and well-being helps us, to cope with the busyness, and difficulties of daily life. Breathe, I am beautiful. I make love to the Universe, but now it's my turn. Breathe, sunny, breathe, share, breathe, sunny, breathe, share.

Spectacular morning: Thomas

The intercom's new buzzer pulls me out of my trance. The word "buzzer" is no longer appropriate, because I've programmed it to sound like birds chirping. I'm refreshed and feeling fantastic.

"Thomas has been waiting," Aimee says. I also had Robbie set the speaker's tone, so Aimee's voice sounds soft and clear, like a smile.

"Please tell him to come in," I say.

I can tell right away, by how he holds his shoulders, that he didn't like to be kept waiting, but the way he holds his head indicates, he carries a lot of feelings of shame, tightly, in his neck. These things I can fix.

"You're thirty minutes late," Thomas says.

"I offer my apologies."

"I came here early, you know, to be prompt. I wasn't sure, if you were even in."

"Now, why would you think that? Did Bill Sloan ever do that to you?"

"Yes."

"Ah, then let go of it." I feel my main work, with him, is to get him to let go. If a car cut him off in traffic, or someone is rude to him at Dunkin' Donuts, he should just go ahead as if nothing happened. I won't work on having him smile, and tell them to have a nice day, because it would be impossible, at this point of his healing.

"You know, I need to remember that. You've told me that I'm supposed to exhale too, right?"

180

"Breathing is an important part."

"I tried to meditate, but my mind is too busy. I start thinking about my job, and the things I have to do for you. Oh, and by the way, doesn't the office look great? A bit weird, but great."

"You, Dan, and Robbie did a wonderful job, but we're getting bogged down here. Let's get to work. I want you to sit on the foot stool, over there, by the table."

"Why?"

I tell him that I'm going to work on his neck, and I'm going to need to pull something out of it. The type of Reiki, I will be attempting, is a very powerful physical form of the teaching.

"Careful. I don't want to end up in the hospital," he says.

"Release your worries." I pull his head up to align everything. When I manipulate his neck, I let out a yell, which startles him.

"What the hell?"

"Shh...it's part of the healing process, it happens sometimes. How does it feel?"

"You're going to put me in the hospital! The way you're bending my neck..."

I tell him to be quiet. He doesn't like it, but he obeys. He's definitely coming around. I feel his shame leaving slowly, like water dripping. I press down on his head, so it is almost flat against his shoulder, and his shame starts to pour out, like water shooting out from a powerful geyser.

He grimaces, "Whoa, oh...you're hurting me."

"One more minute." My face is getting sprayed by all his shame, and then, as if nature has shut down the geyser, I am done.

He sits up, flexes his neck. There is color in his checks, and he smiles. It is a rare and wonderful smile. "Wow! My neck hasn't felt like this in years." He moves his head side to side; slowly at first, then with more confidence. "Wow!

"See?"

"Kate, you're amazing! When I met you, I thought you were crazy, and cute, and I just wanted to get into your pants. I don't feel that way at all now! How did you fix my neck?"

I tell him, no one said I wasn't crazy, and that what I have learned, I offer as a gift to others.

"Some gift. This appointment cost me one hundred bucks," he says, then smiles.

"You don't have to pay me, if you're tight for money," I say.

"No, I'm joking. This is exactly what I needed. I feel free, and it's weird, but I feel happy. I feel like I don't have to be so shitty about everything now. Just because of my neck?"

"Not exactly," I say. "You'll figure it out."

Sunny afternoon: Lunch—cool beans, fresh crisp organic apple, pure water which has been blessed
Open soul to feelings of warmth, like sunshine

Warm, sunny afternoon: Stella/Pearl

I ask her if I can call her Stella, since there is no need for me to call her Pearl.

She seems angry. "Of course you can call me Stella; that's my name. Where's Bill? I have to talk to him." She looks around. "What have you done to this place? Bill and I picked out all the furniture. It was perfect."

"Hello," I say. "I'm Kate. What can I do for you?"

"Well, I'll tell you what you can't do. What you can't do, is talk about my kids. Nor can you talk about my current husband. Nor can you help me, in any way. I don't come here for that. I come here to talk to my husband, Bill."

"Ex-husband. Unless you're still married?"

"I am, but not to Bill. So, what can you do for me?"

"I can do some healing work with you. I'm probably going to need to burn some more sage."

"Is that what I smell? I thought I was in a hookah den. Will Bill be back next week? He won't be burning any sage, or any of this other bullshit, that's for sure."

"Bill has opened up, a little, to the process," I say, and can't help smiling.

"Oh, God," Stella says. I know what that means and say, "You must have opened something for him. So will he be here next week?"

I need to stop any, and all, negative thoughts. My spiritual awareness has led me to situations like this, and right now, I need all my openness in love, to get through this. Stella is very dark. I'd love to help her, but also to help the person called Pearl. She is here for a reason. "Stella, Bill is gone."

"Fired?"

"He has a new opportunity: to be a successful therapist on TV. Didn't you sign the form? He's going to be in contact with you soon."

"I'm not counting on that. I'll have to go see him, or maybe someone will e-mail me. Either way, Bill and I will always be connected, in some way."

"Yes, it's funny how the Universe connects people."

"No, space shot! It's because we have kids! Careful, if you offer Bill free love, he's going to take it, and that's all he's going to get, out of someone like you."

"Hmmm," I say. "Hmm."

"Fine," she says. "So, let's get back to me..."

Warm, sunny, such a wonderful afternoon: Grady

I've heard of the plans for the television show, through Bill but not through Grady, so I'm interested in seeing what he thinks the chances are that the show will succeed. This might affect Bill's treatment. Either way, I can heal both of them.

"Ah, Sonny and Cher," he says. He looks calmer and less sweaty than usual. Many times, I've seen him in the waiting room, all scratchy and red. "Do you know, that's a copyright infringement? I work in the television field."

"Grady, I know you do." I place my hands on his forehead and he immediately starts to sweat. "You have a new show you're developing with our friend."

Grady leaps out of my hands, like a wet fish held in a boat. "It's going to be great! *The Doctor Bill Sloan Show.* It's going to blow late night out of the water."

"Bill's not a doctor."

"Legal just cleared that. Boston University has sanctioned giving him an Honorary Doctorate, which we'll give him at the station, right before we go on. The trade-off, is all Bill has to do, is mention them on the air."

"Ah, I see. Grady you know healing and therapy is based on honesty and openness. I don't think you're off to a good start."

"Come on. It's Bill Sloan. He's real and believable. We're going to conduct a market research study, one of those *"Do you think this man is real and believable?"* types of deals. You'll see. It's totally going to fly. Are you going to appear on the show?"

"Yes I am." This makes Grady grin. "So Grady, do you think this is going to be successful? Do you have enough time to set this up? I mean, Bill is out of a job for specific reasons. You're going to need some damage control, about the ins and outs, if all that information goes public."

Grady jumps in the air a few inches. "Yes! It's going to change programming history. The other networks are going to throw up their white flags. It's going to put them out of business. It's going to put other therapists out of business!"

"Grady, will you lie down for me? I want to channel this energy back into you, kind of like a big letter *U*. This will keep you energized for a long time"

Grady walks to the edge of the table. He places his hands on it, then removes them. He steps up and puts a corner of his big, round butt on the brown, padded cushion, but then slides off, and walks a quick circle. I give him a little, *come on,* look and finally he gets on, and lies back.

"I am a Love Sharer," I say. "I want you to accept this Reiki with a discerning attitude and an inquisitive, yet accepting spirit. Do not question a spiritual healing practice, which promotes physical, emotional, mental, and spiritual well-being. When we receive Reiki, we are accessing the source of subtle energy itself, and this is something that never changes. The way Reiki healing expresses itself in a person changes over time, but Reiki itself does not change." I put on my *Spiritual Transformation* music CD, but Grady is asleep before I can begin.

Warm sunny sensational afternoon: Ethan's father

Ethan's father comes in with a piece of paper, for Bill. "It's the permission slip," he says. I tell him I'll get it to Grady. "If only I'd known you were here," Mr. McGrath says, "I'd have Ethan come and see you. He talks about you all the time."

"Does he?"

"He calls you Wonder Woman."

"Is he available? Can your wife drive him here? Time is not important."

Ethan's father makes a call, and it's decided that Ethan can come see me later. I'm supposed to see Dan at that time, so I immediately text him a list of things I need for the office, knowing that this will keep him busy past his scheduled time. *Oh, shit, I just texted, and thought about scheduled time.* Quick meditation.

Later, on a warm, sunny, sensational afternoon: Ethan

I'm deep in meditation when Ethan, and his parents bound through the door.

"Wonder Womaaaaaaan," he sings.

His mom says, "Honey, she looks nothing like Lynda Carter." To me, she says, "I told him not to say that."

"You are beautiful," I tell Ethan.

185

"I'm going to ask your parents to leave us alone for a little while, is that okay?"

He nods.

"He's having a tough time," Ethan's dad says, as he and his mother head for the door. "Plus, you know that thing…" his dad blushes slightly, when he looks at me and whispers, "sexual stuff."

"I understand," I say. Meanwhile, Ethan is running around the room. He is full of joy.

They leave, but the door is still cracked open and I see his mother's shadow peering in. I ask Ethan to close the door, and he pushes it hard, so that it slams in her face. "Are you ready?" I ask him.

"You're Wonder Woman and I'm Superman, like the old shows. Superman flies out the window and rescues people. Do you think George Reeves was fat?"

"Who?"

"He's an actor. You can Google it and find out tons of stuff."

"Ethan, I don't do the internet. Electronic devices disturb the Energy Fields in the Universe."

"Really? I'll Google that."

"You ready to lie down?"

"You going to do magic?"

"Something like that."

I put on soothing music. Ethan remarkably names the artist on the CD. "Shhhh," I say. His breathing is fast. "Pretend you are going to sleep," I say.

"I pretend every night to do that, but I never sleep."

I place my hands a few inches above his head and pass them over his body. He is settled. I sense his rage, his frenetic energy. His brain works at a speed, I've never felt before. I try to push back the racing thoughts, and release the distracted ones. This is hard work. Ethan's energy is ripping through his body, like someone being tased, except without the instant lack of bodily control. His energy bounces around inside him, almost as if each point within him is

186

one billion nuclei, with the energy of thought found in his every supersonic electron. It's all within this dark flowing river. I need to clear out the horrible, terrible layers of this.

I wipe the sweat off me. It's been thirty minutes. This is having an effect on me—my training has warned me of this, but I'm not listening. I should see Ethan again soon, and not take it all in at once, but I know there is not much time. I'm fighting, kicking at it. Ethan is beating me, his darkness is where I've been physically, and mentally, and I'm spinning, spinning inside. The room does not feel real. I pick up, that Ethan believes he's a member of an alien race called the Skrill, which comes to Earth, to steal the minds of humans, to be sold into slavery. It's Episode 210. I don't know how I know this, as I've never seen the show. I'm fighting it, I'm fighting Ethan, breathing quickly, trying to force back the negativity that Ethan is a mind stealer from outer space, who must succeed. If Ethan fails, the Skrill will use insanity-inducement procedures upon the Earth. I feel weak; I feel I used to be Wonder Woman, but I'm only Diana Price, and Ethan has weakened me.

Beads of sweat fall off me and onto him. "Ethan, we need to stop now. Time's up." I have barely survived.

Ethan gets up and smiles. He is calm. Gives me a hug. He opens the door. "Mom? Dad? Are you ready to leave?"

Wonderful dusk: Dan

Dan doesn't have any of the things that I asked him to buy. His head is clear of worry, which is wonderful. I ask him if he remembers what I wanted, and he sighs, sheepish. "I wrote the list, but didn't remember to look at it. Where was I supposed to go?"

"Braintree. I need Angel and Oracle cards, Chakra crystals, healing rings, and information on companies that sell fountains."

Dan pulls the list out of his pocket and starts to write the new list on the back, but I reach out and stop him.

"No. Use your memory. I also need some new relaxation music."

187

He nods. "I'm going to find all of this in Braintree?"

"At a place called Open Doors, but there's also The Crystal Boutique, The Pendant Boutique, The Pendulum Boutique, and The Chakra Boutique. There are so many exciting boutiques, I feel like I'm bursting with joy!"

"I can't remember all those," he says.

"Don't worry. I just gave an extra hour of love to someone in your time slot. Isn't that wonderful?"

"Are you going to do that with me? Heal me with love?"

"No, I need to go give some love to some animals tonight. There's a wolf sanctuary in Ipswich I'm planning to visit. I looked into adopting a wolf, but unfortunately, when you give them the money, they only give you a picture of a wolf. I was so disappointed that I didn't get one to take home. I could love a wolf!"

"Oh, I remember that place!"

"You remember something! That's wonderful!"

He tilts his head, confused. "Kate, I remember something else: a show I watched last night, about people who keep wild animals in their homes as pets, but then the animals attack them. Snakes and buffalo. Those aren't good pets."

"All you need to do is relate to the animals, show them you love them, and give them calming Reiki. It's exactly what I do here, with my clients, but I don't think any of you would harm me. Animals only harm, if they feel like they are being harmed. Give them love and they love. Would you like to meet the one, they call, Weeble?"

"Weeble?"

"Yes, it's the name of the wolf that I was going to adopt. I want to drive there, under the light of the moon."

"The sanctuary is open that late?"

"No, not exactly."

Outside the office...

Bill: Dream states

After a few days off in a row, Bill is in a sleep pattern, where he has difficulty waking. He may sleep for most of the day, but it's not depression, as Bill makes no conscious decision to remain in the bed. It's almost as if, he has been sent into a trance, where his soul and his mind become one with the mattress. He used to enter this dream state as a boy, and once his mother called for an ambulance, because she couldn't wake him. It was a school vacation week, and Bill was dreaming about flying over fields and skies. The emergency workers wondered if he was in a coma, but when they moved him from his bed to a gurney, he said, "I'm hungry."

This morning, Bill had a dream he was on a school bus, heading to his office, to collect his notes. His notes were extremely important. The driver was a diminutive woman, with blond hair, wearing a gray sweatshirt. She was not a "little person," but she was too small to view out the windshield, and she had to sit on the floor, near the gear shift, in order to get enough leverage for the stick, in order to shift gears. She was on the highway and the bus was moving, but she couldn't see where she was going. Bill reached into the inside pocket of his jacket, and pulled out an organic Pop Tart. It wasn't in a wrapper, because that would be bad for the environment. He took a bite, and the pastry was crisp; the apple filling was fresh and tasty. He offered a bite to Thomas, who was sitting next to him. Thomas took a bite, directly over the spot Bill had bitten. Thomas said, *"That Pop Tart is better than any morning toaster snack I've ever had."* Then, he handed the pastry to a potential new client, who turned it around, and took a humungous bite from the opposite side. This was the point, at which Bill woke. He was worried that there would not be enough to satisfy his own appetite.

"I don't care what this means," he thought. "I'm not a frigging doctor."

It was early afternoon, and he had seventeen voicemail messages from Grady. *Grady needs to be treated for relaxation,* Bill thought. He knew he had to go to WHDH, and start production meetings. He knew he, and Grady, needed to discuss money. He knew syndication would be brought up. There was great potential here, but the show needed to get off to a great start, so it could grow, get a better time slot, and be picked up by markets in other cities. Bill wondered if guest stars would be interested in making appearances, like celebrities used to, for example, when they appeared on *The Muppet Show*. It would keep the show fresh. These Hollywood types didn't even need to discuss their problems; they could plug their newest shows or movies. He would tell Grady that he needed to relax. Bill would return all his calls, after fixing some lunch for himself. There were no cold cuts at home, to make a sandwich with, because he'd given them all, as treats, to the dog. *What a wondrous animal,* he thought.

Hanna: Field Day

Comealy's Farm, at sunset, is a place of peace for Hanna. Today she is there to regroup, to think about a list of things: A television show, a spiritual store in Cranston, Rhode Island, and the lastest series of men in her life, not in that order, or in any order at all. The shopping in Rhode Island, seems to be wedged into her mind, as has the advice from Kate, the strangely-odd woman, now occupying Bill's office. She thinks, "I'm not going to buy into this," as she inhales deeply, exhales slowly, and sees the sun setting over the field. She would like to live in this field forever, if the weather was good. Food could be delivered to her, and there was a comfortable bed.

Hanna's legs are crossed and her eyes are closed. It is getting darker, as her eyelids are no longer fire-engine red on the inside.

When there is a tap on her shoulder, she doesn't come out of it immediately. She's not asleep, nor is she awake. What is she? Randy taps again, and she exhales. He holds a bottle of Jameson Irish Whiskey by the neck, and the liquid swishes when he moves it from his right hand, to his left. He reaches down, and touches her cheek, and Hanna, gives a small startle. She opens her eyes, looks around, and gathers her bearings.

"Hello," she says, "are you mad at me?"

"Nope." Randy slugs from the bottle. "You want some?"

"You drunk?"

He smiles, "Do you want some or not?"

"I don't know what to say. I'm sure you're mad at me. I didn't try to be rotten, but when I couldn't deal with things, I just ran. I don't know what I'm doing, but I know I should have spoken to you, instead of leaving a note. It was a shitty thing for me to do."

"It was. But you were going through a lot, so I decided not to be pissed. I also can't help thinking, I was his friend too; that his death affected me, too."

Hanna reaches for his hand, and he places the bottle into it. He knows her well. She drinks, and feels the warmth from the alcohol, thinks the colors in the sky are more beautiful than anything in her life. "It's not fair that I like you, Randy, and that selfishly I still want to be friends with you, but also, I want to be more than friends at the same time. Then it's not fair, that I still want to push you away. I'm working on not doing that."

"I hope you find out what you want."

"I'm going to be on television," she says.

"I didn't know television was something you wanted to do."

"It's not, but the whole Bill Sloan therapy-show-thing, is kind of screwy anyway. I'm just going to go with it, maybe keep it at the mind-fuck level."

"Is that healthy?"

"No, but it'll feel good fucking with him. I've been doing a lot of things lately, just to feel good. Speaking of which, would you be

191

interested in taking a drive to Rhode Island, at some point? It would be just to shop." Hanna suddenly feels embarrassed, by the specifics, of her trip to Cranston.

"I'm sure I could be talked into it." Randy pulls the folded break-up note Hanna gave him out of his pocket, and hands it to her. They sit in silence, until the hay bales begin to become darkened silhouettes, followed by the complete black and moonless night.

Kate: Noted

In the car with Dan, Kate reaffirms that love is the most important thing, and that fantastic Thursday notes will no longer be collected during her appointments. She says that they're counterproductive and take away from the process. She makes Dan drive, as a way to overcome his fears. She asks Dan, what he thinks about ending note taking, in order to run a successful spiritual calmness and awakenings practice. He doesn't answer. His eyes are glued to the highway; the headlights are the only illumination on the way to Ipswich. If he thinks about animals leaping out, he begins to sweat, and his hands won't stop tingling when he grips the wheel.

They are both dressed in black. Kate tries to tuck her hair under a knit hat, but her hair is too thick. She lets it fall freely and sees the distress on Dan's face. "You're doing fine," she says. "The biggest step was to ask your mother to borrow the car."

"She's had the Caprice Classic for twenty years," he says. "It's her baby."

Kate taps on the Plexiglas barrier, Dan has installed, between the front and back seats, which he modeled after a taxi. "You did a nice job on this. Does your mom know?"

"No. I don't think I'll say anything to her. The barrier isn't screwed into anything that will be damaged, once I pull it out."

"Just be calm and believe no animal can harm you, since you've already been harmed."

"Just be careful of the wolves, Kate. I still remember what I saw on Animal Planet."

"No animal can harm me, either," Kate says, and as if on cue, a deer jumps out onto the highway, its white underside reflecting in the headlights. Dan screams, in blood-curdling terror, and stomps on the brakes, temporarily locking them, but stopping the Caprice successfully, the nose of the vehicle bobbing. The deer stops for a moment which feels like an eternity, and five years of Dan's memory rushes back to him.

"How beautiful," Kate says. "Dan? Are you all right?"

"I'm good. I think my brain was jarred a bit."

"Good."

Thomas: Stretching exercise

Thomas stretches his neck, grateful for how good it feels. The present is a great place to be in. If only he'd done something about this sooner!

He's been living in his sorry past and worrying about the future. Bill used to take him to these mental places which pushed his buttons, making him think about his trauma, and he'd react with anger. Thomas is ready to share himself with the world. When a man in a suit walks past, he smiles. "Good day, sir," Thomas says. When the man doesn't respond, Thomas calls out, "Fuck you, too!"

Stella: It takes two and some other crazy facts about multiple personalities

They say, it takes two people to form a perfect union of one. Stella, has now been married twice. So, three people made an imperfect union of two.

It also takes two to tango. Al Pacino tangoed in *Scent of a Woman*. He had two eyes, but he was blind and could not see. If it takes two people to tango, then it takes four eyes. But it only took

193

two eyes, because half of the couple could not see. Neither character wore glasses. One person wearing glasses is said to be four-eyed.

It Takes Two was also a film, starring Mary-Kate and Ashley Olsen, who played a single character on a show called *Full House*. Stella knows it is possible.

"It Takes Two, Baby." Marvin Gaye and Kim Weston sang that. Most people thought it was Tammi Terrell. That would make three. Tammy Faye Bakker and Jim Bakker were a perfect two. Tammy Faye had two names, but they shared the married name, Bakker, which had two "ks", where usually it took only one. Bakker's sex scandal involved two other people. Both he, and preacher John Wesley Fletcher, drugged and raped Jessica Hahn for "about fifteen minutes." Note: John Wesley Fletcher's name contains two names before Fletcher. Hahn's fame, lasted more than fifteen minutes though.

Fifteen minutes can be divided by two, to give you two exact periods of seven and one-half minutes. The average shower in America lasts seven and one half minutes. This means, the average water consumption of a shower is anywhere from fifteen to fifty-two and one half gallons of water, based on how much water flows from your shower head. Stella has one head. It's up to her to remove half of the two people within it.

Anything divided by itself becomes one.

Grady: Notes on *The Dr. Bill Sloan Show*: What might interest viewers?

Grady has a manila folder marked, *Confidential Client Records/Client Profiles*, which Bill Fed-Exed him. WHDH told him that he needs to briefly outline the first show, and propose what the viewer will find interesting. WHDH wants to run the show, but they want to make sure the show has focus, before they invest. Initial ratings are extremely important for the late-night slots in determining their future success rates. *Why don't they trust me?* Grady wonders, as his faulty mind analyzes, and over-analyzes WHDH's request. Each profile is only a few paragraphs, and he thinks of calling Bill, to gain more insight. This thought causes him to scratch his chest under his button-down shirt, until the skin there, is the color of fresh sunburn.

He calculates eight, five-minute segments; seven clients and a wrap up. There will be twenty minutes of commercials for the one-hour show, but Grady notes to remind the Advertising Department that they should not sell ads to companies who normally produce Infomercials, as WHDH would then have, a constant and open option to replace *The Dr. Bill Sloan Show.*

Segment One, Hanna Sertin: Either focus on her youth, dating, sex appeal, or her recovery from the loss of a loved one. The Survey of American Television Viewers indicates, a preference for young women in sexy outfits.

Segment Two, Kate Hummingbird Warrior: Focus on her wackiness, her attractiveness, and her spiritual way of life. Show her full name on the screen as much as possible. Do not focus on, or discuss, her Love Sharing Treatment with those who Bill Sloan currently treats. This would create a viewer conflict and potentially confuse the audience's loyalty. The Survey of American Television Viewers indicates, late night audiences have lower IQs than most prime-time viewers.

Segment Three, Thomas Mercer: Focus on his anger management history, and try to find out how he deals with things day-to-day. This is a gold mine for on-location scenes. Possible plants may be set in the community in order to set this guy off. Audiences surveyed, enjoy physical violence over verbal arguments.

Segment Four, Pearl Sloaney: Focus on the life she has with her current husband and the interactions between them. Audience surveys indicate, viewers root for marriages that appear to be bad, but have the potential to work out. This creates something to root for, or against.

Segment Five, Grady Simon, (me): I don't know what to focus on. Audiences will find this segment dull.

Segment Six, Ethan McGrath: So much to focus on. Spend as much time on this segment, at the expense of all other segments. Audiences will relate and root for a cute, intelligent kid who is struggling with the mental problems of an adult. Make sure some of is presented in a humorous way.

Segment Seven, Dan O'Shay: Focus on his memory loss by giving him memory tests. Audience surveys indicate, if characters cannot do a mental task that the audience can solve at home, they become entwined and amused with the character, or they become disgusted.

Grady stops scratching, looks at his notes, and attaches them to an e-mail directed to WHDH. Hopefully, by tomorrow, the show will be approved.

Ethan: Studying the trends

At 2:15 AM in Boston, five of the local stations have paid programming. Channel 2 re-runs *Frontline* and CW56 re-runs their 10 PM newscast. TV38 runs *My Name is Earl* and WHDH has a regularly scheduled show, *Poker After Dark,* which is costing them a lot to syndicate. Ethan read, in *The Boston Globe,* that soon all of the stations will be opting for paid programming. The controversy around this is, that even though the shows are getting ratings, there are questions about them. Are people watching them, or are they using them as sleep aids? If Ethan ran a network, he'd have superhero shows and movies, which would stimulate people enough to watch and not sleep. If he were an advertiser, he'd demand the TV stations put up a message that read, "Are you still watching?" and people would have to use their remote controls to reconnect to their show, or else a loud alarm would sound on their television. Why would you pay a station to run your program or commercial if no one was watching? Ethan thinks people will sleep to *The Dr. Bill Sloan Show,* as well. The concept is dull, it's not vibrant or exciting, the way superheroes are; after all, they fly, use magical powers, and solve crimes. He has to speak to someone about this, as it is of upmost importance that the show does well in the ratings. The show would make people understand him and view him as a man. His father would say he's just a boy, but he can't tune out all of the other stuff.

One time Ethan got an F on a project he did about the pyramids. He failed, because people didn't understand how urgent it was for him to make the project completely authentic. The pyramids were made from mud-brick, and Ethan needed the exact ingredients in order to properly give *his* representation the exactness, that was required. It was an impossible task. He built the miniature rollers, which could move the miniature mud-brick pieces. That was no problem. It was getting the exact materials from Egypt, which hindered Ethan, who wrote, called, and e-mailed representatives from there, to request access to the exact materials. No one responded, so he failed. His dad contacted the school and produced Ethan's requests for materials, but Ethan's teacher told him, he could only give him a grade based on the finished product.

During his research, Ethan also read a theory that the pyramids were built by aliens, so in his attempt to rebuild the pyramids, he tried becoming an alien for a few weeks. He no longer understood the English language being used at his school. Ethan needed *The Dr. Bill Sloan Show,* for people to understand all of his internal make-up, in order to be completely legitimate in the world. Then, and only then, would he get better.

Dan: Finding it

Dan's head feels clear for now. It's remarkable that he knows the who, what, where, and how of this situation, all at the same time. He knows that his car is parked at Wolf Hollow, and he knows exactly why he's here. He remembers checking out the place on-line, and finding out that educational lectures are given each day, followed by the opportunity for all guests to howl at the wolves.

Kate says she needs a wolf, but Dan knows about the importance of keeping wolves in packs. Dan tells Kate this, but she says these wolves are different; they're not wild, they've been domesticated and given human names. "By adopting one," she says, "I will be able to teach it the ways of the wolf." She smiles. "We're doing the right thing. It's not stealing. Without the wolf, we are, and I am, nothing. Think of all the healing this wolf will help me do in the future. I've already cleared it with Robbie."

"So, what's the game plan, do you have tranquilizers, or what?"

"No! Not for the wolf." She shakes her head, remembering her mother telling her that she wished they made tranquilizers for children, so they'd be knocked out, from morning to night. She'd said that nearly every day.

"Well, so...how will we?"

"I'm going to relate to them in a spiritual way. Hopefully, Weeble will follow me into the car. Then, I will re-name him Hopi."

Dan adjusts his cap. "And the chain link fence?"

"Wolves can jump," Kate laughs. "Hopi will hop. Just keep the car door open and the engine running."

Dan waits in the car for an hour. He wonders if Kate has been killed. They're so far out in the sticks, no one would know about it for days. He cut the engine thirty minutes ago, but turns the key when he sees Kate walking toward the fence. Does she? Yes! Behind her trots a small, gray and black, wolf. Kate climbs up the fence, and motions for the wolf to jump, and like a circus act, the wolf leaps into her arms, causing her to teeter slightly at the top of the fence. When she drops him down, Dan steps out of the car, opens the door, and Hopi jogs right in, settling himself in the back seat. Kate pats him and gets into the front seat, next to Dan. Dan is so surprised, and relieved, and impressed that he can't even speak. Finally, he says, "We don't even need the plexi-glass divider."

"I told you," Kate says, "I have a way with wild animals."

Dan looks in the rear-view mirror, and he could swear, Hopi is grinning.

Chapter 13: The Doctor Bill Sloan Show
Episode One, April 6

11:45 PM: Alarm clock
Get up
Guzzle 32 ounces of Starbucks, a Red Bull and a bruised banana
11:48: Wake up

1:00 AM: Grady

A drab woman dabs powder and foundation on my face. I have a pre-show meeting with Grady and the Director of the show, but they're both late. When Grady appears, it's obvious, he's been scratching the top of his head, the spot under his thinning hair, which he seems to have much less of.

"Have you heard the theme music? Have you heard the theme music?" He flips a switch and an up-tempo song begins; featuring a multitude of singers with over-dubbed voices" *For your peace of mind, turn on Bill Sloan.* The song sounds more like a jingle, and my name sounds slurred: *For your peace of mind, turn (for your) on BilsssanSloan.*

"What do you think?" Grady asks.

"It sounds… weird. Is this the best you could do?"

"We didn't have much time, so we sound edited an old ad from a debt consolidation company. It used to say *"For your peace of mind, for your bills and loans."* The production team did a nice job, wouldn't you say?"

"No."

"Well, don't worry. We're going to the studio this week to create our own version. We've hired all the singers and everything. It'll sound great."

"Hmm…" I say, not unlike what I might say during a therapy session.

"And what do you think of the set?" He asks. "We had it made up to look exactly like your old office."

"Yeah, it's kind of scary."

"Don't be scared. It's the magic of television. So, here's the layout. We go live at 2:15, as the late show line-ups and news programs start fifteen minutes past the hour. Then we have, in order: Hanna, Kate, Thomas, Pearl, Dan, and Ethan."

"What about you?" I ask.

"No, I'm not in this."

Robbie appears from the hallway. "Oh, yes you are. It's part of the contract with *Mental Health Solutions.*"

"I don't want to be on the show," Grady frowns.

"You have to do it. It's in the contract you signed." Robbie just happens to have a copy, and hands it to him.

"What's he doing here?" I ask, glaring at Robbie. I just don't like the guy.

Grady flips through the fifteen-page document. "Robbie is the director," he answers. "Okay. New order: Hanna, Kate, Thomas, Pearl, Dan, me, and then Ethan. We'll interview each of them, cut to a commercial, and then when we come back, show the audience the filmed segments, which will run into more commercial time. The live segments will last about three minutes each, but if time is getting tight, we will cut my segment out and go right to Ethan."

"We can't do that. There may be billing issues," Robbie says.

"We can do anything. It's fucking live TV, in front of a few hundred live fucking people in Studio A, and about a million at home!" Grady roars.

I've never seen Grady so feisty and competent, and suddenly I kind of like him.

"Show time!" he barks at me. "Be professional, but don't use too much psycho-jargon, or large words."

I nod. Makeup done, I get up and head down the hall, toward the green room, where the guests are waiting. Hanna is wearing the dress she wore at the funeral, and Randy is sitting next to her, holding her hand. Kate is sitting on the floor, with a large dog that almost looks like a wolf. Ethan looks bright-eyed, but his parents are dozing. Stella mouths the words, "Good luck," and Thomas mouths, "You'll need it," and laughs his loud, annoying laugh. Ethan holds his stiff arms straight out, as if he's an airplane. The last thing I note is the window in the green room which has a view of the brick wall from the adjacent building. I never understood why windows exist with such poor views. Why even put a window there?

2:15 AM: Hanna

After the theme song ends, I proudly announce to the audience, that the show they are about to see, involves real people and situations, and that each person, on the show has agreed to participate, as if these were actual therapy sessions. The show is brought to you by Boston University School of Psychology, where I am a doctor. Then I look into the camera and give the viewers at home a brief background of Brad's death, and how Hanna came to see me afterwards, and then I introduce her.

She walks in, slowly stepping over the cables. She looks tentative and demure, but when the audience applauds, she smiles a little. When she gets to me, she makes a move to kiss me on the cheek, but I deflect it. I don't want to compromise my role, as a professional psychologist.

She lies down on the couch. I can tell she's nervous. Memories of lying on top of her come to me, and I try to blot them out; meanwhile, there is an awkward moment of dead air.

"Are you comfortable?" I ask. The audience laughs.

"Yes, but it feels kind of strange, like somehow I'm in a dream."

"In what way?"

"Compared to the first time I started seeing you, when everything felt like a nightmare."

"In what way?"

"It's like… I mean, I needed to deal with Brad's death. I sort of, like, became a different person. I went from feeling lost, to feeling dependent, to feeling recovered, to being filmed at home and in town, to being here, in a familiar office, in therapy on television. I think it's kind of (bleeped)-up."

"I'm sorry," I say.

"Don't be. You've only been, directly, involved in all of them."

"No, I'm sorry we had to bleep you. So, tell us about Brad. Who was Brad?"

Hanna's mouth twitches, as if she's about to yell, but she catches herself. "You should know. You were his therapist."

"Yes, but that had nothing to do with his death. Brad was a very troubled man, but I want to talk about you, and how his death affected you."

Hanna answers in an annoyed tone, "Well, it's very important that the problems in my life get resolved pretty quickly. I know I have problems with relationships, who I see, and why I see them. It's important I recognized the reasons I saw Randy, and you…"

"Yes, me for therapy!" I chime in as Robbie motions it's time for a commercial break. "I need to ask you, are you seeing Randy again?"

"Yes, but this time it makes more sense. I understand it."

"Hang onto that thought, Hanna. We need to break for commercial. When we come back, we'll see clips from Hanna's week, and we'll meet Kate, who heals people with her hands. Don't go away."

Grady runs in and says it's going great. "Let's crank it up a notch with Kate. Just so you know, the ratings have dropped a little since the show went live."

"They have?"

"I don't want you to worry about it. People don't know why they are tuning in, and probably found the show by accident. It's to be expected. The goal is to hook them, so they stay tuned and return as viewers. Hanna, get up—we need the couch for the next guest. Sit in one of the chairs, next to Bill." Grady pats the chair closest to me.

The intercom squawks, "Bill you're back live in three... two... one..."

I look at Hanna. Her face looks as if it's about to boil over.

2:33 AM: Kate

I introduce Kate, as Kate Hummingbird Warrior, and the audience chuckles. I hope they find her adorable and quirky, and she looks sexy, as she walks on set with her big dog. She's wearing a thin, white cotton top, and tight stretch pants. The outline of her breasts is visible under the bright lights. So far, so good: two beautiful women and a dog.

"Who's this?" I ask, offering my hand for him to sniff.

"This is Hopi."

"Is Hopi a therapy dog?'

"No, you're the therapy dog. Hopi is a wolf. I freed him from the cages of men."

"But...wolves are not indigenous species to Massachusetts." The Director of the show motions to me, with a cutting motion. Oops, *indigenous* is a large word. "What I mean is, wolves usually don't live in Massachusetts. How'd you get him?"

"He's a beautiful animal, and he's now free. He lives in my house."

205

"Is owning a wolf a part of your peace and tranquility, Kate? I've been seeing you, as your therapist, for over a year and I really can't quite figure out why you need to…"

"You see me, because you love me," she says with warm sincerity. The audience lets out a combination of nervous laughter and a gasp. From the booth, Grady gives me a thumbs up.

"Well, I don't love you in *that* way. I care about the well-being of all my clients," I say. I sense, rather than see, Hanna shaking her head. Hopi pivots in a small circle and faces me. Now that I know he's a wolf, I'm not as comfortable having his mouth near my hand.

"Easy, Hopi. Sit, boy." I look at Kate, but her eyes are closed; her chest rising and falling, she is in deep thought. "Kate?"

Slowly, she opens her eyes. "Hopi exists within his own free will. I don't own him. You should try to love Hopi," she says slowly and softly, as if in a trancelike state.

"Kate. I want our studio audience to know that you often change the direction of your own therapy with me in order to project information that you are, at a certain level, helping me, too. I want to be clear, that I am not an official client at your practice, Sunny and Share, in any way."

"I see you, to help ground myself," she says. "And I come here, because you need me. The members of the studio audience will find out soon enough." There is more laughter, but it's not the nervous kind anymore; I think they might be laughing at me.

"Time is running out. We should go to the tape," I say.

"It's a commercial next," Kate says.

During the break, Grady runs down to the set again and says that the show is great, but I'm playing it too straight. If something strange happens, I should go with it, keep it interesting, and exciting. I tell him, I thought I was doing that. "Do it more," he says. Hopi squats to defecate, three… two… one…

2:31 AM: Thomas

Before Thomas is introduced, Grady tells me the Advertising Department messed up, and Kate's clip was in fact a commercial for Sunny and Share. Many of my clients appeared in it, undermining the shit out of my authority here. He gives a peppy clap and tells us all, to shrug it off.

With no time to regain my dignity, I introduce Thomas, who has to step around Hopi's pile, in order to walk past the guests, and sit on the edge of the couch. "That stinks," he says, and the audience laughs.

"No, it's beautiful," Kate says.

Robbie has crawled out on the floor at Hanna and Kate's feet, below the camera shot, in an attempt to retrieve the excrement, and put it into a bucket, without being detected on live TV. As the fecal loaf is touched, a growl can be heard, but I'm not sure if it came from Kate or Hopi. The audience gives a collective "Ewwwww," which is going to appear quite nonsensical to the viewers at home. Robbie, then peels back his latex gloves, and removes them, with an audible snap, which is also picked up by the studio microphones.

"Now, now," I add, "I think we're ready to talk about Thomas, a man who deals with any emotional low, or conflict, with anger. Isn't that right Thomas?"

"You don't know everything, so, (bleep) you!"

"You know, the station is not going to allow that, so anytime you swear, they'll cut it, and no one will know what you are talking about. No one will, then, know your story, or what you are going through. Your problems will be marginalized. Now, let's hear what you have to say about your problems."

Thomas raises his voice. "I didn't agree to any of this. I didn't agree to have one, or two, (bleep)ing cameras following me around during the week, either."

Grady sends one of his minions down, who hands me Thomas' release form. "It's all right here," I say. "Is this your signature?"

"Sloan, I agreed to appear on television, that's all. You know, in a moment of great therapy with you, I told you, I've started to cook. Can I give out my new recipe for Tuscan steak?"

"This isn't the Food Network. I think we should talk about your issues, what's going on right now."

"(Bleep) my issues!"

"Thomas, your language needs to be cleaned up. Now, you did agree to be on the show—"

"You're a pretty angry guy, yourself, aren't you, *doctor* Sloan? Where'd ja get that fake Southern accent? You didn't have it last time I saw you!"

I open my mouth and shut it.

Thomas goes on, "And I don't want you playing my (bleep)ing taped clip!"

The studio audience murmurs for a few seconds, then is silent.

Thomas, breathing like a bull, turns to Kate. "I'm sorry for my regression," he says. "It was a bad one."

I'm glad when we cut for a commercial. Grady comes down and he's thrilled with the last segment. I tell him, I didn't like it. I hear Kate reassuring Thomas; she tells him he's making progress, and that he's still a newborn fawn in the woods. Thomas nods, as his chest expands and contracts, the breaths no longer as loud as when he was agitated.

"So, we need to run the tape of you, Mr. Mercer, from Monday," Grady says. "It's an interesting segment. It's must-see TV!"

"Fuck that, and fuck that slogan, asshole! If people see this, I could be arrested. I didn't agree to that!" Thomas yells.

"Thomas?" Kate says softly.

"And since we're on break, you don't have to bleep me, so fuck you again!"

Grady wheels around, away from Thomas, and says, over his shoulder, "We're running it!" I feel oddly proud of Grady and the ratings value of the Thomas segment. I also feel powerless, ineffective, and like the world's biggest asshole.

2:39 AM: Pearl

For a split second, I'm confused about who to introduce. I've never had to introduce my ex-wife to anyone, because I'd successfully avoided her, for years, after the separation. So after I say, "And my next guest..." I wait until Robbie yells out the name "Pearl," from up in the booth. "Pearl," I say. I see her at the edge of the set, but she doesn't come out. "Pearl! Pearl!" a member of the television crew yells. I see her say, "Who?" and then I say, "Welcome, Pearl."

She strides out. For some reason, she looks shorter than I remember. But she looks good; professionally made-up and very pretty. Her hips swish fast when she walks, and like a sports car on a test track, she swerves around the diluted brown spot, where Hopi released his bowels. When she leans in to hug me, like all the other female guests, I stick out my hand instead.

"This is a real (bleep) storm, isn't it Bill?" she says. "You got a show."

"Well, I'm not here to talk about me. I'm here to talk about you," I say, wishing I felt more in control. "Tell me, what's going on with your marriage?"

"Which one?"

I wait out the audience's gasp. "Well, you and Carlton. You remember him...he's your current husband." The audience laughs. "You told us backstage, that the two of you, are not getting along." This is a technique, Grady had instructed me to use, where "secret" information is given to the studio audience as if I had an intimate relationship with them.

Pearl's face shifts. "Could you repeat the question?" I rephrase it, and she says, "I didn't talk to anyone backstage, but I wouldn't say, we are not getting along, but rather, we get along well, separately. That's the relationship in a nutshell. He thinks, I have mood swings, and I think, he's too even."

"Well, you do have mood swings. But it's important to understand what you feel about him telling you this."

Pearl thinks a little bit, which creates the unwanted "dead air" and then it looks like she's about to have one of her mood swings, but then she gathers herself, and responds with poise, "It seems to me, that I avoid him when we have discussions like this. We don't tend to fight, from what I remember. Then, it often seems to me, that the day has disappeared."

The camera wheels in for a close-up of Pearl's arms, and I notice finger bruises on her biceps, and a long, flat bruise around her left wrist. The Floor Director has begun the count down, so I say, "We will have some interesting footage when we return, but it'll take two, to see."

Grady runs down the stairs. "*It'll take two, to see?* What the hell does that mean?"

I tell him I've been working on some catch phrases I'd like to use, to head into the breaks, kind of like how *Love Connection's* Chuck Woolery used to say, "be back in two-and-two."

"No catch phrases. People hated Chuck Woolery. When I first broke in at WHDH, we canceled *The Love Connection*, because we lost viewers, when he said his catch phrase and they'd switch channels, before viewing our sponsor's ads. In other words, don't do it again!"

Grady storms off, and Pearl says to me, "You're right Bill, it does take two, to see."

2:47 AM: Grady

Grady remains in the camera field, while we run Pearl's clip and plops down on the couch. There is a low rumbling from the studio audience, as they sense a mistake. Grady told me, if I made a mistake on set, I should plow through, as if nothing had happened, so I begin to introduce Dan, as my next guest, but Grady interrupts.

"I'm next," he says. I tell him that on the prep sheet it lists: Dan, Grady and then Ethan. He's the segment after Dan.

"Oh, that's right," he stammers, "I messed up."

"It's okay, we can switch the order. We're able to make adjustments in life."

He sits, looking dismayed. "But the memory-loss product's ad is going to run right after this, and it's a tie in to Dan's segment on the show. I really messed up!" The audience laughs loudly.

"I think people won't have to make much of a jump," I say. "And before *I* forget, Grady, here is a television producer, who has a severe anxiety problem, caused by his high-stress job. We can talk about this. What other shows have you worked on?"

"Well, there's this one, and before that, there were a few others."

"Like what?"

"I don't remember." He lies back down. "I'm too stressed to remember. I work more on programming and the scheduling of time-slots. I'm just here tonight, because this show is something I came up with."

"Oh, I see. So, you haven't worked on shows such as *Oprah*, *Jeopardy*, and *Judge Judy*?"

"No."

"None of the big ones."

"No, I've worked on a lot of shows that didn't bring in high ratings."

"So, what are you saying here? Will my show not become a big one?"

"I think your show has great potential. I mean, I think it's a great show."

"Do you like the Q & A?"

I can tell when people are not telling the truth, or are saying things just to say them, and that's what Grady is doing now. On the positive side, he was a ball of fire tonight on the show, and is now back to being relaxed; the way he would be in my office, talking in

211

almost a dream-like way, his eyes closed. I let him breathe a bit and wonder, if perhaps, it's not all that positive. Grady was really on top of the show but now he seems sick.

Suddenly, Dan barges onto the set. "I remember! I remember, I have to be here! I'm late, I'm late!" Grady is startled upright, and inhales with a loud, wheezy "Hhhhhaaaaaaa"; the kind of sound a person would make if they were shaken out of a shallow sleep. There is a stain of sweat on the couch, and Grady is very pale. "Did I miss my segment?" Dan asks, as we break immediately for commercial.

I assure him, everything is just fine. As the ad for *Brain Reload* plays, and images of elderly individuals winning at Scrabble are shown, Grady breathes heavily, says, barely above the commotion on set, "We are successfully invalidating the show, as something not to watch. We'll check the audience surveys immediately, and see what we need to do before next week." Then, he gets up and ambles off the set, escorted by Robbie, who wipes sweat from Grady's head with a small towel.

2:57 AM: Dan

"You're not late," I reassure him gently, the way Dr. Phil would, but I'm rattled that he's here and I didn't get a chance to introduce him. "This is live TV. These things happen. So, we moved you back by a few minutes."

"Oh, good. I'm excited that I remembered to be here."

"Well done." I look into the camera. "My next guest, Dan, suffered a serious head injury, and as a result, has short-term memory loss.

"The antelope horn pierced my skull," Dan elaborates, rubbing the dent on his forehead.

"Your car hit an antelope," I explain to the audience.

He nods. "So they say. I don't remember anything. But Kate's been helping me. She wants me to connect with my memories. Like when I hear the word *antelope,* sometimes I remember stuff. Hey," he suddenly notices Hopi. "I know him." Hopi walks over and licks his hand. "I love you," Dan whispers, as Kate softly hums, her eyes bulging in excitement.

"Dan, when we met, you were very angry. You used to walk down the street shouting at people. Including me. So…how have you benefited from our therapy sessions?"

Dan looks back with a blank expression. "I don't remember shouting in the street, but I do remember coming out of the fog I was in. I don't remember seeing you for therapy, but I know your name and address, because it's written on my calendar every Thursday."

"Maybe what I do with you, whether you remember or not, helps stimulate your brain capacity and opens up some of those areas, which had been closed off."

"No, I think it's the Reiki."

I can see Grady throwing up his arms inside the booth. He's got a blood pressure cuff on, and as he gestures, the thing you squeeze, swings around like a tetherball. "Well," I say hastily, "let's move on from that. I'm going to give you a set of five words and then I'm going to ask you, at some point in the show, to remember these words. Are you ready?"

"Sure."

"All right. The words are pelican, milk, laser, cashew, and Bill Sloan. Can you remember those?"

"Huh? What am I supposed to do?"

"Listen carefully. I'm going to have you remember a list of five words. Ready?"

"Sure."

"Pelican… milk… laser… cashew… Bill Sloan."

"Isn't that six?"

"No, Bill Sloan is one word."

"Oh yeah, the theme song. It sucks."

I hold back, sigh. "Try to remember those words, and we'll get back to you after the next segment."

We break. Grady returns to the set with some people I've never seen before. Am I going to get fired again? "Hi," I say awkwardly.

Grady says very slowly, "Bill, these are members of the WHDH medical team. Once again, your guests are undermining your authority…every time they mention getting helped by someone else, the audience is going to start thinking we've given the wrong person the show." His speech is calm, but it looks to me like he's about to run down the hall and jump through the window.

What can I say? He's right. I do a combo head nod/shake and shrug.

He exhales. "We need to fine tune the show during the next week. Okay?"

"Okay. So, we have one more guest. Any suggestions?"

"Yeah. DO A FUCKING INTERESTING, EDGY, SAD, FUNNY, EMOTIONAL, ENTERTAINING GODDAMN SHOW THAT'S GOING TO BRING IN HIGH RATINGS!"

3:04 AM: Ethan

Grady wants ratings, I'll give him ratings, I think, anticipating that Ethan will burst onto the scene; high energy racing around, and speaking more like a man, or a savant, than a boy. Instead, he walks out slow and calm, as his parents beam just off stage. I wonder if he has taken some medication in the past hour, which has created this remarkable transformation. He stands at Dan's chair and motions everyone to move down one, and when they do, sits next to me.

"I guess you wouldn't feel more comfortable on the sofa?" I ask.

"Nope, I just need to sit here."

"Ethan, I have to tell you something. An hour ago, you were high as a kite, and now, you're cool and collected."

"Mr. Sloan, this show is important to me. It needs ratings and people shouldn't sleep to it. You need a better theme song."

214

"I think the quality, and the music, of the show is important to me too," I say, and the audience chuckles. "Do they look asleep to you?"

"I had my medications adjusted, so I'd be awake. I told my doctor I was going to be on a show in the middle of the night and he said no. He tried to call you, but you didn't pick up."

"I must have been doing something else" flies out of my mouth, like the way a knee moves when tested by a reflex hammer. The audience chuckles, but this time I wasn't going for humor. "What else did the doctor say?"

"I told him how much I wanted to do this show, how it will make me look, and feel, normal to everyone. I want to have friends. I don't have any. You can't, when you're manic, like me, or when you're depressed, that makes it even harder. The pills keep the seesaw balanced right."

"Seesaw? What seesaw?"

"You told me about the seesaw, and how happy and sad energy are on each end. It's straight right now, right this second, no one is going to jump off, no one is going to come crashing down."

"Oh, I remember now," I say, "but I didn't say anything about energy."

"I did," Kate pipes in.

I face the camera, "You see, when you have a bi-polar disorder, there needs to be a balance between the highs and the lows…" I notice Grady jumping around in the booth, pointing at Ethan, so I quickly stop the definition. "Now, back to Ethan. It's very brave to know things are not right, and that you want to look, and feel, normal. I've seen you racing around the Green Room, at nearly full speed, and now you sit in front of us like nothing is even wrong."

"I was nervous," he says. "I had to get rid of that energy, in a way that's not destructive. At Waysworth, they teach me to do it in a different way. Like, when things get too much, I'm supposed to do other things, which are safer than running around, pretending."

"So what were you doing?"

"I was pretending to fly, you know, to be a superhero. Because pretending is safer than really being one."

"Ethan, I want to share with the audience something I've never shared before. When I was a teenager, I lost my younger brother to this disease, called mental illness. He was a few years older than you are right now, but when he was nine, he struggled like you do. But do you know what? He did not have the support you do. He did not have a therapist, nor should I say, three therapists, and he did not have a school, set up the way Waysworth is. I wish I could work with them more directly, but they never return my calls. I'd like to tell you, I miss my brother, and I will make it my top priority to make sure what happened in that situation, will never happen to you."

Ethan looks at me. "The words are pelican... milk... laser... cashew... Bill Sloan," he says. "Right, Dan?"

"I remember that," Dan says.

At the commercial break, Grady comes down and tells me, Ethan's was the best segment of the show. It's the first time Grady has been completely satisfied with the show all night.

"Why can't the rest of them be as honest, and forthcoming, as Ethan?" he asks. Kate places her hand on Thomas' shoulder.

"Because they have problems."

"Well, you're the therapist. Figure out how to get them to act that way, by next week. It was the best segment, but it was still a tiny bit dry. Your reveal was good, Bill, but not enough detail. We'll work on this during the days before next week's show." The commercial ends and WHDH shows Ethan's clip.

Let's go to the clips...

Hanna

Scene 1: The camera shows the top of Hanna's dresser, the makeup dust, various eye liner products, and the note to Randy; the one he gave back to her. "Suicide makes you want to push everyone you love away," she says to the camera. Her kid is sitting on the floor, in the living room, watching *Sesame Street*.

"Elmo? Elmo?" he says.

Hanna walks over and turns the television off.

"ELMO? ELMO?" "We have to go, honey," Hanna says. As the camera follows her into the kitchen, to pack the baby bag for a car trip, the kid says, "Elmo?" and Hanna says wearily, "You can't get too attached."

Scene 2: Hanna, driving, turns to face the camera. "I can't remember the last time I was in Rhode Island." The camera scans to Randy, in the passenger side, and then to her kid, sitting in his car seat in back, pulling the string on his fuzzy Elmo doll. "Elmo love you," says the doll. When they arrive at White Light Books, a Honda FCX Clarity cuts in front of her and takes her spot. The audio bleeps out what Hanna says, as she moves to the next spot.

Scene 3: Hanna, Randy and the kid walk into White Light Books, and a staff person asks if they want a Professional Capability Report. Hanna doesn't respond, and Randy is left looking at the staff person. Hanna moves to the book section and flips through a copy of *Archangel Raphael Healing*. Her kid has two healing stones in his hands.

Scene 4: Hanna and Randy sit on a red and white checked throw blanket, in the shade at Comealy's Farm, her left hand holding

Randy's right. There are three stones on the blanket. Hanna picks them up and shifts them across her palm, like dice. One says HOPE, and one says LOVE, and one is blank.

Kate

Scene 1, A commercial: Kate sits in padmasana (lotus pose) with Aimee on her right, and Robbie, struggling in an easier crossed leg position, on her left. Hopi circles around, behind the three of them, and in the background, Dan and Thomas stand straight as soldiers. The sound of a paina (acoustic guitar), harps, and flutes, played over the lap of the ocean, can be heard on the soundtrack.

"Hello, I'm Kate Hummingbird Warrior, and I am a Love Sharer. I openly give the spiritual energy from my heart, spirit, and soul, to each and every one of you, here at Sunny and Share, located in downtown Boston. All you have to do is come in, and we'll do the rest, whatever you need, to cleanse the negativity out of your life."

Kate turns to Robbie, "Hello, beautiful man."

Robbie's head and upper torso fills the frame. "Come on down!" he says with a big round house gesture. "There will be no initial billing during the initial consultation." Robbie stiffly points at the camera, as the words "NO BILLING!" flash upon the screen. "No bills mailed to your house," pointing again, "and best of all, no bills in any way, shape, or form. All cost will come to you, by way of a spiritual suggestive donation."

"Oh, I liked your improved delivery," Kate says to him. "Not very calming, but you can work on that at Sunny and Share. Just like we work on Aimee, during her coffee and lunch breaks, to become a better person."

"Kate Hummingbird Warrior has taught me that becoming a better person is about opening yourself up, completely, to love," Aimee says. "And it is my job to spiritually suggest a donation for an hour here at Sunny and Share, should be between $35 and $250, depending on how you are feeling, after working with us."

"So come to Sunny and Share," Kate says, as Dan and Thomas walk up to stand behind them, to say in unison, "Where mind, body, and spirit are open to you, for you, and around you, AT ALL TIMES." After a one-second pause they all say, "Namaste," and Hopi lets out a howl. Kate laughs, and says, "I love you."

Thomas

Scene 1: Thomas's truck weaves its way through the traffic lanes on 95, cutting off a white Toyota. His truck has *Sunny and Share Production and Construction* painted on the door. The man in the Toyota is obese, bulging out of his Celtics jersey. The Toyota accelerates past Thomas, and the man gives him the finger, and strongly mouths the magic f-word to Thomas. He waits until he's is barely clear of Thomas's front bumper, cuts over quickly, without signaling.

The video has been edited, as a split screen. One is of the interplay between the two cars, and the other is of Thomas' face. He's not angry; the confrontation has made him giddy. "Ha, (bleep) you too!" He stomps on the accelerator, and the truck bolts to eighty-five miles per hour, and he mimics the guy in the Toyota, starting with the finger, the shout, and ending with a near collision. The can you match this, plays like a game of H-O-R-S-E. The audio picks up one of the cameramen saying, "Don't do this," but if that sound-bite was to be edited out, then the near-miss on the highway, would have been cut as well.

The car accelerates, nosing its way, inches from Thomas's rear bumper. Thomas taps the breaks, then stomps them a few times, as the two vehicles start bucking in synch, like some strange, high-speed automotive ballet. The shot of Thomas's face is no longer giddy. Now it's angry, and as red as a run traffic light. There is a constant bleeping, which has taken over the audio, as the cars continue to honk, and Thomas continues to swear. Then Thomas slows down, decelerating to forty-five miles an hour. The Toyota swings around Thomas, like the Celtics picket-fence play they run for Ray Allen, moving over an extra lane, to ensure Thomas won't bump him at close range. Another car moves quickly in the far passing lane, and nearly collides with the Toyota, which has encroached into his space.

Thomas lies back now, but keeps his opponent's car in his sight for a few miles. When it exits, Thomas moves in closer and follows him to the stop sign, at the end of the ramp. Thomas jumps out of his truck, followed by the camera crew. The sound of six feet running, sounds louder than it should be. The driver begins to jaw at Thomas, and Thomas pulls him out through the window, and lays him out with two punches. The first produces shock and fear on the face of the other driver. The second causes him to collapse. Thomas shoves his flat palm into camera one, and yells into the second one to, "Get the (bleep) away from me". Thomas pulls the truck around the two camera men, leaving them on the shoulder, scanning with their cameras, up and down like robots. The sound of piano, harps, and flutes played over the lapping of an ocean, can be heard from the stereo system in Thomas's truck.

Pearl

Scene 1: Pearl and Carlton are in the middle of a fight. "What do you want from me?" Stella yells.

"I want you to not be so unpredictable."

"Why don't you divorce me?"

"I didn't say that."

"I wish you would get upset, show some fucking emotion!"

"I don't do that."

"I hate you! I went to you because I thought you were safe, but instead, you're a fucking bore!"

"That's enough."

"Why don't you do something? Come on!" Stella picks up a book and hurls it at him. It strikes him on the chest and thumps to the floor. He stands there, unaffected. Stella picks up a heavy glass ashtray and hurls it at him. He ducks, and it leaves a divot in the wall behind him. Carlton shouts something at her, but she charges, hands out, and claws extended, as he grabs her arms. They wrestle briefly, and then he swings behind her, pulls his left arm around her, and firmly grabs her bicep. Stella lets out an, "ow," and they tumble to the rug, him on top of her, his right arm pushing her head into the carpet.

Scene 2: Stella is in the bathroom, showing her arm to the camera, and with her voice echoing into the microphone, says, "There's going to be some bruising here," she points to her forearm, "and here." She shows the camera the red finger marks on her arm, and the camera zooms in for a close-up. "We're not getting along too well, but I'd like it to work out. Don't tell him that."

Grady

Scene 1: Grady and Robbie sit in Grady's office. His desk is covered with papers, which jut out in all angles. "Be careful what you say," he says to Robbie. "This is all going to be on the show."

"Interesting," Robbie says.

"Did you read the research?"

"Yes, I found the statistics were interesting, as well."

"Interesting? It's going to be the basis of success or failure!" Grady says.

"They hate the theme music. Research says, it's cheap and cheesy sounding."

"There is nothing we can do about that. We only had six hours in the studio to create that... crap, we're being filmed now!"

"Don't worry. It'll all be part of the show. Also, it seems *Doctor Bill* has some issues with gaining the trust of our target audience.

221

According to the charts, Bill Sloan is trusted by 17%, based just on his photo. That's pretty low, and the comments aren't very complimentary either. There seems to be a creep factor."

"Yes, but what are the fucking numbers, when his photo is shown along with his background information?"

"They are at 29%."

"Now, check this out, when they show the photograph, with a label of Dr. Bill Sloan, the numbers go up again."

"Yes, they are at a 35% trustworthy rating. It's getting up there. Did we successfully get the honorary Doctorate, from Boston University?" Robbie asks.

"Yesterday," Grady says. "I had it right here, and we're going to use it on the set. We'll tack the diploma right to the drywall."

"Great. Hey, wait a minute," Robbie says. "Did you see this page?"

"No."

"When he's just Bill, average old Bill, the trustworthy rating goes up, to over sixty percent!"

"Shit! We can't market that."

"Why not? Grady, we can be subtle and call it the Dr. Bill, or even, the Mr. Bill Show. What do you think about that change, getting us a better initial audience tuning in?"

"Dr. Bill, is too much like, Dr. Phil, and Mr. Bill is a fucking clay animation, who gets tortured! Fucking A! This is what I get for hiring a research agency."

"Can we give Hanna, or Kate a show? Maybe a children's mental health show, with Ethan? The approvals are high for those."

"Forget it," Grady says, and looks into the camera. "I trust in Bill Sloan. He's a decent man, who cares, and is able to get the most out of some very entertaining people. Solving people's problems, in an entertaining way will bring tons of viewers, looking for help and also to be entertained at 2:15 AM every Thursday. We hope, Bill Sloan will project the kind, and gentle man, we all know him as, here at WHDH."

"Bull (bleep)," Robbie says.

Scene 2: Grady is in his living room, his head in his hands. The room is plush; the maroon curtains, exactly matching, the maroon of the oriental carpet.

Joe sits next to him, his arms around his shoulders. "We tried going on vacation, we tried getting you help, and you're still a mess. Do you think it's time, to do something else?"

"Like what? I refuse to fail. I've worked my whole life to succeed in the television industry."

"More therapy?" Joe asks, flicking his coiffed hair away from his face, with the back of his fingers, so it hangs perfectly again.

"I'm seeing someone else, in a therapeutic way, I don't want to mention now on camera. It will be counterproductive for, *The Dr. Bill Sloan Show*, plus my problems are not about me, they're about television."

"You can talk to me about it anytime, or any place. I'm always open to you if you, are feeling stress, and feel like things are not working in your life." Joe is the cooling water, poured on Grady's inner-fire.

"I feel I should keep seeing Bill, but not on television, and the woman helps, but if they film it, that will affect Bill's ratings," Grady says.

"I don't get it. You never mentioned a woman."

"It's something neither you, nor the show, would understand."

Dan

Scene 1: Dan places his forefinger into the dent on his head. "Of course I don't remember when it happened, but I'm surprised it prevents me from remembering a lot of new things." The camera scans around his apartment and there are *Things To Do* sheets thumb-tacked to the walls. "I wish I didn't have these tattoos on my arms, because they once stood for something, well... I don't remember now. Look at this raven. It's funny—I remember the original raven, but someone told me, the raven is my animal totem. I don't remember what it stands for, but I have it in a book." He opens a copy of *The Spiritual and Mythical Powers of Animals* and finds a tabbed section. "There's this god named Odin, who was regarded as 'the leader of souls.' Odin had two ravens—Huginn, 'thought,' and Muninn, 'memory,' who flew about the world, delivering messages, gathering knowledge, and reporting back to him. So I've been told, I'm related to the raven, that I need outside carriers of my memories, which will plant them back into my head. It makes sense, and I no longer get mad, because I know the raven is on the way."

"What about your therapy?" a voice off camera asks.

"I have a note on that." Dan walks to a calendar and pulls a note off it. "His name is Bill Sloan and I see him on Thursdays. I used to see him in the afternoons, but it says here, I now see him at 2:55 AM. I don't think that's right. I'm asleep at that time."

"And the therapy?"

Dan looks at another note. "Says here, it's useless. He has me memorize lists. I wrote one down, book... cactus... wheelbarrow... pepperoni... Bill Sloan. I can't tell if I'm supposed to order a pizza, or go see someone. We also do card matching memory games, but I don't know why it's important."

Scene 2: Dan is lying on a massage table, in a brightly-lit room. A modulated, slightly-scrambled voice is heard, asking him, what he remembers. "I remember a raven coming and perching, on the dent on my head. It told me, I drove across the country because I was in pain. The pain I put out in the Universe, I got back. But the Universe, being what it is, created something, which wouldn't allow me to remember the pain. Now, with you in the Universe, I'm ready to remember the information that will be brought to me"

"Anything else?"

"Yes, something about the snake soon becoming as still as a statue."

Ethan

Scene 1: Ethan sits in the middle of the floor surrounded by compact discs, vinyl record albums, and a laptop, which plays his mp3 music. Surrounding him, are over one hundred toy action figurines. He looks up, speaks: "I'm doing this, all for the ratings. I'm trying to save television, and television will help me save myself." He sets up some of the album covers into large versions of card houses. He uses the compact disc liner notes, to make patio, and shingled roof areas. "You see," he goes on, "music is important to people. It's as important as super heroes. If you're feeling a certain way, it can save your life, which saves the world." He grabs Superman and flies him, in a circle, over his house of music. "You can't make anything out of digital music," he says; followed by a reflective, "Do you think the fans of The Who, or Great White, planned what was going to happen that night? I think the crowd was there to have a good time, and then, it's like when you're planning something really important in your mind, and something snaps you out of it, suddenly your world can't be saved. Those people died, and there was no Superman. They couldn't even be Superman to themselves, when they needed to."

Ethan looks sad and vacant, as if every synapse within his brain is full, but something keeps pumping neurons through the circuits; overloading him, leaving him unable to react. "I'd like to tell the audience, that in my mind, I think I'm Superman, just as I am also Kryptonite to myself. I want people to see it happen on the show, and it'll all make sense and help the ratings. If I can make sense of it, then everyone else should be able to. I'm just planning on going out on TV, and being normal. If I'm normal, I don't have to fly like Superman, not the one in the Kinks song, 'Superman', but I'm actually in a different Kinks song, called, 'Over the Edge'. It's on the album, right here."

Ethan holds up the record and sings the lyrics: *Everybody is a victim of society, comedy, tragedy, vaudeville and variety, pantomime players in the grand tradition, winners and losers till the intermission.* "If I'm normal, I can get better. It's the only thing I hope for. I tell my parents, and the people at Waysworth, about hope all the time, but it's something, I feel like I'm begging for, rather than working toward. I don't tell Mom and Dad that." He sighs. "I believe, *The Doctor Bill Sloan Show* is very important, not just for me, but for everyone; the way The Who, or the Great White concerts, were for their fans. It's going to be a very important program, but I've been told, by my parents, to not worry about that, and take a more fun approach. No need to put the cart in front of the horse, they say, unless the horse is in bad shape, then the cart is on its own. I try to listen to them, as these records are theirs. They must know what they're talking about."

Chapter 14: The Doctor Bill Sloan Show
Episode Two, April 13

11:45 AM: Alarm clock
Spring up from the bed
Guzzle 32 ounces of Starbucks instant coffee, Red Bull to go
Sprinkle an additional packet of coffee powder on a green banana
Now awake
Floss

1:00 AM: Grady

I walk into Grady's office, and sitting behind stacks of papers on his desk, is Robbie. He has the feedback from, The Survey of American Television Viewers. "We need to talk to you about last week's show. We might need to make some adjustments, before we go on the air."

"I don't want Robbie here," I say. "Every time I see him, he's up to something, and he *fired* me. He never gets the name right, either. He was fine, when he was cleaning my toilets, in the old office, but now I want nothing to do with him."

Robbie stands. "Okay, I'm leaving. But you should know, I'm still cleaning shit out of toilets—except the toilets are different in many ways. When the time comes, I'll gladly give you what you deserve, once again, but I'm rooting for you, Bill. Your show is in my best interest. But if things happen, which are beyond my control, I'll do what I'm paid to do. Imagine if I'd fired Johnny McNamara before Game 6, in 1986? It would have been a whole new story in Red Sox history."

"See you later, Robbie," Grady says, taking The Survey of American Television Viewers report, from his hand. He waits until Robbie leaves, then frowns. "They don't like you. They want you to be firmer. They want you to yell at people, who are admitting to screwing up their lives."

"That's not really ethical, but I can be more edgy and confrontational. There's a psychological technique, which covers that."

"Ethical?" he repeats; he rubs his head, then indulges in a scratch, leaving the skin red. "Come off it."

I should be offended, but I'm not. "What else did they say? Did they like the guests?"

"They thought that Hanna was dull. So, either we sex her up, or we focus on her recent dating history. Kate comes off as attractive and wacky. The audience loved her. What I want you to do is try not to play into her Love Sharing Practice, unless you're making it an obvious rivalry, got it?"

"Got it."

"Now, Thomas. According to the SATV, the audience didn't like him, but they enjoyed the confrontation between the two of you. The survey says, he's the only character, the audience liked less than you."

Did Dr. Phil ever have to deal with people hating him? "No one in the entire world likes Thomas."

"Kate does. There was also an internal survey of your guests; or should I say, clients. Most of them didn't care that they were participants on the show, and none of them liked you. Except Kate. How did you manage to have a practice?"

"Can we go on," I say. "I'll be more edgy and confrontational this week."

"Good," he continues to flip through the report. "Okay, hardly anyone liked Pearl. They wanted more details of your and her marriage, and they wanted her to switch back and forth, between her two personalities. Like a circus freak. Audiences love freaks."

"I have no control over which personality she is in."

"Well, you're going to have to GET some control. The show is good, but it's fighting ratings. We need ratings NOW, or this may be the last show."

"What! The last show?"

"Try not to think about it. We're on in about an hour, so keep it together." He looks back at the survey. "My segment went well, because the audience liked the behind the scenes television moments, but WHDH had a comment, which I'll share: *Grady needs to get the fuck off the stage, until it's his turn to be on stage, as a guest.* Okay, I happen to agree with that." He pauses and takes a deep breath. "Not that I even wanted to be on the show. I mean, Joe was mortified."

"We can talk about your problem on the air."

"Yes, but here, try this." He hands me a small ear piece. "I want you to wear this during the show. It won't be visible, and you will receive instructions directly from the booth."

"I don't know…"

"WHDH really wants you to. I think it means they're showing commitment to the show."

"Fine. I'll give it a try, but I don't like it."

"Right. Right. Now, moving on. Okay, Dan. The audience loved the memory games, but he never responded to them, and I think that, it kind of pissed them off. I think, him not remembering anything, is a gold mine. Let's go for more of that. By the way, Dan's response to the survey, was that he hates memory games, and thinks they aren't relevant to anything. He gets really frustrated… so, we should have more memory games!"

"Fine. Now what about Ethan?"

"Ethan was the subject of more tweets, e-mails and comments than anyone else. They like a boy who is on the edge, and is fighting for normalcy, and sanity. Try to amp that up a little."

"Okay."

"Oh, and we're not showing clips after each guest. The audience didn't like the format. So, we're going to insert the clips during the guest segments, while they're being interviewed by you. Robbie will let you know when the clips will be shown."

"Fine."

"And the theme song has been changed. It has kind of a punky feel, to portray you as being more edgy. I think it satisfies yours and our artistic needs. Want to give it a listen?"

"No, but I'm confident the show, this week, is going to get high ratings."

2:15 AM: Hanna

The new theme song plays, and I check the monitor. They've added washed-out images of my clients, and the names, *Hanna, Kate Hummingbird Warrior, Thomas, Pearl, Dan,* and *Ethan,* over a clearer shot of me, in action, talking. The music is more repetitious and annoying, now that it is "punky." Personally, I'd rather have piano music.

I open with, "That music is really horrible," and the audience laughs. In my earpiece, Robbie's furious voice: *"Don't say that!"*

"Okay, I'd like to bring out Hanna again. As you remember, Hanna is a young woman, whose boyfriend died recently, and she's handling that in a way, that many young women handle emotional loss. What you didn't know, is that she had another boyfriend at the time. Hanna!"

Hanna has an aggressive stride, and when I stand to meet her, she neither hugs me, or shakes my hand; just sits in the chair to my right."

"Get her on the couch. The audience likes her lying down."

"The couch is available," I tell her.

"You bastard!" she says, and the audience answers with a long, sustained, uniformed, "Ooooooo…"

"Why am I a bastard, when I'm just telling people the truth? Isn't being honest important to you?"

"I can't believe you mentioned that, to them," she says motioning to the audience.

"Great inclusion of the audience, Bill. Go with it!"

"Hanna, I want you to remember, that time lines are important. The person you were involved with, before Brad killed himself, is still in your life. Isn't that true?"

"Yes, but I can't explain it, now, in five minutes. There is NO WAY I can explain it, so it makes any sense," Hanna says, looking fierce, then under her breath growls to me, "You are trying to tie my behavior into Brad's death? What the fuck!" I can't hear Robbie telling me, to get Hanna to do something.

"What?"

"Get her to speak up."

"I'm not going to repeat that," Hanna says. "I didn't do anything wrong, and I'm not going to be made to feel like I had anything to do with this death!"

"Well, we have a little surprise for you. You see, Grady, our producer, has asked both Randy, the other man, and Brad's parents, to join us on stage. So here they are, Randy Lawson and the Flaggs."

When the guests come out, Hanna stands and pulls Randy close. "I don't know what the fuck is going on," she says.

"Be prepared. This is going to get good."

"Don't worry," Randy tells her. "I'm just taking their thousand dollars, but I got your back, babe." The sound and random feel from the group, is the same vibe you might find from a line of large people at The Olde Country Buffet, bustling to get in. Finally, they position themselves, Hanna next to me, followed by Randy, and then Mr. and Mrs. Flagg.

"I just want everyone to know, we're not here to blame, or to judge, anyone here. This will be an open session of communication, between some of the important people from Brad's life."

"And some of the people, Brad proved to be unimportant to, as well," Mrs. Flagg says.

"Now, Connie," I say.

"Call me Mrs. Flagg," she replies curtly.

"Now, Mrs. Flagg. There is no need to accuse Hanna of that; after all, she is the mother of your grandson." I turn to the audience, "Who couldn't be with us tonight."

"I meant you, you dumb (bleep). You were the treating doctor, and it was more than apparent, he was unimportant to you."

"What? No! You know that's not the case!"

"No?"

"No! At the time, I wasn't a doctor. But now, I am. My Doctorate, is supported and brought to this program, by Boston University, a private urban research university, established in 1869, offering a breadth of undergraduate, graduate, and professional programs, through its 17 Schools and Colleges, and more than 250 fields of study."

"*Way to work the plug in.*"

"That's not what my wife meant! We blame *you*, Sloan!" Mr. Flagg jumps in. "We knew about Randy and Hanna, but all we wanted, was to be in the life of our grandson again, and it just wasn't happening. When Brad and Hanna were together, Hanna and the baby would stay with us, and then after the funeral, we never saw them. By the way, your little speech at the funeral, indicated you knew nothing about Brad. If you had done your job, he'd still be with us!"

"*Gain some control here.*"

"I'm sorry you feel that way," I say, but to my right, I notice Randy getting up, off the chair, and Hanna's hand gripping his pants by the belt loop.

"He's right!" Randy yells. "You acted like you needed to fill up your obligation, by attending and speaking, so your plate would be clean..."

"I don't understand what you're getting at," I say.

"And then YOU started dating Hanna, and made her feel like (bleep) about me and her! Don't you think it might (bleep) up her (bleep)ing head?"

At this point, everyone on the set is standing and the sound coming from the audience is the same one, which a crowd at a courtroom would make, after a "Not guilty" ruling is made, at a trial for a heinous crime.

"You do understand, because of your swearing, this will be edited out," I say. "And I never dated..."

"*LOOK OUT, LOOK OUT!*"

Randy lurches toward me, and has me by the lapels of my blues sports coat; as he throttles me, I see Hanna walk off the set. Then, there is a wave of black shirts upon us, with the words *Dr. Sloan Security*, printed on breast pockets in large block letters. We break for commercial.

2:24 AM: Kate

The set has been cleared, and Grady brings me a new blue suit coat to replace the one Randy tore. My knees are shaking. "No need for the clip," he says. "They walked off, and they're threatening to quit the show. But don't you worry: if the ratings are up, we'll beef up their payment. No one has stopped watching DBSS tonight." Grady is wearing the blood pressure cuff again; his thin hair matted with sweat.

"DBSS?"

"Doctor...Bill...Sloan...Show. It's TV shorthand. Okay, stay focused, and listen to the instructions from the booth. We're on in thirty seconds."

When the music is brought up, Kate, her hair flowing behind her, like a long blond river, walks out with Hopi. "I notice there

233

might need to be some Love Sharing techniques to be worked on," she says.

"*Don't go there!*"

"We're not going to go there…exactly," I say.

"Are you planning on going there, inexactly," she teases and smiles, flirting, but not trying.

"*Don't encourage anything but the rivalry between you two.*"

"Where we are going to go is, to compare my way of doing things, to Sunny and Share's way. It'll be kind of an educational discussion, not adversarial. I'd like the studio audience, and the audience at home to see which is better."

"Oh, that sounds wonderful. I'd like to educate people about Sunny and Share, and the Love Sharing therapy we conduct."

"You see, I fix people's minds, the way a mechanic fixes cars," I say. "You go to a garage and have the old engine, that's not working properly, taken out and replaced with some new parts, which work the way that they should. From what I gather, Love Sharing, involves a physical Reiki massage, and other types of physical activity."

Kate laughs. "You're so silly, that's just a part of it. What I do is spiritual healing; I help people find inner peace, so they have confidence they're attractive, both inside and out, and deeply loved by the Universe. The whole process, puts a smile on their face."

"I bet. Is it true, that you have been stealing some of my clients?"

"Hmmm, did they leave you? Have they stopped seeing you, Bill?"

"Well, no."

"Then, I have not stolen anything. What I offer is a better, more well-rounded, additional service. Even Hopi is involved, as he has great spiritual powers."

"So, to get Hopi's services, how much extra would that cost?"

The audience laughs.

"*Careful…watch where you're going.*"

"We take our donations on a scale of whatever people think the service is worth. During a Reiki session, I use the energy to suggest it should be in the ball park of $150, and you know what? People come up with that number on their own, just like that."

"We have some old clips—they're blockbusters against her therapy."

"Okay, we're going to show some clips, Kate."

"Oh, the ones you took of Dan, teaching Hopi to hug him, are amazing."

"Bill, these are not from last week. The first is from Camden, New Jersey."

"Well, just have a look," I say.

Clip one is shown, and it's a grainy black and white surveillance tape from ACME Supermarket. There's a woman is in an aisle, frantically adjusting boxes of pudding. Kate's mother. The manager is trying to get her to quit: *Ma'am, the store is closed!* She refuses to leave, and they begin to skirmish; the boxes knocked off the shelves during the restraint of Kate's mother. The clip is cut to the final scene of Kate's mom being led away in handcuffs.

"I know that woman," Kate says, sounding as thin and weak, as the barely audible audio from the ACME film.

"Bill, move to the next clip. I think you'll recognize this."

Clip two is equally grainy, and it's taken from the corner of my old office. Kate is sitting on my lap, and we're face to face; she throws her head back as I penetrate her; my mouth on her breasts. It's too late to stop the clip, but I stand and shout, "Stop! That's outrageous!" anyway.

"Sorry man, had to show it. I found it last week. Say the therapy, HER therapy, is outrageous!"

"Her therapy is outrageous!"

Kate is sitting in her chair with her eyes closed. Her hand is lax and Hopi, sensing that he's no longer being held, stands too, and approaches me. Nervously, I offer my hand for him to sniff, but he chomps down. I retreat and he lunges for my crotch. At the same time, some guys from security run to the stage and wrestle him to the ground.

Kate opens her eyes. "No, not the wolf! Not the wolf!"

In my earpiece, the command, *"Get him!"* but I don't know if Robbie is instructing security to grab Hopi, or Hopi to attack me! We cut to a commercial, and the medical team comes up and wraps my hand.

As security starts to drag Hopi off stage, Kate stands, regal and sexy. "No," she says. "Hopi stays."

"He's dangerous," a security guy says. "We need to put him in a cage or something."

"No, he'll be fine. He was protecting me. I'll keep a tight hold on his leash. Okay, Grady?" She sends him a smile, and he caves right away.

"Okay, the dog can stay."

"Dog, my ass," I hear Robbie say; *"he belongs in a zoo or something!"*

"So, Grady," I reflect, "you just happened to have security and medical people here?"

"For your own protection, after we pre-interviewed your clients and the surprise guests," Grady says.

"I wasn't planning on a show like this! I wanted a revamped Dr. Phil rather than a Jerry Springer type."

"Must I remind you that we had less than a 1.0 rating last week? Don't tell me you didn't know anything about our plan, because you told me you were going for more edgy. If the ratings maintain and viewers stick around, we might have another week of this."

My hand throbs. I sigh. "Okay, fine, fine, I got it. Keep it edgy. Has Hopi had his shots?"

2:32 AM: Thomas

Thomas walks out with a shit-eating grin on his face. "Dumb ass, music," he says.

"They'll edit it out," I say.

"The music or the word ass? Robbie already told me the word "ass", will not get bleeped, so, ass, ass, ass, you're a (bleep)ing ass."

"Settle down," I say. Edgy is one thing, but this is just stupid. "I think you're misdirecting your anger to—"

"Think so, Doc? Oh wait, you're not a doctor."

"Yes, I am. My degree was given to me by Boston University, a program of enhanced learning where—"

"Shut the (bleep) up, Doc. Now, I want to say something. I'm pissed. Remember when I said, I didn't want, or agree to, being filmed."

"Yes, but there's not much you can do about it."

"Well because of *The Doctor Bill Sloan Show*, I was arrested, found guilty, and put under house arrest. I had to use a CELLx House Arrest Bracelet. When you're not in a rush, and the clinker is not an option, ask for CELLx. It'll keep you in check."

"Um, what?"

"Cha-Ching. Ten thousand dollars, right there from CELLx! If you had any (bleep)-ing ratings it would be one-hundred thousand."

"Thomas, we need to talk about your anger issues."

"No, but wait. You might think, how did I get on the show tonight, if I'm under House Arrest?"

"No, I wasn't thinking—"

"Well, funny you should ask," Thomas says, looking directly into the camera. "For a limited time, Ken Savage's DVD, or downloadable information video, *How to Remove a House Arrest Bracelet*, can be yours for the low price of $24.99."

"*Deflect this! NOW! CELLx and Ken Savage didn't pay for us to talk about their shit!*"

"Excuse me?" I say.

"But wait! If you act now on this special TV offer, Ken will give you, the two foot steel prying rod, at no extra cost...but that's not all! We are ready to offer you, two free leather straps with rivets, which can firmly re-attach the bracelet, back on your ankle, when you return home. You get the video, the steel rod, and the leather strap all for $24.99." Thomas takes his eye contact away from the camera and back on me. "Ch-Ching, fifty grand!"

The words no sooner leave his mouth, when the security team walks back on stage. "We've been asked to secure you, for violation of your parole," one of them says.

Grady comes on stage, too. "Don't worry Bill, we knew all about this. We couldn't have Thomas doing something illegal, on the show, so we called his parole people. We didn't want to let you in on it, because we wanted your reaction. It was great television."

"I see."

"Don't worry about next week. We can fill in the time, by either giving the others more time, by showing clips of Thomas at home, or he could phone in. Another option, is to have a local celebrity guest star in that slot."

"Guest star?"

"Yes, don't worry about it," Grady says.

2:42 AM: Pearl

Grady remains on set, sitting and panting on one of the guest chairs, as I introduce Pearl to the audience.

"There's this breakthrough moment, in the movie *Sybil*, when Joanne Woodward, playing Dr. Wilbur, brings all sixteen characters of Sybil's personality into the room and fuses them into one healthy person. She calls in Vickie, Peggy, Marcia, and Patty, all with distinct personalities, ages, problems, hopes, and dreams, to reintroduce them into the body and soul of the singular Sybil."

"*Bo-ring...*"

I ignore Robbie's chanting. "Later, it was claimed Wilbur fabricated most of the research, which makes *Sybil* more like a novel, as many details of the real case were changed, to make it more interesting,"

"So?" Pearl is looking away into the audience.

"But the technique of joining the characters together is useful."

"*Ohhh... yes, do this, this'll be awesome!*"

238

"I don't know what you're talking about," Pearl says.

"Well, I'm not going to try that technique. All I want to say is that...YOUR NAME IS STELLA. IT'S STELLA AND YOU ARE MY EX-WIFE! PEARL IS SOMEONE YOU USED, IN ORDER TO TRICK THE SCREENER, TO GET INTO MY OFFICE, TO TALK TO ME. SNAP OUT OF IT!"

Pearl has a funny look on her face, and her lips look wavy, like she's chewing gravel without any teeth.

I lower my voice. "Don't you remember? We have two children, and you have a different husband. You are slipping into the Pearl and Stella characters, as if they are real! They are NOT; there is only one of you. Pearl? Pearl? There's only one, and it's Stella!"

Pearl is sitting still and looks dazed. "Pearl? Stella?" she repeats.

"Yes." I shake her gently.

"Great segment! But we need to break."

"We'll be right back," I say. "It'll take two, to see."

Kate's eyes are closed and she's silent. Stella isn't moving or speaking. They're both so... still. "Did you teach her this?" I whisper to Kate. "Is she meditating?"

Kate opens her eyes. "Oh, dear. I think she's in some kind of shock." Hopi sits up too, and awaits her next command. "Good boy," she says.

"What do you mean, shock? Like, she's in a trance?"

"If she's in a trance, she won't be a good guest! Our ratings will drop!"

"Not a deep one. Hopi knows what to do."

"We're back in three...two...one..."

"Ladies and gentlemen," I say, "my guest Pearl seems to be in a state of suspended animation. This is something I've never seen before, but we're hoping that Hopi, the wolf, will participate in some kind of healing, and Kate here will facilitate."

"No she won't! This is YOUR show! You've got to be involved! This has to be about you!"

239

"So under my direction, Kate, here, will use the animal, to pull Pearl out of her current state. Kate and I have discussed how the wolf is going to do this, and we're going to need absolute silence, as the thoughts that will be conjured up, within Pearl's unconscious are the ones she and I have been working on in therapy, for the last few months."

"*Good. Good.*"

Kate has her hand on the top of Hopi's head, and it's almost as if the wolf has been restrained again. I follow, as she walks Hopi over to Pearl, and Hopi begins to lick Pearl's toes. The look of frozen fear leaves Pearl's face and she smiles. "Oh, Carlton." The audience applauds.

I motion toward Pearl with my left hand, saying, "See, there you have it," and Hopi wheels around to nip at it. "Hopi is still in training," I hear Kate say, as I grunt the introduction for the next commercial.

2:50 AM: Dan

Dan walks past Hopi, then Grady, and pats both of their heads. "What happened to your hand?" he asks me, seeing my bandage.

"Were you not watching backstage?"

"Yes. I saw Kate and the wolf heal that woman."

"Under my direction, of course," I say.

"Not really. Hopi did all the work."

"I don't know if we should believe someone who can't remember basic information, like word chains, or what they had for breakfast."

"I had granola."

"You did?"

"Yes. I have it every morning, so it's easy to remember what I had for breakfast."

"So, that only proves you are redundant. Admit it, you can't function, because of your memory loss, and if you could remember, you would realize, it was only after seeing me that things got easier to deal with in your life." Suddenly, I hear Kate whisper the word *antelope* and Dan breaks into a big grin.

"Pelican, milk, laser, cashew ,and Bill Sloan," he says.

"What?"

"Those are the words, I was supposed to remember."

"Not good for the show. Regain the control, Bill!"

"Oh," I say, "Those were last week's words. This week we have *coffee, cheese grater, pigeon,* and *Michael Collins.*"

"Who?"

"Michael Collins. He was an astronaut on Apollo 11."

"Is this some kind of trick? That's totally not fair!" Kate says. "Everyone forgets him!"

"It helps the brain to heal if someone, like Dan, can connect with the irony."

"Dan, Dan," she says. *"antelope."*

"Yes, I remember Kate. I am remembering things. You are the one healing me. You brought me back to life."

Hopi yips, and Kate says, "Good boy."

"Ladies and gentlemen, welcome to the Kate and Hopi Show," Robbie's voice says sarcastically.

My hands clench the crease of my pants, "No, Dan! You should not be able to remember things, not here, not now, not this week, please!"

"Not because of that dog!" Grady shouts.

"Me, you, and Grady, need to talk at break."

3:01 AM: *Grady*

During the break, Grady's words come out like they're shot from a cannon: "Let's get this straight—this is my life, Bill, and you're blowing it! If this fails, I'm basically done at WHDH! And then what? What do I tell Joe? What will I do? Even the people like you, who were supposed to help me through these problems, have blown it!"

A nurse has moved in from side-stage, and has begun to inflate his blood pressure cuff. "Robbie, we're going to need to monitor this," she says. The doctor opens Grady's shirt and affixes sticky pads onto his chest, hooking him up to a portable heart monitor.

Watching him, I feel a mix of sadness, anger, guilt, and defensiveness. "I must say, it's pretty important to me, too. What will I do, if this thing blows up?"

"I don't give a rat's ass about what you're going to do, but what you *will* do is, attempt to create award-winning television for the next fourteen minutes, before we go off the air. Is that something, you have in you?"

"I've got your section, with a clip of you and Joe, having brunch."

"That's not going to cut it."

"And, I have something I can try with Ethan. It's a bit risky, but the risky segments have done well tonight. Are you sure we're in trouble?"

Grady starts at his head, moves down the side of his face, to his neck, and scratches, until he's red all over. "I don't have the numbers, but I'm sure some of the shenanigans, during this hour, will not bode well with keeping an audience, I mean, you practically told everyone at home, you're unreliable, unlikeable, and unethical."

"I think we can save this."

"You'd better pull out all stops, or we'll be canceled. We can't be canceled!" The heart monitor beeps out a warning.

Robbie, standing next to me, says, "Pull out all stops!" and I simultaneously hear it in my earpiece. Everyone is still on stage when the commercial break ends, but Robbie directs the camera into a close-up of my face.

"Ladies and gentleman," I say, "being an executive at a local TV station, where your job and career rely on the success of a certain project, can be stressful and bad for your health." The camera swings to a shot of Grady's red face. "But, I'm going to show you a clip, of Grady and his partner Joe, enjoying cantaloupe, waffles, and a dozen eggs, last week at The Four Seasons Hotel brunch. Sounds relaxing, wouldn't you say? Watch how Grady here, shovels forkful, after forkful, of eggs and bacon into his mouth." The audience groans, as the screen reveals the empty plates in front of him. "Now, I'm not a doctor in this field, I'm an honorary one in another field of study, according to Boston University, but my point is; anything that may happen to this man, is based upon his own choice, and he is solely responsible for his own health. One might blame the success and failure of any given television show, but a medical doctor will agree, a lot of health issues are based on diet. Isn't that so, doctor?" The doctor on stage nods his head.

"We'll have more in a moment."

3:08 AM: Ethan

The audience applauds loudly when Ethan hits the stage. He's wearing a loose, bulky sweatshirt and jeans. He walks out slowly, but his face reflects a sense of urgency that I've never seen before. "This is, *the all important*," he says, as he shakes my hand.

When the applause dies down, I announce that Ethan said something profound during our handshake, and ask him if he'd like to repeat it.

"Are you going to save me?" he asks.

"Uh…what you said when you shook my hand, Ethan, was 'This is *the all important.*' I'd like to know why, in your words, this is so important."

Ethan has a funny look on his face. "No, it's not important, but it's *the all important.*"

I wonder if the audience understands the distinction, the way I do. Someone with bi-polar disorder uses certain key words and phrases, to indicate things as life or death, even if they are not life or death situations, and '*all important*', seems like one of those to Ethan. The phrase is magically significant to him. "The show," I say, "in the grand scheme of things, is not *the all important.*"

Grady begins to cough. My earpiece is silent.

"The show is a part of life," I continue. "It's entertainment, and though it's important to some, what should be important to you and I, based on what you said, is the feeling of being normal. Is that correct?"

Ethan nods.

"So far, the show isn't important to too many people...the ratings suck!"

I keep going, "That said, it's important to note, son, that the same way your mother is, you are also. The seesaw will never stop, and you will be this way the rest of your life."

Ethan stiffens. "No," he says, "this will save me. You said this show will be magical."

"We're going to be canceled." Robbie's voice in my earpiece is so loud that everyone on stage hears, *"We just heard—WHDH says, it's over."*

I pull out the earpiece and jam it in my pocket. "I did say, this show would be magical, Ethan, but I don't think it's going to save you or anyone else, in the near future. I think you need to deal with the fact, you might not ever be normal, and if the show's canceled, you will always be this way. You need to try to accept and adjust."

Ethan stands, and pulls a Superman cape from the back of his shirt, and begins running around the set, in a small circle, each time around increasing the circumference, until he bangs into a camera, and nearly trips on a cable. He rights himself, then runs faster, and faster.

"Ethan, stop!" I suddenly realize the importance of, *the all-important*, and what role I've had, first by giving him hope, and second, by pushing him to this point. Ethan finishes a wide circle, and runs offstage toward the Green Room. I've pushed him over the edge and he's breaking. He must be stopped, but I don't know what to say, so I yell out the first thing that pops into my head, "Ethan, I love you, like I loved my own brother!"

The camera follows him, speeding down the hall, slamming against his father, who tries to contain him, knocking him over, like a bowling pin.

Grady has turned magenta and is grabbing his chest. I too, am feeling an overwhelming need to black everything out. I can no longer see, but I hear the dark urgent command, "We need a doctor! The boy jumped out the window!" This is followed by, the cries and screams in the studio, which increase in volume and overtake me, like the sounds of the wind from a tornado. I'm left covered in the debris of what I've done. It covers me, like a heavy blanket, until I no longer feel like an object on this earth.

Part 4: The Healing

Chapter 15: The Catatonic State of Bill Sloan, April 14

7:22 AM: Deep in subconscious, somewhere an alarm clock rings
Can't move
Think I hear Todd Rundgren's, "Healing Part II"
Think about today's schedule...You are thought itself, and only that
8:45 AM: Blank state
9:45 AM: "0"
10:45 AM: ...
11:30 AM: Deep in subconscious, somewhere, there is a lunch—sandwich,
apple, juice box
12:45 PM: _____
1:45 PM: ( )
2:45 PM: ~~000000~~
3:45 PM: xxxxxxx
4:00 PM: Ethan

Chapter 16: Sunny and Share's Fantastic Emergency Appointments

Wake from the sun shining in my window
Invigorate Self in the spring breeze, blowing in through an open window
Feel freedom

Morning reflection. Glorious morning (really)

It *is* a glorious morning, damn it! Breathe. At 3:30 AM, I told all my clients, the cast of *The Doctor Bill Sloan*, to return to the studio in the morning. Through this, we will learn to heal, be beautiful, and find the love. We need to start working on, post-Bill Sloan therapy. Dan and Thomas, have started redesigning, and painting the television set, so it looks exactly like my Sunny and Share office, at *Mental Health Solutions*, except they're bringing in seven extra massage tables. Thomas has been told to cover Bill, with a drop cloth, so no paint spatters on him. Bill, is now officially my patient, and I've ordered him to be treated on site.

I don't own a television, but I know what I would find on all the stations, (except WHDH), if I did: reports about *The Bill Sloan Show* fiasco. I have a voicemail from *Animal Planet,* saying they want to do a show on Hopi, and a voicemail from Robbie, letting me know that Grady's heart attack was minor, and that he'll be fine, but is no longer employed by WHDH. Robbie also asked, if I wanted to pay for my commercial clip, filmed for the Sloan Show, to repeat in a loop next Thursday at 2:15 AM. I need to empty my mind of these things.

Breathe.

I stand and rub my hands together, "Heavenly Father, Thou art omnipresent; Thou art in all Thy children; manifest Thy healing presence in their bodies." I raise my hands, outstretched, and I should chant, *Aum*. I'm having trouble; the word in my head seems hollow, so I wish to leave it, and to move on.

Breathe.

"Heavenly Father, Thou art omnipresent; Thou art in all Thy children; manifest Thy healing presence in their minds." I rotate my hands around the light I've created for Bill, Hanna, Thomas, Grady, Dan, and Ethan. Ethan is dead.

Breathe.

"Heavenly Father, Thou art omnipresent; Thou art in all Thy children; manifest Thy healing presence in their souls." I repeat the act of rubbing my hands together, but I can't say, *Aum*. I can't do it. I'm here by myself. I am alone. I need to go to WHDH immediately, and heal them all. There needs to be love right now, instead of occupying myself with me. What have I learned in my life? I need to apply it. I need to help Bill Sloan find love. I need to heal him.

I need to not reset Bill Sloan before I can love him. The test will be to love him, and help him love himself, so he may break out of total sensory deprivation, and re-enter the world. I say, *Aum* abruptly, and walk to the kitchen, to cut a slice of raw steak for Hopi. "We have a lot of things to work on today, Hopi," I say.

Glorious Morning: Bill

When I walk in with Hopi, I see Bill sitting on one of the guest chairs from the set, and the show's theme music is on continuous loop, making the place sound, and feel, like a carnival. Bill looks waxy; his mouth is an emotionless, straight line. I speak over the horrible music, my voice echoing: "That needs to be turned off, it'll keep him stuck in this state." Dan shuts it off. I take out a CD I brought, and put it in the player. Hopi is tugging on his leash; wants to pull me back out, through the door. The hallway, leading to the Green Room, has been roped off in yellow tape.

Robbie is pulling double duty, working for me, and WHDH, and as he heads into the control room, he says, "I don't know what to do with Bill, to get him out of this state. I checked the internet, and the first thing Yahoo Answers says is, low doses of Electric Shock Therapy, but the second most popular answer is, getting a puppy."

"Plus, he's in the way of us working, and stuff," Thomas says. "I say, we put him in the dumpster."

"I'm trying love and Hopi," I tell them. "He's better than a puppy. He's a big, healing wolf."

The plastic, painter's drop-cloth, wrapped around Bill's shoulders, makes him look like one of those fake heads, you find in beauty training school. The cloth makes a loud, rustling noise when I remove it, but he doesn't stir.

"I should have never taken this TV job," Robbie says. "Things were going fine when I was working in your office, Kate." I hear his voice from the control room, but also through Bill's earpiece, which I remove.

I turn up the volume of the CD; we need all the wonderment we can get. Then, I put a chair directly in front of Bill, and sit. "I know you can hear me. There's overwhelming negative energy, the size of a cinder block, in you right now, and we need to smash it open; free it, so you may come back to us. We all want you to come back. We all love you." I stop. *Do "we"? Or is it just me?*

I look at him; his immobile face, his blank expression, and I feel it. Love. Why? How did this happen? I hate him, too. I need to get past that, past the hatred that's going on. What I need, is the belief there is love, and that Bill fits in with the world. That's what everyone needs; it's how I treat everyone.

"More on this later," I say to him. "Think about the music cracking that cinder block, so we can break up that energy. It's what is messing with, and shutting down, your system. There is no love in a cinder block."

Robbie yells down, that Hanna has been waiting for me off stage, and she should be seen as soon as possible.

Could be a Glorious Morning: Hanna

Hanna doesn't want to be here. She says, it's really fucked up that the studio has been redecorated to look like my old office, down to the wall, with bright lights attached to orange brackets.

"Is that really what you want to say?" I ask. "Use your innermost serenity, to say what you want."

"No, I have other things on my mind." Hanna looks at Bill. "Is he going to be okay? Not that I don't think he doesn't deserve this."

"Sweetie," I say, "we need to get you well. Then, he will be well. It'll benefit you, him, all of us. It's what Sunny and Share does."

"You know," she says, "in a way, he was right. I did bounce through different men, to help get me get through things. Yes, Brad and I were over long before, but I didn't have to be with Randy, then him, and then back to Randy. I think Randy deserved better, but I couldn't help what was going on; the guilt of my son without a father. I just don't know. Bill did manage to bring that out of me. Fuck, look at him. Will he be like this forever? I do feel bad. Well, sort of. Can you do, like, electric-shock or something?"

"I'm going to help him using my own methods."

"This is fucked up. Why am I in conflict? Look at what he did! He brought out Brad's parents, then that boy, that poor boy."

"I have a stupendous, wonderful plan, which will help both of you," I say. "Robbie, could you help me move the massage tables closer to Bill?"

Robbie comes out and pushes the tables close together, in a circle, so when Hanna lies down, I'll be able to touch her and Bill's heads at the same time. I've never tried joint Reiki before, but I feel, if Hanna is open to it, and if I can keep Hopi in contact with my leg during this, we'll start breaking through the walls, we need to break through.

"Close your eyes and go to a place of love."

"Comealy's Farm?"

"Go there."

Bill: Blank state, 9:15 AM

Bill senses something, like a heartbeat, like a drop of water against a sidewalk, like rain plopping on his forehead. It starts soft, but each molecule is dense, full of Kate, and growing in intensity. There is the smell; the smell of cleansing, fresh rain in the spring.

He can smell Hanna, too; he knows her perfume, he knows everything about her. But when he was with her, he kept that information hidden from himself, because he didn't want to get close to anyone. He feels her sitting on the grass at Comealy's Farm, leaning back on her arms. Bill is sitting with her. It is the first time she had taken him there. That night, she threw her arms around him, and their lips pressed together, softly at first, then their heads jockeyed for the best leverage possible. She had trust then.

Bill almost stopped. He knew, she was lost. He knew, she was looking for closure; she needed to come to terms with Brad's suicide. He knew, she was coming on to the therapist, who hardly knew her, and all the while, she was wondering, if she still wanted

Randy; but she was too scared, to want two things, at the same time. Bill knew this. The sun had gone down hours ago, while they were at dinner, but the night stayed cool and clear. Her love making was intense; her hair falling down, like wet tendrils, after she came (much quicker than Bill). When he came, minutes later, she said she needed to go. He knew, there were issues to work on, but he didn't work on them.

Bill can feel Hanna, here, now. She is relaxing, and it's raining on both of them. Their clothes are soaked. The tiniest corners, the most miniscule corners, of the concrete begin to weaken.

Reality hits Bill, like the flashes of a thunderstorm. He can't move, and pushes back against the flashing: the hard physical makeup of concrete, is the furthest thing from Comealy's soft lure; the crib of nature. The rain pounds hard, like a heavy thunderstorm, and the water springs, back up, from against the ground. It's so full of Kate, that it explodes in the sound of, "swoosh, swoosh, swoosh". If Bill just lets go, he can be drowned by all this love, such love he has never had. Hopi is licking his face. The concrete pushes back harder, the solid ground forms immoveable mud, and everything stays solid and hard underneath, as the rain slackens down, from torrential, to heavy, random drops, in dark puddles.

Is it a Glorious Morning? Me

The time I take for me–to go to the woods, to meditate, to relax, and love–isn't available today. I took some time in bed this morning, before coming back to WHDH, but it was only for a few, short minutes. I need time to recharge, otherwise, all this healing work will overcome me mentally. There isn't enough sage in the world, that could possibly be burned, to cleanse this energy.

I am having stress about what I see and think, in the real world. Right now, it's about not having a useable Green Room, and seeing both Thomas and Stella, waiting at the side of the stage. Hanna is on the table, eyes closed, and Bill remains in his state of stone. I have increasing love for him. I have five minutes; not too much time to rev up the power, but enough to re-place my hands on them.

9:55 AM: Bill "0"

Bill feels Kate's presence again, but it's faint, and cool, in the way mist from an open refrigerator escapes on a scorching summer day. He wonders, if he's in a morgue, lying in cold corpse storage. Everything about this seems flat and strong, it's all locked in. The tic of coolness, is like a fly on his nose. He wants to swat it, his brain is giving him the message to swat it, but he can't move. Kate's hand is ice cold. *It should be warm*, Bill thinks. *Before, it was warm, like a heating pad.* Kate is deep in meditation, pushing out humming noises, and Hanna lets out a sigh. Hopi rests his snout on Bill's lap. Bill is gathering the sensations, necessary for his recovery. Bill wonders why he's just starting to feel. He thinks of his dead brother, but his next thought, toward Ethan, is blocked. He's back in a blank state.

Somewhat of a spectacular Morning: Thomas

"Thomas? You're next." I call.

He walks on the stage, and confronts me. "Why the hell are you helping out this asshole? Just let the authorities get him and have him locked up, in an institution, for however long it takes. I hope that's forever."

"That's not what we do at Sunny and Share. What have we been working on?"

"Fuck that. I'd like to kick him in the head!" Thomas shouts. Hopi stands, and rears back, ready to face off against Thomas.

"Whoa," Thomas says. "He's never done that before. He should know, I care for him."

"Exactly," I say, "and he's in a healing mode that he's been trained for. He is gathering energy, through this healing, directly from Bill. Hopi will remain in the Reiki circle."

"But why help Bill? He embarrassed you on television by showing clips of your mother, then clips of you and him, having sex."

"You choose to see that, but I choose to see, how it will help Sunny and Share. We've already received hundreds of new referrals, because of the show. I'm thinking of franchising. Isn't that wonderful?"

"That's great!" Thomas nods, then frowns. "Why doesn't this kind of luck, happen to me?"

"It can, and it's not based on luck. It's based on all the work I've done on myself, in my life, starting with visiting the happy, spiritual, and comfortable places, in my life. Thomas, I've already started to reach a place in your head where you were happy. I can do some intense work with you on that. Can you go to, say, when you were in college, and in love?"

"But didn't I fail there?"

"It depends on how you look at it. I can perform Reiki, and put love into that moment, where you were most at peace. We'll channel the energy around you, feeding Bill, then Hanna, and of course Hopi will benefit, and put out energy as well. Let's get started. Lie down on table three. Oh, and why are you not in jail?"

"The authorities dropped the recent charges, based on the circumstances around my appearances on, *The Bill Sloan Show*. They viewed my behavior as reasonable."

11:15 AM: Bill "... hum"

Bill hears the hum started by Kate. It builds like a tornado, far off in the distance, coming closer; like a train blowing through a station, multiplied by many thousands. Bill knows the sound of a train's roar is distorted by a phenomenon, called the Doppler Effect.

The Doppler Effect? How is he receiving this information, in his closed-off state? He is unable to explain how, or why, but he is.

258

He's far from the tornado, but it's coming, and he wants to cower in a safe place. He feels like he's waiting. He knows it's only a matter of time before it's on top of him, and then he'll be directly in it. If he survives, there will be the ransacked destruction to deal with; the cleanup, and the after-effects. He hears the hum, and the sound of twigs, and dead leaves, being picked up. The sound is building, the funnel is forming. Kate's hands control the surges of wind.

He fights the cracking of his catatonic armor. He must avoid the destruction, and think of the science. He thinks, *Doppler radar measures the wind speed of heavy thunderstorms and tornados*. He can feel the relative motion of him, Kate, Hanna, and Thomas. Small cracks are starting to form in his defensive wall. Bill feels these people, and their energy, seeping into him. The love and healing is being sent. He can feel the change in electromagnetic fields, which is the energy all around him. The Doppler Effect is measured in low-earth-orbit satellite systems. Bill feels like he is a LEO satellite. He feels everything is moving relative to each other, and to points on him. He feels his mind affected, relative to the earth, relative to the far reaches of outer space. He has thought of the science, and it too, has made him crazy. He feels himself cracking. Small amounts of sand, from the cracks, are being sucked away and thrown around in the hurricane.

He continues to fight. He knows, if he loosens, he'll have to deal with the mess caused by the hurricane. As a LEO satellite, he feels Ethan, viewing the world as an alien, and the speed of the world measured by Ethan's Doppler. Ethan's soul is upon him, inside his thoughts, even though Ethan is not linked in the circle in WHDH's studio. Bill has created the tornado, from the lives of all his clients. He needs to, not crack, not loosen, because the devastation is just too great, but somewhere, in the darkened subconscious, there is love pulsing, from Kate, and surprising love, from Hopi, Hanna, and Thomas. These are unlikely sources. He couldn't stand them, and they couldn't stand him, but in this moment, they are bonded, by love and sharing. If he were able to, he'd try to test the waters, but right now he can't even stick a toe in it. He knows, he must be in or out, and right now, he can't be in. Not yet, anyway. He wants to scream out, with the mighty force of every natural disaster ever, but he can't.

Warm, sort-of-fantabulous afternoon: Robbie

Robbie asks, if he can join the circle. "I went somewhere, to change my life, and now, I need to do something else positive, for others. If I hadn't fired Bill, none of this would have happened. May I join the circle, Kate? May I?"

12:15 PM: Bill: "_____"

Somehow, Bill knows Robbie is there. *Is it lunch time? Did I miss lunch? After Thomas, is lunch, on Thursday, always. Lunch has always been the same, even as a child. Why can't the apples, ever be good?*

Every hour, someone joins the chain, and Bill feels their initial darkness. He feels like saying, "Hello my name is Bill, and I'm stuck," but he can't. It's right on the tip of his brain; he can almost push it out of his brain, and through the mechanics, of his jaw and airway. He can almost say the damn thing. The energy is there, on a slow simmer, and additional energy, from each new person, is softening him.

There are two fields of energy close to Bill. The first, emulates from Robbie, and it is his strength which is most surprising. The second, is the combination of Kate-Hanna-Thomas-Robbie; forming a circle, like the one Ethan started, when he began to run last night in the studio.

Bill also feels something warm on his lap—partially lying on him. He wants it to be Kate, but he swears it's something else; warm blooded and furry. Bill has a sudden thought--he is as friendly and social as this creature, but it confuses him, because he's never been given any advice, that has worked, in his own life. Maybe he is a snake, like Kate said, but she's a wolf, and she teaches others about sacredness, and spirituality. He wants to believe, he is not cold blooded. The circle is warm, and Bill is not sure how it happens, but his body twitches in a single jolt. The drop cloth rustles, he tries to move again, on his own, but his everything clenches once more. Love may be softening him, but Bill suddenly wants a sandwich.

Warm, sunny, so tired afternoon: Stella/Pearl

Stella delays coming out. She says with a smirk, "I was waiting for an intro." She looks like she's aged ten years, since last night. She needs to take a breath. She shakes her head at the sight of Hopi, lying half in Bill's lap. "I can't believe this is the same wolf that took a bite out of Bill last night."

"Hopi is in healing mode. Remember, you were like Bill is now, and Hopi worked on you."

"I was not!"

"You were. Bill tried to shock you back from it, but it was Hopi, who helped you come out of it."

"I remember the wolf, and then I remember the show's horrible ending. I couldn't sleep at all. I had to stay up and talk to Carlton all night. He's not much of a talker."

"I think we can work on this," I say. "I want to tell you, Stella, is a fantastic person, and she will be the one, who is going to be left."

"Why are you referring to Stella in the third person?" she asks. "Am I a fantastic person, or not?"

"I think you are."

"I don't think he is," Stella says pointing to Bill. "We've had our ups and downs, but he was never as crazy as he's been this year. I just hope he's all right. Maybe now, he can spend more time with the kids."

"Yes, last night was awful, but the Universe is all about love and healing. Look at all of the people, and creatures, who shouldn't be gathered here today, lying in a circle for themselves, and for Bill. This wonderful event would not be happening, if not for last night. We can't take back the tragedy, but we can love, and we can heal. This is why you came back this morning, Stella. Today, we're going to mold all of you into one, in the healing circle; the energy will swirl around exponentially. It is what I've been working toward, and it'll be fabulous, and wonderful and totally, totally fantastic. I can't wait until the end of the day, today." I can feel my own energy building again.

"Whatever happened last night, I don't want to happen to me, ever again. I'd like to have a good life with Carlton, and with Bill. He's the father of my children. I want him to be well."

"We can all be well together, you, me, Pearl. Are you ready to work?"

1:11 PM: Bill "( )"

Bill was always able to sense when Stella was near. He remembers that time she snuck up on him in the basement, when she didn't really sneak up on him. He knew she was there, the entire time. He was the one who could hide. The only time she took him by surprise, was when she booked that first appointment with him, under a fake name, to get past the screener.

Bill feels Kate pulling both Stella and Pearl out, each with half energy. Stella does not resist; she is letting go. Stella and Pearl are two energy fields, who, when merged, will become one large energy field. But, Kate is not only trying to merge Stella and Pearl. She's going for a full merge of everyone in attendance, to heal Bill. He has another small, involuntary twitch, and he realizes, that the warm presence on his lap, is Hopi.

He feels the merging and it's like the release of valuable items from a locked safe. Stella is doing fine. She didn't need to be shocked out of it, the way he attempted last night. *Shocks form cracks in my concrete*, he thinks. He is surprised he is thinking. It is as if he

262

has been held under water, and is beginning to float up. Another twitch, and slowly he starts to swim. He feels the thrusts of, "love-love-love", working on areas that have been frozen. He's starting to feel, and he feels Kate, and everyone else, without judgment. Only calm. He gets an image of Kate, sitting in the woods, and there's nothing more to it than that. He can sense Stella's confusion, and reluctance to accept what is happening to her, but it seems to be the same thing that's happening to him. He thinks, *We're finally working on ourselves; finally, we have all begun our work.*

Warm, medical issues of an afternoon: Grady

"I'm so sorry," I say to Grady, as he and Joe come into my studio. Grady is still wearing a hospital johnnie. "You are the one person who really doesn't need to be here. I'm trained to give you energy, but in your condition, it would have been fine if you'd stayed in the hospital."

Joe says, "The doctors told us, he's had minor heart attacks before. He has to take it easy." He shoots Grady a look, as if to say, "You shouldn't be here." This, I can deal with, as long as he doesn't collapse.

"Oh, you poor man," I say. "We will take it easy. One part of this treatment, will take everything easy, let everything go, and the other part, will be using positive energy on your medical condition."

"I don't know what I'm going to do," Grady moans, then looks around the room. "I can't feel sorry for myself. I'm certainly better off than *him*," he says, pointing to Bill. "And the rest of them... Jesus."

"They're all beautiful, and they're all getting stronger. I'm getting tired, and weaker, but everyone else will be doing fantastic. They have a lot of work to do, but that's what I do at Sunny and Share."

"You sound like that commercial again. Did WHDH ask you to expand on that, as a late night show?"

"Grady!" Joe yells.

"Oh, I know," Grady says. "I'm not supposed to think of show line-ups, or the fact that I may not be working here anymore. I thought a lot about it, while I was on my back last night, and honestly, if it were to happen, I'd be all right with it. I just need to take care of myself."

"Exactly," I say. Grady will be easy to work with; he seems to have grasped some very important concepts.

"Let's see how it goes," Joe said. "I don't think I'm ready for you to retire."

At my feet, a muffled voice: *Grady Simon…Grady Simon.* The earpiece. I look up to the production booth and see a WHDH executive, talking into a microphone, and then he pulls a switch, opening up the studio to his voice. "Grady Simon," the suit says, "WHDH is offering you a chance to resign from your position. You have the rest of the day to think about it." The microphone is shut off with a loud "click."

Grady hangs his head. The love he needs can overcome this, it can overcome anything.

"What are you going to do?" Joe says.

"I need to take care of myself," he says again.

"Would you like to join the circle?" I ask.

"Yes, it's a good place to start. I got a lot out of the time I had to think last night, so I might as well get on my back again."

2:18 PM: Bill "000000"

1. Heart. Nothing more than a pump made of muscle. It pumps the blood, and all the other vital materials, and removes the waste we do not need. The brain requires oxygen and glucose, and if it does not get it, then a person will become unconscious. If the heart stops pumping, then the body will shut down. Suddenly, Bill is getting information; a lot of it. The blockage is shifting.

2. Heart. The band Heart covered The Who's, "Love Reign o'er Me", which was a song where the singer begged for love, and he craved a drink of cool, cool rain. In Cincinnati, people rained and poured over each other, trying to enter the few arena doors that they opened for the concert. People in the back ran up, and threw their bodies forward, into the crowd. Eleven fans died. They were crushed to death. Ethan knew that. Bill doesn't know, how he knows that.

3. Heart. It can be broken. Bill's is broken differently than Grady's. Grady's heart is partially broken, not only from love, but also from physical wear. There is an answer to, "How do you mend a broken heart?" It's happening, right now!

4. Heart. There is the symbolic heart. It's a drawn, red, object that connects the spiritual, emotional, and moral core of a human being. The heart was once widely believed to be in control of the human mind. The word is poetic and connects to the soul. The heart is love.

5) Heart. Bill sees the colors pink and green. Kate is like a maestro, conducting a symphony. The colors come pouring from the Heart Chakra. Bill knows, the love center, from our human energy system, is often the focus of bringing about a healing. Kate's busy on this, but with all the love, there is also this: hurtful situations, which affect people's emotional well-being include divorce or separation, grief

265

through death, emotional abuse, abandonment, and adultery. All of these are wounding to the heart chakra. Bill feels wounded, but he also feels Kate on him, in him, and through him and the Reiki circle; like a healing wind, sifting round and round. He knows the concrete is bursting open, forming rubble. From all the crumble, will eventually come sand. Bill is receiving information, on the process, he can't fully understand. He is open, to just letting it happen. The rubble lays over his soul. Bill would like to trample it down, and crush it up some more. He feels strong enough to pick it up and crush it with only his bare soul.

Sunny afternoon outside, no available windows inside: Dan

When Dan arrives, I'm sitting on the chair Bill sat in, during the show. I feel tired. If only, I could keep my eyes closed, but I can't–Dan is tapping me.

"I knew I had to be here, today," he says. "I'm remembering a lot of stuff, Kate! I remember hitting that antelope. Last night, I heard your voice, saying that word, while I was in bed. I stomped on the breaks. My comforter fell off the bed." He shakes me, "Kate, wake up!"

"I'm so tired," I say. "I haven't given out this much energy in one day ever before. It's so glorious, so glorious."

"I want to remember more."

"Antelope," I say.

"I remember last night," Dan says quietly. "There is an advantage of not doing so."

"We just have to tie some things together," I tell him. "I'm almost done healing here and you are almost done too."

3:10 PM: Bill "xxxxxxx"

Bill remembers pitching a blue, rubber ball to his brother; a ball always out of the strike zone, and his brother never able to hit it. It either bounces five feet before the garage door, which acts as the catcher, or misses the entire garage completely. *You're not trying*, Bill says. He keeps throwing, until his frustrated brother is swinging at anything, his head pulled violently out of line of the ball. *Miss. Miss. Miss.* They both miss.

Bill's brother says, he's doing the best he can. Bill says, it's not good enough, to which, the brother says, *"Nothing ever is."* Bill doesn't say anything. He concentrates on the one perfect pitch, he can grove, and that his brother can hammer. *You don't have to pitch anymore,* the batter says.

Bill remembers Ethan when he first walked in the door, with an "I can't do this therapy stuff again" expression. Bill knew he had to throw balls that were hittable. Then there was Hanna, Kate, Thomas, Stella, Grady, and Dan. Did he ever have control? Kate has them all reeled in. These people are not his problem, but they all wish to be healed, and as one, all wish for all, to be healed. Bill feels Dan, remembering Bill. *Well, asshole,* he finds Dan thinking, *if my brain can be healed, then so can yours.*

The cement lifts and clears, and Bill becomes his thoughts and breaths. He has become everyone's thoughts, and breaths.

Sunny, late afternoon outside, almost sunny and shared: the McGraths

I feel like crying when Ethan's parents are brought over by the WHDH executive, who tells them how sorry everybody is at WHDH. They nod without speaking. They seem calm; I expected more emotion. If I can reach them, in love and forgiveness, I will have done my greatest work.

But it's not about me. It's about how great the Universe is.

"I'm sorry. This is very hard," I tell them. "Thank you for coming in. It's important you get some healing."

267

"Ethan," Mrs. McGrath says, "saw your light. I can see your light, too. It's an aura, it's definitely there." Her eyes are wide, with wonder. "I can't believe I'm feeling this. My medication keeps everything very flat. I would never tell my psychiatrist about this, but I know it's real."

"He was making progress," Ethan's dad says, "but he elevated this television show up, so unrealistically…that the show would fix him and fix everything. It just ended up in a way that made sense, if you knew him, but doesn't make any sense, whatsoever, to anyone else. Waysworth, by the way, has sealed his records from the media."

"I think his mind needed to be quieted," I say.

"Do you know, we were contacted by a lawyer?"

"Oh, that's not my business, unless I'm trying to heal lawyers. But that'll never happen," I say. "Too much paperwork."

"We'd never sue," Mrs. McGrath says. "Although, I blame Sloan for a lot of this. He wasn't the one who created Ethan's brain, but he wasn't able to adjust it. Don't get me wrong, because we are *very* fucking angry. But there's not going to be a lawsuit."

Ethan's dad cuts in, "A trial will bring her ailment into this, and it would be, even more, painful. The case would all be about biology, instead of the cause of Ethan's fatal snap, and why nothing was done to derail that. We would sue Sloan, WHDH, and the entire television industry, if we thought it would make any difference, but I don't think it would. I don't think it would bring us any closure."

I can feel the sweat on my neck under my hair. The talk of biological connections between Ethan and his mother, brings up old wounds. I rejected my mother and found myself fighting her biological influences, with what I've learned in the spiritual world. "I know this won't change anything, but if I could give both of you a super Reiki charge, within the circle, it would benefit you."

"Ethan liked you," Mrs. McGrath says. "He felt something from you, and I can't deny that now."

"Yes, he really did like you," his dad says. "I wish you could have saved him."

4:00 PM: Bill "Ethan?"

Bill is an open channel, receiving energy from Kate-the McGraths-Dan-Grady-Stella-Robbie-Thomas-Hanna-Hopi. Their love swirls round and round; it's all in the circle. Bill remembers, it's four o'clock. He sees Ethan every Thursday, at 4 o'clock. Bill starts to worry about his commute home, at about this time. Where did the day go?

He feels like he's in a dream. The warmth of each soul is erupting into fire. They are stronger than when they started, either healed, or in the process of healing. He feels them each distinctly, and as a whole. He has absorbed this concept through Stella. Pearl is now joined within her, just as all of their energy has been joined, within him.

He has absorbed through Hanna, that there are safe places to take yourself, that don't involve others, and there are other places you need to let yourself go to. No one can harm you, if you find a safe place for your soul to go. Accept those places, and accept people like himself, and Randy, for the positions we all find ourselves in.

He has absorbed through Thomas, to let go of the past, and to let go of anger. He doesn't have to like Thomas, in fact, even with all Kate's current work, he still hates him. Let go of your anger and hatred, and love, love, love.

He has absorbed through Robbie, that you can be whatever you want to be, even with all your flaws. Life is something you can be actively involved in, without relying on fantasies, until you reach a new potential; a new life.

He has absorbed through Grady, that if something ends, it's not the end. Grady will bounce back. He knows healing can be medical and spiritual. It's okay to rest, retire, or reinvent yourself.

269

He has absorbed through Dan, that you can never forget, that you can regenerate. There are certain natural prompts, which stir real truths, and real memories. Bill can hear the word *antelope*.

He has absorbed through the McGraths, that the ability to forgive, even the most tragic of circumstances, is through love and acceptance of people, and situations. He knows that he may not be forgiven completely, but there is hope and love, shared, over hate.

He has absorbed through them all simultaneously, and also through the singular Kate. He now knows why, and how, Kate sees him. She's not the whacked-out person, he was treating, but someone who has been changed by him, and by his existence. Kate sees him–and always saw him–as someone who needed her; a person, who needed to be healed by her, and who was needed to love her. They dance through each other's light as Bill awakens, and as he does, he wants her, and all of the energy he has absorbed from her and the others, to change him. The warmth of her hand is bringing him back, sweeping the crumbs of his crushed concrete block, and he wants to bolt upward, to shout something but he lies there and allows himself to go back to Thursday morning, at 3:18 AM.

"Ethan, stop!" he yells. Ethan runs in a tight circle, he expands in width each lap, and Bill understands the importance of it all, and what role he had in pushing him. Ethan finishes a large circle and runs straight toward the Green Room. Bill wants him to stop so he blurts out, "I love you, like I loved my own brother," Ethan knocks his father down, like a bowling pin. Grady grabs his chest, and I hear a dark and vital order, "We need a doctor! He's jumped out the window!"

Bill jumps and the drop cloth springs off him, to the floor. "I'm not a doctor! I'm not a doctor!" he yells. Hopi licks his face, and everyone comes out of their trance.

The Crossing of Right Paths: Ethan, R.I.P, April 20

AT THE FUNERAL, Ethan's parents give a eulogy, in which they remember Ethan as an imperfect son, who was pretty much perfect, in every way. Mrs. McGrath tells the story about when he jumped off the seesaw, after speaking to Dr. Sloan in therapy, bruising her. Everyone laughs.

Then, Kate gets up to speak. She mentions Ethan's freedom, and his innocence of spirit, and how that makes his animal totem one of a primate. "Human nature is easily seen, in the characteristics and habits of monkeys and apes. We love to watch their behaviors, because they remind us so much of ourselves, and Ethan, really was like everyone else, which was, exactly what he wanted." Some of Ethan's Waysworth classmates are crying.

Bill Sloan steps up. He calmly silences the murmur by speaking of his history with Ethan, the treatment, and the struggles, Ethan had to endure. He respectfully mentions bipolar disorder, and how difficult it is for someone with that disability, to shut off their thoughts. Then, he relates it to the sadness of his own loss: "I knew what was going on. You all saw what happened, but I never wanted it to end the way it ended, and I'm sorry. I loved Ethan, and all I can do is own, and accept my responsibility in all of this, and try to love others. Remember, you can lead, by taking the right path, as a follower. It's better than being the leader, going the wrong way."

Afterward, the reception is attended by all of Bill's former clients. Hanna hugs him, while Randy hangs back. "This is hard," Hanna says. "It's almost as if, we're going through everything all over again."

"It's weird, all of us, here," Thomas says.

"The family wanted us here. They feel the show was the last connection to Ethan's life," Kate says.

"We're so much better, and more prepared, as people," Bill says, "but this is a difficult day for us all."

Thomas moves to stand directly in front of Bill. He looks him in the eye, for a good twenty seconds. "That was really big," he says. "Your eulogy was very good. I hope things work out well, for all of us."

"I hope so too. Here's to another chance," Bill says, raising a glass.

Stella overhears, and repeats the phrase. "I'm going to try to do it the right way with Carlton. Kate made me realize, that I *do* love you Bill, and the children and I, want you in our lives. This time, in a healthy way."

Dan rests his hand on Bill's shoulder. "I'll always remember what you did for me: you introduced me to Kate. I'm a new man, because the Universe put you in my path, and through you, Kate."

"You did it, the healing, yourself. Bless that power and that glory."

Kate walks from the outside of the circle, to the inside, and whispers to Bill, "I'm so proud of the love in you. I'd like to leave here, soon so we can be in that love."

"I'm ready," he says quietly. "I love you very much."

"Thank you," Kate says. "Don't you know, the correct response to, I love you, is not to repeat 'I love you' back, but rather to say, 'thank you.'"

Bill takes her hand, and they walk out to the parking lot, where Grady and Robbie are waiting.

"Don't leave just yet!" Grady yells. "Kate! I want to ask you if you're interested in a show of your own, in the Thursday, early-morning time slot. Your likeability rating is very good."

"Didn't you get fired?" Bill turns to Grady.

"I'm a consultant, thanks to Robbie's advocating."

"That's wonderful," Kate says.

"Well, Kate, what do you say?"

Kate pauses, thoughtfully, then her words come out slowly. "I think I'm going to say, no thank you. Even though I am full of love for both you and Robbie, and for everyone else here, I'm only one person within the Universe, who recognizes it took a lot of hard work, for me to get to this point of comfort and love. I must reflect on that and give myself the proper credit."

"We'd do that," Grady says. "We'd run proper credits, at the end of the show."

"Oh, not that," Kate says. "But people, in general, never think in the way that I do. They are constantly evolving, without an end point." She places her hand, in the hand of Bill Sloan. "Come on Bill. It's time to go home."

About The Author

Timothy Gager is the author of eleven books of fiction and poetry. He has been published in over 300 print and on-line journals. His work has been nominated nine times for The Pushcart Prize and has been read on NPR. His book of poetry, *The Shutting Door* was nominated for The Massachusetts Book Award. He lives on www.timothygager.com.

The Thursday Appointments of Bill Sloan is his first novel.

A Message from Timothy Gager

Dear Reader,

I hope that reading this book has been a good experience for you. If it has, maybe you can think of other people who would appreciate it. Here's how you could help them and me. Many books are competing for readers' attention, and the most important way for a book to get more notice is for readers to write favorable reviews and post them on Amazon.com.

The more positive reviews or comments a book gets, the more it moves up the ranking for exposure when people search on Amazon. When a book has ten reviews it becomes eligible to be included in the "also bought" and "you might like" recommendations. These listings add to the number of books likely to be purchased and read.

If you don't have time to write a review, please take a few minutes to read and rate reviews posted by other readers. Just the act of "liking" a review moves books up the queue in which they appear.

Thanks in advance for your effort to boost the distribution and exposure of this book! I really appreciate it!

Made in the USA
Charleston, SC
15 August 2014